Trained together at the Athena Academy, these six women vowed to help each other when in need. Now one of their own has been murdered, and it is up to them to find the killer— before they become the next victims....

Alex Forsythe:
This forensic scientist can uncover clues others fail to see.
PROOF, by Justine Davis—July 2004

Darcy Allen Steele:
A master of disguise, Darcy can sneak into any crime scene.
ALIAS, by Amy J. Fetzer—August 2004

Tory Patton:
Used to uncovering scandals, this investigative reporter will get to the bottom of any story—especially murder.
EXPOSED, by Katherine Garbera—September 2004

Samantha St. John:
Though she's the youngest, this lightning-fast secret agent can take down men twice her size.
DOUBLE-CROSS, by Meredith Fletcher—October 2004

Josie Lockworth:
A little danger won't stop this daredevil air force pilot from uncovering the truth.
PURSUED, by Catherine Mann—November 2004

Kayla Ryan:
The police lieutenant won't rest until the real killer is brought to justice, even if it makes her the next target!
JUSTICE, by Debra Webb—December 2004

ATHENA FORCE:
They were the best, the brightest, the strongest— women who shared a bond like no other....

Dear Reader,

We invite you to sit back and enjoy the ride as you experience the powerful suspense, intense action and tingling emotion in Silhouette Bombshell's November lineup. Strong, sexy, savvy heroines have never been so popular, and we're putting the best right into your hands. Get ready to meet four extraordinary women who will speak to the Bombshell in you!

Maggie Sanger will need quick wit and fast moves to get out of Egypt alive when her pursuit of a legendary grail puts her on a collision course with a secret society, hostages and her furious ex! Get into *Her Kind of Trouble,* the latest in author Evelyn Vaughn's captivating GRAIL KEEPERS miniseries.

Sabotage, scandal and one sexy inspector breathe down the neck of a determined air force captain as she strives to right an old wrong in the latest adventure in the innovative twelve-book ATHENA FORCE continuity series, *Pursued* by Catherine Mann.

Enter the outrageous underworld of Las Vegas prizefighting as a female boxing trainer goes up against the mob to save her father, her reputation and a child witness in Erica Orloff's pull-no-punches novel, *Knockout.*

And though creating identities for undercover agents is her specialty, Kristie Hennessy finds out that work can be deadly when you've got everyone fooled and no one to trust but a man you know only by his intriguing voice…. Don't miss Kate Donovan's *Identity Crisis.*

It's a month of no-holds-barred excitement! Please send your comments to me, c/o Silhouette Books, 233 Broadway Ste. 1001, New York, NY 10279.

Best wishes,

Natashya Wilson

Natashya Wilson
Associate Senior Editor, Silhouette Bombshell

Please address questions and book requests to:
Silhouette Reader Service
U.S.: 3010 Walden Ave., P.O. Box 1325, Buffalo, NY 14269
Canadian: P.O. Box 609, Fort Erie, Ont. L2A 5X3

PURSUED
CATHERINE MANN

Published by Silhouette Books

America's Publisher of Contemporary Romance

Special thanks and acknowledgment are given to Catherine Mann for her contribution to the ATHENA FORCE series.

SILHOUETTE BOOKS

ISBN 0-373-51332-1

PURSUED

Copyright © 2004 by Harlequin Books S.A.

Visit Silhouette Books at www.eHarlequin.com

Printed in U.S.A.

CATHERINE MANN

Bestselling author Catherine Mann writes contemporary military romances, a natural fit since she's married to her very own air force flyboy. Prior to publication, Catherine graduated with a B.A. in Fine Arts: Theater from the College of Charleston and received her master's degree in theater from UNC-Greensboro. Now a RITA® Award winner, Catherine finds that following her aviator husband around the world with four children, a beagle and a tabby in tow offers her endless inspiration for new, action-packed plots. Learn more about her work, as well as her adventures in military life, by visiting her Web site, http://catherinemann.com.

To my daughter Maggie, a kick-butt kid with an indomitable spirit, sharp mind and tender heart—truly a Bombshell heroine in the making. I love you, kiddo!

Chapter 1

"Negative G forces coming. Hold on to your lunch."

Captain Josie Lockworth, USAF, upped the throttle and pushed forward on the stick of her T-38 supersonic jet. Out of courtesy only, she offered the warning to reporter Shannon Conner strapped into the back seat.

Not that she had anything against reporters. Hell, she'd flown with top-notch embedded journalists in the Middle East. Her best friend was even a television correspondent.

This reporter, however, could only be called a hack. Her news network soaked up scandal like a thirsty rag. Josie couldn't afford bad press derailing her multimillion-dollar military test project. Forget the money, actually small change as far as the government was concerned.

Her mother's honor had been held hostage long enough.

The T-38 pierced a low-lying cloud. Blood rushed up to her head with negative G forces, the reverse of positive Gs that pushed blood down. The body tolerated fewer negative Gs before passing out. One negative G. Two. Three. Spots danced in front of her eyes on the mountainous horizon of the California desert.

Adrenaline sang through her veins. Sweat popped along her back through her T-shirt. Her flight suit clung like a second skin. But then the uniform was already as much a part of her as any epidermal layer.

She pulled back on the stick, glancing up at the mirror to check her passenger. Shannon was awake but slumped in her seat in the tight cockpit, one strand of blond hair sneaking out of her helmet to stick to her pale face.

No hurling yet. A twinge of respect trickled through Josie's steady focus, even a bit of sympathy.

But she did need to keep the reporter busy and disoriented. How better than nonstop acrobatics in a supersonic and nimble airplane? Shannon had insisted on the full-out flying experience. And Josie always delivered one hundred percent.

Tucking sideways, she slipped through a mountain pass. Through her clear top canopy, she watched the sandy landscape scroll past.

Josie forced oxygen in and out. Her huffed exhales echoed through the headset Darth Vader style. Near silence swallowed the cockpit, the only sound the rasp and drag of breathing through the oxygen mask since they'd left noise behind with speed.

As always, she flattened her frustration with the

familiar routine of flying. The trainer jet zipped along over a range near Edwards Air Force Base, approximately one hundred miles northeast of Los Angeles. Not much time left in this flight until she landed where she worked in a military detachment at the nearby Palmdale testing facility, also known as Air Force Plant 42. For a test pilot, steely nerves were mandatory, leaving no room for cranky emotions jangling her at a critical second. And during test missions, *any* second could be critical.

Okay, so this wasn't a test and she was pissed.

That someone like Shannon had been allowed access to Josie's current test project just proved higher-ups were only paying lip service to endorsing her work. Someone wanted this resurrected project that had once been her mother's to fail. Damaging press could facilitate their cause.

And yeah, yeah, she mentally rolled her eyes at her annoying voice of reason. Part of her still resented Shannon from their prep-school days at the Athena Academy for the Advancement of Women.

Advancement? Shannon had tried to advance Josie right out the front gates on a trumped-up charge of stealing.

Good God, as if.

Her stomach, which held strong against negative Gs, grew downright queasy over the notion of taking so much as a post office pen. But back then, Shannon had convinced everyone Josie was off her rocker, like her washed-up military mama. Who could expect reasonable behavior from a Lockworth lady?

Anger fired hotter than an afterburner, jangling the singing adrenaline off-key. Her combat boots braced on the rudders. She kept her right hand loose on the stick, her left on the two throttles, flicking up to adjust dials then landing back on the stick. Not a HOTAS—hands on throttle and stick, with all the buttons attached. In the T-38 she had to take her hands off the stick and throttle to work the controls. But for Shannon, she'd give a new spin to the HOTAS—Hands On Tummy and Sickbag.

She ran the stick fore and aft, gliding the T-38 through the sky in a porpoise-style swim along the rolling mountain range. Push for a hint of a negative G at the top of the sine wave. Pull for the kiss of a positive G at the bottom of sine wave. Push, pull. Push, pull.

"Uh, Josie?" Shannon's thready voice echoed over the headset. "Where's the eject button again?"

Crap. She'd gone too far, something she never did anymore. She steadied the stick. "Just a little PIO—pilot induced oscillation. My fault, and nothing to worry about. I've got it back under control."

Time to get herself under control, as well. She needed to tamp down the old impulsive Josie in favor of her more structured self she'd cultivated after her mother's breakdown. "We're on the straight and narrow now. As long as you keep your eyes forward, all will be normal."

Unlike looking to the side, where everything blurred with speed.

She hugged the terrain with skill and calm. No one would ever have reason to accuse her of weakness or emotional instability. She knew how hard she would have to fight even a whisper of that label, since her mother had been locked away after "the incident." But with this test project, Josie hoped to clear her mother's name and shake free of that dark legacy.

"Doing okay back there?" Josie's gaze flicked up to the mirror again.

"Just fine," the ever-prideful Shannon replied, brown eyes wide, makeup still impeccable.

Pride, Josie could understand. She had her fair share of that. Sad thing was, Shannon really packed a genius brain under all that uptight pettiness. Given the right direction, she could have been an incredible asset to the Athena Academy alumni list—if she'd made it to the twelfth grade instead of being punted out on an honor violation.

All a moot point since, more important, that genius brain could twist things against Josie in a heartbeat if the intellect wasn't otherwise occupied. And if her navigational calculations were correct, they were seconds away from a guaranteed distraction.

Bingo. Right on target, there it was, a nifty distraction for any brain. "Bet you wouldn't expect to see that out here."

"See what?"

"A nudist colony." She hoped her words didn't convey the grin she couldn't stifle.

Silence echoed over the headset, then, "You're making that up to get me to look over to the side where it's tougher to keep oriented with the motion. You just want to freak me out again."

"I'm only playing tour guide." Oh, yeah, completely in control again. "Not that I have anything against nudist colonies, but I can't help wondering. Why have one in the desert? I mean think about it. Wouldn't the sunscreen sting in sensitive places? And sitting on a metal lawn chair, a guy would really have to watch his butt and be careful of his, uh, well, hoo-hah hanging out there."

"And this helps me with my story how?" Broadcaster-neutral tones livened up with an extra touch of bitchiness.

"I'm trying to show you some of the local scenery. But if you don't think it will work, no problem. Besides, hoo-hah might be too technical a term for your viewers."

"You're so not funny."

This whole damned flight wasn't funny. And the threat Shannon posed to her career was downright terrifying, but Josie had to find moments of levity where she could. "You're right. I totally understand if you don't want to look. It's much easier to keep your lunch down if you're focusing forward." Now wasn't there a nifty life lesson there? "Watching out the side is only for folks with steely nerves."

She'd tossed down a gauntlet and Shannon would undoubtedly accept the challenge. Wait. Wait for it…

"Oh my God." Shannon's face went waxy in the mirror. She jerked back around front, gaze fixed on the horizon.

"Been that long since you saw a hoo-hah, huh?"

Shannon's growl echoed through the headset.

Josie concurred on a number of levels. Sadly, it had likely been even longer for her, since she didn't have time for a man lately, much less his hoo-hah.

Not that she would admit that to Shannon.

The woman resented her, always had. Right from their early teenage years at Athena Academy, Shannon had envied Josie's connections through her grandfather, past CIA director Joseph Lockworth. Poppy had been directly responsible for starting the prestigious all-girls prep school designed to empower women, many of them going on to government security jobs. With only two hundred students from grades seven through twelve, the bonds forged among students were tight and lifelong.

She still sweated bullets over how Shannon's little stunt had almost cost Josie her dream. Luckily, her best friend Tory Patton had worked her own investigative skills and proved Shannon was responsible for stealing the class's petty-cash fund and setting up Josie.

Josie's hands fisted tighter. She should just get over it. Besides, she had the Athena diploma. She could afford to be magnanimous. Adult.

Easing back the stick, Josie skimmed a more scenic route along California's desert valleys cut by the ridges of the Sierra Nevadas with the Kern River running through. She cranked an east turn away from the river valley, out of the Sierras back over flat land of dry lake beds and creosote bushes, closer to her Palmdale testing facility near Edwards AFB and closer to dropping off Shannon.

Josie continued a tour-guide litany while her passenger stayed silent for once. Thank God.

A road splitting the desert stretched straight and long ahead of her, marred only by the dust kicked up from a motorcycle bearing down toward the test facility. She lined up along the lone band of road, pacing, gaining ground on the rider. And why not? Everything in an aviator's life was a chance for competition.

Fringe rippled from the arms of the biker's leather

jacket giving off a Mad Max air that fit well with the scattered miners, desert rats in rusted trailers. Wild and untamed, like the old Josie who was no longer allowed free rein. The taboo element entranced her all the more for being forbidden. Even while she rambled her scenic explanations to Shannon, Josie couldn't look away from a sight and yearning that held her attention beyond any hoo-hah.

Her headset crackled with a cleared throat. Shannon's interruption yanked Josie's attention back to the cockpit.

"Too bad you couldn't get Tory to cover your dog-and-pony show. No doubt she would have televised anything you wanted. That loyalty among classmates is something else. You two even covered for a pregnant friend once—what happened to Kayla and her kid anyway? Did she ever find a man to marry her?"

Okay, that ripped it. The old Josie still humming just below the surface kicked her adrenaline level up into a freaking aria. "For a smart woman, you sure do say some mighty unwise things at times."

She could put up with someone smacking at her. But her innate sense of justice, which had once earned her the label "Josephine, the Tattletale Queen," really balked at letting an injustice go unavenged.

Nobody messed with her friends.

"You know, Shannon, I don't think I'm lined up just right. We need to go around." She clicked on the radio. "Palmdale Tower, Bat two-zero on the go."

Josie popped the jet into afterburners, dumping raw gas into the exhaust stream like a pilot light on a stove igniting, pumping up the speed. *Thwump.* The plane jolted from the swift kick in the ass. Exhilaration trilled within her like the final high note exploding free to reverberate through an auditorium.

Her eyes flicked to the mirror. Shannon's face had turned cucumber.

"Ah, hell, Shannon—" she couldn't quite suppress the sarcasm "—I probably should have told you I was going to do that."

Shannon grappled at the face mask. Her throat worked, then cranked down in a swallow. Impressive move, holding back the volcano of vomit that would have spewed up through the mask.

Enough payback for one day. Point made. The last echoes of justice faded, leaving an emptiness inside her that grew increasingly difficult to ignore.

Josie leveled off at five hundred feet above the runway. "Palmdale Tower, Bat two-zero requesting left closed."

"Left closed approved. Repeat base."

"Bat two-zero, left base with gear."

The control tower responded, "Bat two-zero, clear to land. No traffic."

Coming in. Landing. One hundred and fifty miles per hour at impact, the tires screeched in protest of the brakes. She kept the nose up to bleed off speed, as well until…*poof,* the plane's nose tilted down and kissed asphalt. The plane taxied down the runway at a sedate pace.

Hand easing back on the throttle, she slowed, pulling off onto the hammerhead toward Shannon's waiting television cameraman. "Palmdale, Bat two-zero clear the active. Going to ground control." She switched frequencies. "Palmdale ground, Bat two-zero. Clear the active. Request parking."

"Bat two-zero, taxi via Alpha," ground control responded. "Back to spot sixteen. Caution construction. Right-hand side of Alpha at Bravo."

A blue pickup truck slid in front of her with a "follow me" sign in back to lead her onto the tarmac. The sun's rays baked through the clear canopy, desert temps still notching in November. Her flight suit stuck to her back against the leather seat as she followed the truck past the guy waving wand flashlights toward the parking spot—

And toward a uniformed man, the major, her boss, standing and waiting.

Not good. The murky cloud over her day went opaque.

Major Mike Bridges had no doubt made the trip out to the flight line to coincide with her landing for a reason. Since he stood by the hangar housing her two modified test models of the Predator unmanned spy drone, he must be here for her. A problem? If so, she needed scoop-hungry Shannon Conner out of the way before any discussion.

Josie whipped off her helmet and deplaned. Wind tore across the treeless expanse, lifting her short hair, drying the sweat on her body with gritty gusts. Her combat boots smacked steamy asphalt three steps behind Shannon, who was staggering toward the nearest trash can. Shannon gripped the metal edges and leaned, her borrowed flight suit stretching across her heaving back. *Wonder if the cameraman will document that part?*

Her boss frowned. Josie cringed, then braced. He'd only assumed command a month ago, so she still wasn't sure where she stood in regard to his approval and respect. Still, she'd followed orders today—show the reporter around and pull out all the stops. Okay, so she'd worked in a little revenge for her friend along with it.

And at a totally sucky time.

She needed to lay low after the fallout from her helicopter diversionary stunt she'd pulled to help one of her Athena grad friends with a mission a few months ago. Another wrong she'd leaped in to avenge and damn the consequences. She'd never quite understood why being right wasn't always the right thing.

Regardless, her flight and fun were over.

A rumble from behind the hangar interrupted her thoughts seconds before a Harley rolled into view. The same low-rider cruiser she'd seen from her plane roared up with the guy wearing black leather.

The motorcycle jerked to a stop by the fence gate. The fringe on the man's arms rippled. The growling engine shushed.

One boot slammed the cement. A muscled thigh in faded blue jeans and black chaps swung over. The second boot pounded pavement. He tugged off the helmet, shaking free coal-dark hair longer than any military regs allowed. The thick mane hit his shoulders.

Definitely not military.

He smacked along his leather-clad thighs, dusting, the action and chaps drawing attention to a hoo-hah package that—

Nope. Not gonna go there even in her mind. Too much talk of hoo-hahs must have her hormones on overload.

Her P.C. call sign might have started out as a Josie and the Pussy Cats reference, but she'd quickly redirected it to Politically Correct. She had rights and wrongs down pat. Checking out a man's hoo-hah was as disrespectful as an ass-check from him.

Even if this guy didn't have a problem with women who flew jets and shot the big guns like other men she'd seen outside the workplace, she didn't have time for a relationship. Hell, she barely had time to do her laundry.

Once she cleared her mother's name, her life would be different. Then she could shake off the ghosts of her past and not worry so much about the repercussions of letting the occasional emotion slip free.

She turned her attention back to the upchucking reporter, reaching into her thigh pocket for a pack of tissues and a peppermint. Silently she passed Shannon the candy and tissues.

Blond hair straggling forward, Shannon snatched the offerings and started restoring order for a camera appearance. "My feature about you is going to suck, you know."

"We both know it was going to anyway." Josie popped a peppermint into her mouth, as well, and clicked it to the side against her teeth.

Life might not always be right or fair, but people were predictable for the most part. There was something comforting about that, even when it brought negative garbage her way. At least she could see it coming and strategize.

After her mother's breakdown and discharge from the air force, Josie had submerged all impulsiveness, clinging to clear-cut reason and stability. Except for a brief lapse today with shaking up Shannon, she'd stuck to her plan. Emotionalism, injustice, any upset in the cosmos launched jitters in Josie's tummy that left her HOTAS.

Her wayward eyes skipped right over to the biker making his way toward her commander. What the hell were the two of them plotting? Her instincts screamed *ambush ahead.*

Chapter 2

Fifteen minutes later, Josie watched the dark blue military truck depart, Shannon Conner, her cameraman and personal agendas safely on their way off government property.

Time to turn her attention to whatever had brought her boss out to the flight line. Biker Boy had his back to her now as he faced her boss in deep conversation. What a contrast they made—Major Mike Bridges with his cropped brown hair and military precision next to the man with wild hair and dusty gear.

Bridges's easygoing smile smoothed the edges of authority. He'd become a well-liked leader in the short time since he'd transferred to California and assumed command of the detachment at the military's Palmdale testing facility. Josie didn't need to see the other man's face to know he was far removed from easygoing. The set to his shoulders, the tightly leashed energy in his loose-hipped stance all lent a dangerous air.

Not good.

Her ambush alert and jitters double-timed. As if the flight with Shannon hadn't already shown her too well how easily unruly emotionalism could slither in to affect her actions. Unacceptable, especially now.

Over twenty years ago her mother had been a young captain in the air force, as well, a test engineer working to improve stealth on aircraft. Her dreams had tanked in a horrible crash that killed the pilot and resulted in an investigation resulting in the blame falling on Josie's mother. Zoe Lockworth had resigned her commission and suffered a mental breakdown.

Josie was stronger than that, damn it. And thanks to an air force now more open to having female pilots, she would fly the riskier test missions for this project herself.

Shoulders squared with military precision, she approached her detachment commander beside the looming hangar. Bridges's gaze zipped up from the conversation. Smoky eyes met hers with a steam quickly banked by professionalism.

Damn. She almost stumbled at the impact. She knew her boss was attracted to her—not that he'd ever made an overt move—and she wasn't stupid enough to cross that line, either. No hoo-hah was worth risking her career, and apparently he concurred.

But if he wasn't her superior? What if their paths crossed later, once she'd made major and moved on to another position? Maybe. There was much to respect about Bridges, his drive, his humor. She'd even been attracted to him the first time she'd seen him days before his command assignment had been announced.

All moot now because he *was* her superior and she did have a job to complete. Besides, she didn't date guys she worked with. She'd seen firsthand with her parents' dual military marriage how tough joint service relationships could be.

She would just continue to ignore his good looks—and the quickly disguised appreciation in his eyes. "Good afternoon, Major."

"Captain Lockworth," Major Bridges called, voice carrying on the tearing desert wind. "Come speak with us for a moment."

. "Yes, sir." She closed the distance between herself and the pair.

The biker pivoted on his boot heel toward her and nailed her with brooding brown eyes that bordered on black. She didn't stumble. She downright stopped for two seconds before regaining her balance and plowing forward.

All right, she was an adult woman with a normal sex drive, but she wouldn't let it or anything else control her. She blinked away the haze and found the hard features in front of her niggled at her brain with familiarity.

Bridges nodded, no exchange of salutes required on the runway. "Good flight, Captain?"

"The reporter got her money's worth."

Chuckles rumbled from her boss. Brooding brown eyes from their guest even twinkled for a flash. Where had she seen him before?

She stared, trying to place…

He quirked a brow at her.

Josie willed away a blush too juvenile for a seasoned combat vet and thrust out her hand. "Captain Josie Lockworth."

His hand enfolded hers in calluses and heat.

"Diego Morel. Pleasure to meet you."

His husky drawl stirred the taste of Southern Comfort on her tongue. A strange notion for a woman who never risked the loss of control brought on by alcohol. And an unwelcome notion.

Realization clicked into a radar lock. Awe stilled her.

No wonder he seemed familiar. She'd seen him around from a distance since she'd begun working at Palmdale, even if their paths had never crossed for her projects. Diego Morel—or Cruiser, as he'd once been known—was considered a god in the testing community. A former military test pilot, he'd flown with dazzling grace, the plane such a part of him it seemed to respond to his mere thoughts.

He'd been expected to take his place in aviation history alongside Chuck Yeager, until a simple undetected sinus infection had caused his eardrums to rupture during a grueling mission that cost the life of his wingman. All was normal for him on the ground, but he suffered vertigo in the air.

The winged god was now earthbound for life.

Sympathy whispered through her like clouds dusting her windscreen. His eyes hardened.

Damn. She needed to hide her emotions better. She'd hated those pitying looks after her mother's problems came to light.

Josie withdrew the hand she hadn't even realized was still clasped in his. "It's an honor to meet you in person. I flew your full-hydraulic-failure, engine-control-only approach profile in test-pilot school. That was pioneering work you did back in the day."

Would he accept her olive branch?

His weathered features smoothed into a smile. "Yeah, 'back in the day' this old Mississippi dog could hunt."

Bridges cleared his throat. "I imagine you're wondering why we're here."

Josie gathered her composure. "It crossed my mind, sir."

"I wanted to be the first to tell you."

"Tell me what?" And why was Morel on hand to hear it?

Curious eyes bored into her back. From whom? So many people populated the runway—maintenance, security, other pilots doing a walk-around check of a plane.

Bridges frowned at the activity, then waved toward the hangar door. "Let's step inside where we can speak privately."

Crap. This didn't sound good. "Sure."

She punched in the cipher lock code and pushed through the side door, leaving the two men to follow. Silence blanketed the metal cavern, disturbed as their footsteps bounced an echo up into the rafters and down again. Her pair of modified Predators sprawled immobile, the dimmed security lights high overhead casting a night-lamp glow on the white-and-gray sleeping crafts. Not overly large, each craft measured 320.4 inches long and 580.8 inches wide from tip to tip, or approximately twenty-six by forty-eight feet.

The UAV—unmanned aerial vehicles—were medium altitude, long range. Flown by a pilot from remote control, they could be guided from countries away, data transmitted instantly through a satellite.

Test models were also equipped with an outboard seat for a pilot to ride along wearing a parachute. An override set of controls had been installed, as well, so that the ride-along pilot could assume command and save the craft if the remote control went to hell during testing. Since the Predator didn't have a traditional cockpit, the pilot perched on a saddlelike seat with a high back, straddling the fuselage. With no clear canopy covering, such as on small jets, he or she flew out there in the open, as flyers had done in the old days.

Prior to entering test-pilot school, Josie had flown the U-2 Dragon Lady spy plane. She'd donned her space suit and popped above ninety-five percent of the earth's atmosphere, penetrating enemy air space to gather intel. And while she would do it again in a heartbeat if called in defense of her country, the Predator's intelligence-gathering methods didn't risk lives.

Except the pretty baby was damn noisy. Actually only a whisper of propeller engines, but still enough to announce its arrival if the heat of battle didn't mask the sound.

That flaw made it the perfect craft for continuing her mother's theories, since her mother had been part of the early work on improving stealth for bomber aircraft. Other testers had taken another scientific path after the fatal failure, and a different form of improved stealth was added to the inventory.

Zoe Lockworth's input was no longer needed in the bomber world. But here with the Predator, Josie could use a piece of her mother's idea involving acoustic stealth. If proven, it would be invaluable to the nation's defense.

Josie stroked a hand along the Predator's sleek

white side. Clearing her mother's name wouldn't give
Zoe Lockworth back her ruined military career. It
wouldn't give her two daughters back the lost years
with their mom as she'd drifted deeper into depression
over the loss of her life's dream.

But it was the only present Josie could offer a mama
who'd been too medicated to enjoy the gift of a clay
handprint from art class. Her mother had recovered her
mind. Now Josie intended to give her back her pride.

Morel cast a threatening shadow across her Predator.

Josie stepped between him and the plane before
turning to her boss. "Sir? What is it you want to tell
me and why here?"

Bridges drew up alongside. "I thought if we're
going to have a scene, it's better that we should have
it in here, away from everyone else."

She prepped herself for the worst. "There won't be
a scene, Major, but could we cut to the chase, please?"

"Your test program went under congressional oversight this week."

Her program had *not* been scratched. Relief almost
staggered her back a step. Then the subtle crosswinds
of his words whipped over her along with suspicions.
Her program was still in danger.

Why? This project wasn't near big enough to be
under congressional oversight, a safeguard usually re-
served for programs budgeted over one point three
billion dollars. Her project ranked more in the twenty-
five-million range.

That her little budget had landed on congressional
radar didn't bode well. "And Morel's reason for being
included in this meeting?"

"You may or may not know that Morel consults for contractors and the government. He's been tapped to report back to a congressional committee on how the program is really going without any sugarcoating by the air force. Nothing will change in how you do business. You'll just have someone walking behind you while you do it."

"A contractor spy." She softened her words with a smile. No scene, but even an idiot would know this sort of news would piss off any tester. These two men weren't idiots.

"That's not the label I would choose," Bridges quibbled.

"A baby-sitter then?"

Her boss shrugged, his classically handsome face neutral. "Whichever label makes you less uncomfortable."

Both sucked.

Although "spy" seemed more appropriate, since she'd never had a baby-sitter who looked like that.

Morel lounged against a support beam. "Listen, little lady—"

"Little lady?" She struggled to keep her voice steady and soft. "I'm the program manager for this test, not some Powerpuff Girl."

He studied her with hooded eyes before a slow grin creased his face. "Lockworth, you might want to be careful about selling short those Powerpuff Girls. If I understand my Powerpuff lore correctly, Blossom's a commander with a bright future and Buttercup is one helluva fighter, like you."

What a hoo-hah. "Well, I'm still not a Buttercup."

His smile turned as hard as his eyes. "And I'm not

a spy. Furthermore, I'm sure as hell not the baby-sitter sort. I'm just here to help out where I can and tell it like it is. A test program that fails before it gets off the ground is still a success because it means a faulty program wasn't launched for somebody to die in the air. Remember that."

Damn. Already he was talking about nixing her program, not to mention the veiled reference to her mother.

Josie pressed her lips together to hold back a torrent of frustrated words. This man held her future in his hands. More important, he held her mother's past. "Of course. My apologies for the spy comment. I was just caught off guard. I'm sure you understand the frustrations of this side of the testing fence. Scheduling is tight enough without extra paperwork. But we'll just plug in an extra coffeepot."

"Coffee? Lifeblood in a flying community." Morel cranked his lazy smile up a notch. "We're gonna get along just fine, Buttercup."

Buttercup? She cringed.

He might be an ass, but at least he'd let her off the hook easily. She had to appreciate that they were back on even footing, playing the diplomacy game. She would bury him in paperwork, data and reports. God knows she was good at details.

Starting now. "Which would you rather do first? A walk around the aircraft? Or should we head straight over to my office for a prelim brief on our progress to date?"

"We can do that tomorrow. How about you bring me up to speed over a beer?"

A beer? She didn't drink and she rarely socialized.

She didn't have time to waste shooting the breeze in a bar, especially during duty hours. Probably why she'd never met this man face-to-face, if that's how he preferred to spend his after-work hours.

Bridges gave her a pointed look. Play the game.

Fair enough. She understood the rules of this boys' club and knew how to play them her own way on her own terms. "We can talk just as well over drinks as we can in the office. I'd be honored to hear a legend's take on the merits of computer simulations replacing actual flight tests."

Legend, my butt.

Grinding her teeth in frustration, Josie forced herself to lounge against the quarter panel of her Mustang outside the Wing and a Prayer Bar while she waited. And waited. And waited longer while Diego Morel took his sweet time parking his bike, stowing his helmet, making sure his Harley was parked just so under the security light.

Holy crap, she'd be ready for retirement by the time they made it inside.

He'd chosen the locale, deep in the California desert, a flyer hangout with an airplane tail sticking out of the roof. Music vibrated through the walls, rowdy voices swelling from the back porch and over. She would have preferred somewhere quieter where he could have his draft and she could order a grilled chicken salad while they talked. But he was calling the shots. And as long as they discussed business, she would be content.

Finally he finished playing nursemaid to his Harley and started across the gravel lot toward the door without a glance in her direction.

Hello? Did the guy not even remember she was here?

Josie shoved away from the car. "Well sure, I'd love to join you. Right this way."

He shot a quick glance her way. "Did you say something, Buttercup?"

Buttercup. She forced herself not to roll her eyes. "Nope. Just tagging along with you. You're calling the shots tonight."

There, that sounded nice, didn't it?

"Hmm. Somehow I doubt that." He swept open the door with a near-mocking flourish.

Josie stepped into the doorway, pausing half in, half out to give herself time to adjust to the blasting cacophony of clanking glasses, blaring music and conversations shouted to rise over it all.

"Great place, huh?" He drank in the atmosphere like a favored microbrew.

"Great." And entirely too packed.

He crowded her space until she had to continue inside. At least now they would get down to business. She scanned the room. The din of voices blended with the never-ending blare of old military movies. Airplane parts loaded most of the walls. He ambled inside, his eyes gravitating to the back door leading to the porch. The wall out there sported hundreds of signatures from test pilots, hers included. She'd scrawled her "Jane" Hancock during the one and only other time she'd been here—a mandatory appearance to celebrate her first test flight.

Through the press of bodies, she spotted a couple pushing back their chairs to leave. "Looks like there's an empty table there in the corner—"

Josie glanced over her shoulder. No Morel. Great. She searched and found him settling on a bar stool in front of one of the airplane "sticks" for drunks to "fly." Talk about frequent flyer miles. This guy must have racked up more than his fair share, given how everyone knew him.

Patience, she reminded herself. And no unruly emotions.

By the time his beer and her water arrived, someone recognized him, which led to another beer with a couple of C-17 pilots in California on a TDY—temporary duty—from South Carolina. Three drinks later, he asked, "Want another water?"

"No thanks. My eyeballs are floating." Enough already. She could be polite while still drawing boundaries. "If you don't want to talk about my project, that's cool. But could you please let me know so I can return to work?"

"No need to head back just yet."

"What does any of this have to do with my test?"

"We're building a working relationship. I'm watching how you operate, getting into your head. Understanding the way you see things will help me interpret your data."

"Sounds to me like an excuse to knock back beers with your pals. But however you want to play the game."

The duo of C-17 pilots stood with apologies and calls of "Catch ya later, dude, gotta find some food."

Morel sighed. "Listen up, Buttercup—"

Josie propped a boot on the lowest rung of his bar stool in an aggressive move forward he couldn't mistake. "That's Captain Buttercup, thank you very much."

"To Captain Buttercup." He toasted her with a pull off his bottle before slamming it back down on the scarred wood of the bar. "Those guys actually had some damned interesting insights on the Predator's performance during a hostage rescue mission overseas. You might not be so pissed if you'd actually bothered to listen."

Damn it, he had a point. Her innate sense of justice was a real pain in the butt sometimes. "Score one for you. But in the interest of fair play—" and she was always fair "—it would help if you included me in these conversations, Major."

"For the record, I'm plain old mister these days. I'm not in the air force anymore." His fist twitched around the flight stick mounted on the bar, thumb absently stroking.

Contrition nipped. Hard. He was an ass, no question, but God, he'd lost so much. She couldn't imagine having her feet nailed to the ground. Like her mother, he'd had his dream taken away. Her mother had gone mad. Had this man perhaps simply gotten mad? Her boot dropped back to the floor. "I'm sorry."

"Don't be. I didn't die. I'm still working tests, just from the other end. I'm lucky and I know it." He motioned to the bartender for another round.

"Okay then." She hitched up onto the bar stool next to him. "I'm sorry for the air force's loss of your flying talent."

His eyes narrowed as he lifted the new bottle toward his mouth. "Watch it Buttercup. That was damn near a compliment."

"Your skill in the air is a matter of record. I've made it more than clear how much I respect your work." Her attention shifted to a crowd back by the pool table. "And speaking of work, *finally*—" She waved to one of her workmates striding toward the pool table and gestured him over. "Hey Craig, come meet the newest member of our team."

The pilot loped closer, red hair, freckles and boyish even nearing thirty. Josie smiled a greeting. "Diego Morel, this is Craig Wagner. He's one of the pilots assigned to my team and a great asset to the program."

"A pleasure to meet you." Wagner pumped the handshake. "While Josie and I were in test-pilot school together, instructors used your quick look reports as models, sir."

"Thanks. But drop the sir. Diego's fine. All this sir stuff is starting to make me feel ancient."

Ancient? Josie studied Morel for the first time beyond just a threat to her program and considered him as a person. A man. Maybe ten years her senior, but still a hundred percent in his prime—even half drunk on his ass.

Craig saluted Morel with a lift of his beer. "You earned the sir label early."

"Ah, you're more diplomatic than your boss, Wagner."

Wagner's boss? Josie frowned. She didn't really think of herself as his boss, although technically she was. He was just a guy whose work she respected. One of the best fliers out there and she needed that. Sure they were the same age and had gone through test training together, but they were friends, too. She hated that Morel was making her question if Craig might be harboring resentments.

Josie dunked another lemon in her water. "Morel is

on loan to us from the subcontractor. He'll be offering feedback on our procedures." She would fill Craig in on the rest later.

"Excellent. I look forward to working with you."

"Same here."

Wagner pivoted on his boot heels toward Josie, creating a pseudo privacy wall blocking her from Diego. "See you for dinner after I get back from the Red Flag exercise?"

Morel's eyes bored into her back. Was he taking notes even now? She couldn't afford to discount his influence just because he'd knocked back a few drinks. "The Friday after you return, at seven, right? I may be a little late but I'll be there."

"Cool, I'll have the grill fired up and ready." Wagner pivoted back to Morel. "Great meeting you, sir. I look forward to working together."

Sir.

Morel winced. "Same here."

As Wagner threaded through the crowd back to his table, Morel motioned for another beer. "Do you and he have a thing going?"

Damn. She didn't need this. "God, no. He's a friend from test-pilot school. Besides, he's married with a kid and another on the way."

She was adamant about no relationships with fellow service members, a big part of why she'd decided to ignore the initial spark of attraction she'd felt for Bridges.

"You're having dinner together."

"At his house. With his wife and their daughter," she paused, then rushed to add, "once they get back from visiting her mother, in case you're wondering why he's here without her on a Friday night."

His skeptical snort did little to alleviate her concerns.

"Marriage doesn't always stop some folks from hooking up, Buttercup."

This guy was beyond jaded, which didn't bode well for her. "Well, it most definitely stops me."

"Good." He didn't bother halting his assessing smile.

She glanced down at his ring finger. Bare. No cheater lines. "With all due respect, are you hitting on me?"

"With all due respect, if I was hitting on you, you wouldn't need to ask."

"Fair enough." She reached to loop her hair behind one ear, her hand pausing mid-motion at the flirty gesture. Subconscious no doubt, but enough to stir the air like raw fuel dumped on engines to kick a plane into afterburners.

Her hand jerked into motion again, completing the hair smoothing with a defiant sweep. "And if you were hitting on me, sleeping with someone in my chain of command isn't allowed."

Damn. Damn. Damn. Now he had her thinking about sex. Was he messing with her mind? Setting her up by seeing if she would take the bait?

"Technically, Captain Buttercup, I'm not in your chain of command. It might not be wise for us to screw around while we're working together. But there's no rule that says we can't." He held up his bottle to forestall her interruption. "Just to be clear on the technicalities."

Either way, setup or not, time to put this guy in his professional place. "Thanks for the clarification. Not that it's a problem here anyway since you aren't hitting on me."

"Of course. Because like I said, you would know." He pulled another slow drag off his beer before thunking it down on the bar. "And for the record, don't get your G-suit in a knot about whether or not I can do my job. I've got more time at the urinal in tests than you have in the air force."

"Lovely," she muttered. "What a hoo-hah."

"Pardon me?"

"Uh, wah-hoo. Like a cheer. Or a toast." She lifted her water glass. "Here's to the success of my test project and all the, uh, experience you're bringing to table. Wah-hoo."

Josie clinked her glass to his bottle. The guy's losses might tug at the sympathy strings, and she understood full well she had to be patient and play nice. But if his incompetence threatened her program, she wouldn't hesitate to bring him down.

Chapter 3

Her head was ready to explode with frustration.

Josie made tracks through the parking lot toward her Mustang convertible. Alone. Luckily, legends were able to nab plenty of designated-driver offers after a few too many beers.

They hadn't once discussed her test. Although, maybe his slack attitude could work well for her program. She could feed him positive data, downplay trouble spots. She would work through any bugs given time, and she needed to pass this investigation in order to have that time.

Winding her way through haphazardly parked cars, she stayed alert for drunks or any other possible threats. The survival knife in her boot pressed a steely reassurance against her calf.

Across the lot, she noticed a vehicle parking beside

hers, even though there were plenty of other closer spots. Excellent night vision clearly identified a familiar red SUV with a "1 Pilot" license plate.

Number One Pilot. She suppressed a groan.

Bridges? Waiting for her again?

After dark.

Damn it. He was a professional, as was she, but she hated this itchy feeling of unease. He likely didn't mean a thing with the parking spot and she wouldn't think twice about it if they were the same gender. However, gossip was hell and with her mother's history she was hypersensitive about negative press.

Just when she'd decided to haul butt back inside, three other figures stepped from the SUV and erased suspicion. A general rounded to the back bumper along with two colonels. Bridges was hanging with the big dogs tonight.

Continuing toward her car, Josie snapped a salute to the senior officers. "Good evening, sirs."

Bridges slammed his door and nodded. "Good evening, Captain. Hold on if you have a minute. I'd like you to meet our guests."

Bridges made the introductions to the general and two colonels who'd flown into Palmdale on an unplanned visit. "I was filling General Quincy in on the kick-ass flight you gave the network reporter this afternoon. Folks up in the control tower said that was some fine flying, Lockworth."

"Thank you, sir. Just doing my job." She might wonder about Bridges at times personally, but professionally, he was a good boss when it came to giving positive face-time for those under his command.

General Quincy's stars winked in the lamplight. "Let's hope positive media coverage comes our way. We could use some additional congressional funding next fiscal year."

Josie struggled not to flinch. "Let's hope, sir."

"I'll be on the lookout for the feature piece." Quincy's attention skated to the bar, thank God. "We just finished dinner at the Officer's Club and I wanted to see if this place has changed since I did some work at Palmdale and Edwards back in the Dark Ages. Do they still have the signature wall?"

"Yes, sir, right out on the back porch. It would be a crime to paint over it."

"Outstanding. I'll bet it's full now." He turned to Bridges. "What do you say we check it out, gentlemen?"

As Josie watched them leave, warning lights blazed in her mind. What was up with their unscheduled visit? There were too many upsets crashing down in one day for her liking.

First the flight with a reporter who hated her guts. Then a congressional oversight appointee who didn't give a crap about anything but shooting the breeze with flyers over a beer. And now the general directly in her chain of command showing up out of the blue on the same day—and talking about her.

Coincidence? It didn't feel that way.

She shook off the paranoia. Wouldn't they have a field day if she expressed her concerns? It was already going to hit the fan anyway when Shannon's story came out if something wasn't done to counterbalance that report.

Starting now. She'd never been one to wait around for fate to stab her in the back.

Fishing out her keys, Josie thumbed the unlock button. She hadn't stood a chance with Shannon's interview anyway. The dazzling flight plan was her only hope of showing higher-ups she'd at least tried to give the reporter her money's worth—even if she'd also taken some personal satisfaction in shaking up Shannon.

Josie slid into her car, locked herself inside and tugged her e-mail pager from her flight suit thigh pocket. Sure she could e-mail at home in twenty minutes, but she hated the solitariness of her place. Probably came from spending years in a jam-packed boarding-school environment.

She needed to send out feelers to her network of contacts and discover what was going on with the congressional investigation. Athena Academy grads watched each other's backs. Nobody messed with their friends and got away with it.

And Athena afforded her some hefty contacts. Only the best were invited to attend.

Their high-powered professions around the world made group reunions in person damn near impossible, so instead Athena alumni relied on the Internet and their government-secure alumni Web site for communication in their high-octane lives. She hadn't even been able to make the recent funeral for one of her older classmates and a personal friend, Rainy Miller.

How unfair and unbelievable to think of Rainy as gone. Nothing about her death made sense.

Josie sagged back against her seat, feeling too mortal. She'd tried to think through everything on her project. But then so had her mother, and still someone had died.

Rainy had also died in a suspicious car accident only days after calling an emergency meeting with Josie and their five closest friends from Athena Academy. Rainy had died on the way to the meeting. Now they were all seeking answers, and the questions were piling up even faster. Most recently, Samantha St. John had tracked down the man responsible for killing Rainy, an assassin known as the Cipher. Unfortunately, Sam had killed him without learning who had sent him to murder Rainy.

God, she was getting morbid and that wasn't her style. She preferred action. She clutched the e-mailer in her hand and scanned through her inbox, which was packed with everything from questions about the Cipher to details of Tory Patton's latest date with the new man in her life.

A reply to Tory would be a good place to start in diffusing Shannon. Josie tapped through a message to her old classmate and closest friend Tory, who worked for Shannon's rival network. Tory would be more than glad to one-up Shannon, since she'd recently caught the traitorous witch buck naked in bed with Tory's former producer and now ex-boyfriend. Things had worked out for the best, though. Tory had hooked up with Ben Forsythe, a man worthy of her. Ben was the brother of another member of the group, Alexandra. Or Alex, as she preferred to be called.

Josie hit Send on her e-mail, then started a second note to her sister, who'd graduated a few classes behind her at Athena Academy. Damn, but Diana had been young when Dad had shipped them both off to the boarding school.

Her fingers paused midway through the message.

She and Diana hardly ever talked anymore, the rift between them widening over the years. Rainy's death should remind them all to reach out more.

Josie fished in her leg pocket for her cell phone. Her fingers closed around her lip gloss. She pitched it in her lap before tugging free the phone and dialing Diana's number. The fact that her baby sister worked in army intelligence out in Arizona would offer enough of an excuse to call that Diana wouldn't go into shock over hearing her voice.

If she even recognized it.

While the phone rang, Josie defiantly swiped on a coating of lip gloss. She'd wear orange tryst if she wanted, and it had nothing to do with questionable looks from Diego Morel or Mike Bridges.

The extension picked up. "Hello?"

"Hey, Diehard." Josie pumped cheer into her voice and worked to recall happier times of horseback races, her little sister's blond pigtails streaking behind her. "It's me. Your bossy big sister. I've got a favor to ask, if you have time to talk for a minute."

The five-count silence was deafening.

"Uh, sure, Josie. What can I do for you?"

Stunned or resentful? Who could tell anymore with Diana?

Josie tucked down into her leather seat for a more comfy chat, her eyes locked on the neon spotlight showcasing the plane tail sticking out of the top of the bar's roof.

"I was wondering if you could track down some insider scoop on a retired air force test pilot, Major Diego Morel."

* * *

Through the air conditioner-fogged bar window, he watched Josie Lockworth's silver-gray Mustang, the car the same color as her arrogant eyes.

The bitch had to be stopped.

"Birddog," as he was called these days, nursed his bottle of beer while others at the table discussed her project and her future, how lucky she'd been to have this chance to resurrect her mother's work. Of course, some made their own luck. He savored the taste of hops and success. His eyes stayed focused on the window, on Lockworth. He kept silent. Listened. Planned while his thumb cleaned condensation from his bottle.

Her test data would be proved eventually. He didn't doubt that. But with Lockworth out of the picture, he could make his own modifications. The success would be deemed his.

He could not allow her to assume the credit—her or her mother. By the time they split all the accolades, there'd be little left to go around. Tough enough to accept defeat if another man assumed the glory, but how unacceptable to be beaten by a woman.

Ego? Sure. But ego was damned important for fliers. The godlike feeling in the air had enabled him to hurtle his body through the clouds in nothing more than a tin can.

And walk away victorious.

It was all about the victory.

He'd been willing to share the fame at one time, until the subtle rejections started from *her.* Never anything overt, but the *back off* was clear all the same. The Lockworth bitch barely noticed his existence.

But he'd sure as hell noticed her.

His eyes lasered in on the Mustang convertible, where a feminine shadow moved inside. Images reeled through his mind of womanly flesh. Lithe, soft.

Naked.

He flexed his fingers along the scarred wood table to capture the imagined sensation of sliding his hand through silky brown hair. Tighter he gripped as if to tug her closer, pulling harder while he pounded deeper. The mere fantasy left him shaking. What he wouldn't give for the reality of having her under him.

Definitely under.

"Birddog, are you with us?"

Hearing his call sign brought him back to the present. Lust still pounded through him, painful, unrelenting and with no hope of relief. Not with the kind he wanted, anyway.

He forced his fingers to relax, his thoughts to clear and flicked away stray pretzels from the table. "Absolutely. How about another round? This one's on me."

Cheers lifted, blending with the camaraderie of the bar. Birddog instructed the waitress to keep his tab open while he assessed his drinking partners. Nobody suspected a thing. And they never would, because he had control of every detail.

He would simply keep closer watch now. The opportunity to stall her project would present itself. He only needed to be patient. Then he would bring Josie Lockworth down fast in a ball of flames.

The conversation with her sister was spiraling downward.

Fast.

Josie tucked the cell phone to her ear with one hand and pitched a Beanie Baby puppy up and down in her other while watching car after car pull out of the bar parking lot. She and her sister had covered work, Athena news and exhausted every superficial conversational topic on the planet. Neither sister wanted to be the one to say they really had nothing important to discuss, nothing important to share, sister style.

And if they dared try broaching a deeper topic, they could very well end up arguing about their parents. Diana defensive of their father and disdainful of their mother. Josie protective of their mother and pissed at their father's emotional abandonment. How ironic that their parents were still together, but the discord between the sisters had never fully healed.

So she continued to pitch the toy basset hound and keep the conversation light, an odd turnabout when she'd never been a quitter or a coward. Why back off in a relationship that should be special?

The whole mortality deal swamped over her again.

Okay. She'd take a shot at communicating with her sister while staying off dangerous territory about their parents.

"How's life treating you, kid?" She mentally kicked herself for the kid comment. What a way to sabotage reaching out from the get-go.

Diana had prickly down to a fine art when it came to being the younger sister wanting to outdo her older sibling. But sometimes it was hard to imagine Diana as anything other than a dimple-cheeked kid with no front teeth.

"I'm fine. Busy at work, but fine, *Josephine*."

Josephine. Josie stifled a wince at her sister's apparent payback for the kid comment.

What a name to be saddled with for life. God, she'd hated the first day of any new school year when the "official" roll was called. Josephine Lockworth. Those early days at Athena seemed so long ago, the initial days when the Cassandra group had formed under Rainy's senior leadership. Sam, with her huge chip on her shoulder. Tory, the motor-mouth attention hog. Darcy, the kiss-ass. Serious Kayla, with no sense of humor. Alex the snob. And, of course, Josephine, the Tattletale Queen.

A smile flickered. It was a wonder they hadn't blown apart the school with their arguments in the early days. But slowly, surely, an unbreakable bond had formed as a group of hardheaded leaders figured out how to combine their strengths into an unbeatable team. Rainy, a senior, had been their group leader. Before she'd graduated, they'd all made a vow. If one called for help, the others would rally. No questions asked. They called it their Cassandra promise—a promise invoked by Rainy's call just before her fatal accident.

Another car grumbled past the bar's front window. "I'm glad to hear work's going well."

Gotta love those deep and intense answers.

Your turn, kiddo. Josie waited.

And waited.

The thickening air damn near smothered her. Unease prickled with the sense of eyes boring into her forehead. Josie scanned the parking lot, rechecked that her doors were locked. She found nothing. Sheesh. She really was paranoid tonight. But then talking to her sister always left her on edge.

Fine. Diana didn't want to talk. Better to hang up and try again lat—

"So what are you doing calling me on a Friday night?" Diana asked. "No hot date with some pilot pal of yours?"

Hot pilot? Her mind immediately winged to both Morel and Bridges. Two hot men in so very different ways.

And both a serious pain in her side right now. So, yeah, She was seriously *hot* under the collar *about* Diego Morel and Mike Bridges, and the threat this congressional investigation posed to her project. "I just finished up a late business-dinner meeting after a flight. What about you?"

"Only me all alone with my big bowl of macaroni and cheese."

"Ah. Comfort food." Some people turned to ice cream or chocolate. She and her sister always dug into a bowl of cheesy starch to fill the emptiness when life got them down. A boxing match between them afterward worked off the calories and steam. "I gotta confess, after my luck with men lately, I wish I had a bowl for myself right about now."

"Mac and cheese beats the hell out of most guys any day of the month. It lasts longer anyway."

A laugh trucked up and out so hard Josie missed catching the Beanie Baby. She adored her little sister's sense of humor, even if occasionally it turned to prickly sarcasm directed at her. She also envied Diana's ability to find the humor in life.

Josie lifted the Beanie puppy from her lap and tucked him into the drink holder, paws over the edge, basset hound eyes sadly pleading from between two floppy ears. "I guess I'll have to wait until I get home to make a batch."

"I wish I could have some of yours." The clink of a spoon against pottery echoed. "How come when you cook the boxed stuff it tastes good and mine tastes like soupy crap?"

"Secret ingredient." Just a slice of processed cheese dropped in, not that she intended to share that her single claim to culinary brilliance could be attributed to peeling off a plastic wrapper.

"Remember the time Dad tried to cook us macaroni and cheese like Mom always did?" Diana's words slipped through the earpiece and past Josie's defenses.

Her throat closed up like she'd tried to swallow down too much at once. Which was a damn good thing since it choked back the urge to snap at Diana's transparent bid for their father.

Diana was always trying to make her remember better days with their father before he gave up and shipped them off to boarding school rather than be bothered with parenting. Just as she was always trying to help Diana remember the happier days with their mom before she checked out mentally.

Josie forced a lighthearted answer. "Yeah, the noodles were so hard my loose tooth popped out."

"He stomped around the kitchen cursing about how the directions must be wrong because somehow he'd overcooked the stuff until it was too tough."

"I remember." And it hurt, thinking of that time. Her father's abandonment afterward hurt even more. At least her mother had illness as an excuse for leaving her kids. "I figured I'd better learn to make mac and cheese or we'd be toothless by Christmas."

"We sure needed comfort starch in those days."

Could that be a concession on Diana's part? "That we did, Diehard."

Silence ticked by with cyber wave crackles. Josie reached to the coffee holder and flipped a doggie ear backward on the Beanie puppy. She rubbed the fuzzy softness between two fingers until finally she surrendered and asked, "Talked to Dad lately?"

"Just last week." Diana's voice gentled with a sympathy Josie wasn't sure she wanted.

Her eyes gravitated to the puppy, the latest in the Beanie Baby collection her mother had started for her. "And what's the news?"

"He and Mom just got back from a cruise. They're enjoying his retirement dollars."

They should have had a double retirement fund at the end of two fruitful military careers. Her mother had been robbed of her career as well as her dreams.

The parking-lot lights dimmed. Or was it only her gloomy mood? Josie glanced over as the lot brightened and dimmed again with the intrusion of passing people finding their way back to their cars. "Yeah, I got an e-mail from their stopover in—"

Thud.

The noise echoed overhead from her convertible roof.

Josie jolted, stared up at the soft top, pathetic protection against a determined intruder. Her free hand snaking down toward her survival knife in her boot, she turned—and looked straight into cold, dark eyes peering through her window.

"Uh, Diana." Josie kept her eyes trained on the man standing beside her car. "I gotta go."

Chapter 4

"Jesus, Morel!" Josie slid her knife back into her boot, phone dropping to her lap. She lowered the window. "What the hell were you thinking, scaring the crap out of me like that?"

Her heart pounded over how close she'd come to drawing a weapon because of some whoo-hoo feeling that somebody was watching her. She was becoming paranoid, and that scared her more than any threat from the outside world.

Diego slumped back against the car parked beside her. "You can quit looking at me like I'm roadkill. I'm not some freaking Peeping Tom."

"Then why are you here?"

He shrugged. "I was watching you through the window. Saw you hadn't left. Got worried something might be wrong."

Her senses itched again, leaving her longing for the security of her knife in her hand. Cars growled and crunched out of the lot, disguising other sounds, while streetlights cast shadows for hiding.

"You came out to check up on me?"

"Sure, why not?"

That was actually kind of…thoughtful. Even if she could defend herself.

Definitely thoughtful…even nice. Both making her more uncomfortable than the pissed off feeling this man usually engendered. "Thank you."

"Sorry to cut your conversation short."

"We were through talking anyway." She tossed her cell phone into the cup holder with a small stuffed dog. "Time for me to head home."

"I need a ride."

So much for him being nice. Now his real agenda rolled out. "I thought you already had one or I wouldn't have left."

"I did. But he hooked up with a waitress. Suffice it to say that for a guy, a willing babe in the sack beats talking with a legend any day."

Definitely roadkill. Just when she'd thought she might have an amicable working relationship with this guy. "How lovely."

"This'll shock you I'm sure, but we men can be pigs sometimes. Not much I can say in our defense." His gaze hitched on the strap of her seat belt tucked between her breasts. He looked back up. "So? Give me a ride back to my place?"

She considered booting him on his butt. Was he sober enough to remember in the morning? "I could call you a cab."

"You could. But I'm not sure they even come out this way, and I'd have to wait at least an hour if they do. Maybe more. Then I'll be dragging ass all weekend, which will probably set back my whole week. For the good of your test project, you really should give me a ride home so I can get more shut-eye."

Her eyes closed with resignation. "Climb in."

"Thanks, even if it is for the good of your project." He settled into the bucket seat beside her and sighed. "Ah, nothing like a fine-performance machine."

Finally, common ground. "This might not be a jet or even a Harley, but a Mustang Cobra with a three-twenty horsepower V-eight engine can come mighty damn close to flying. So where to?"

He recited the address.

She smacked her steering wheel. "Good God, Morel. That's an hour away."

"Do you have somewhere to be?"

"No."

"How about we do the ride topless?"

Anger spiked. "Damn it, Morel—"

"The car top. Down. So we can see the night sky full of a half moon and stars." Grinning, he draped a hand over her gearshift. "What else would you think I meant?"

She knocked his hand off. "I think you meant to rile me and it's working."

"Sorry, Buttercup. Just can't resist." He hooked his elbow on his open window. "Getting a rise out of you is the most fun I've had since I performed a *lomcevak* maneuver in test-pilot school."

She gasped, interest snagged against her will and better judgment. "A *lomcevak?* You actually pulled off that tumbling insanity on purpose? In what air-plane?"

"A Christian Eagle biplane. And did I do it on pur-pose? As far as you know."

"Amazing." She shook her head, hair tickling her chin. "And a stupid risk."

"No arguments from me on that. Do I still get the ride?"

"Yes," she sighed her surrender. She would just have to keep her mouth shut until she dropped him off. "But only if you promise to tell me the rest of that *lom-cevak* story someday."

"Done deal."

She pressed the controls to roll away the roof, then backed out of her parking spot. "You're lucky I've got a full tank of gas and a crummy social life."

Josie shifted gears with smooth force, her knuckle brushing his leather-covered thigh. Hot. Diana's words from earlier came back to haunt her.

Holy crap. This guy *was* hot, in more ways than one. And she had no desire to get burned.

The sooner she got him home the better. She had a pile of her mother's old test-data printouts waiting at the apartment to keep her plenty busy.

Josie nailed the gas, gravel spewing from the tires on her way out of the lot.

Sprawled in Josie's Mustang, Diego stared up at the stars speckling the purple-black sky overhead planetarium style, the desert night clear. A perfect night sky for flying.

If he hadn't nailed his feet to the ground three years ago.

Electric poles whipped past with increasing speed on the desolate two-lane road. Creosote bushes and Joshua trees dotted the inky horizon for mile after mile.

Already he anticipated another beer to rid himself of the bitter aftertaste of the hangar meeting earlier. He was a washed-up test pilot. His life was in the crapper along with his career. This job only proved it.

Baby-sitter, spy, paper pusher, and for a low-budget project at that.

This assignment only proved how far down on the food chain he dwelled these days. The subcontractor he freelanced for kept him around to trot out a *legend* and his medals. Apparently his surliness was starting to chafe, if this job was any indication.

He worked because he had bills to pay. For putting his feet on the floor and getting dressed each morning, he rewarded himself with a race across a dry lake bed on his Harley, the only thing other than his dogs that he'd kept when his ex-wife walked after the accident. For making it through another workday—a necessity if he wanted to keep the bike and feed the dogs—he rewarded himself with a beer.

Long-neck. Budweiser, like any self-respecting Mississippi native.

And with any luck, the bottle was thrust his way in the hands of a hot woman who for some reason didn't know he was a washed-up test pilot who'd killed his best friend.

Bailout. Bailout. Bailout.

Even now, he could hear his own hoarse shouts. His wingman, flying alongside, had ignored the order during that last test, vowing he could recover, the instrumentation reading agreed. The poor bastard had flown right into the ground trusting his data.

Data Diego himself had supplied prior to take off.

Shit. Screw thinking about that. Rewind back to the image of a hot blond waitress thrusting a beer his way along with her bountiful breasts. Except his brain kept overlaying the image of a buxom blonde with a smart-mouthed brunette, one with minimal curves and maximum moxie,

Josie Lockworth might not be his type, but no question about it, she was hot. Self-assurance echoed from her, whether she was gliding on long legs into a bar or steering her Mustang convertible along rural desert roads.

He remembered well the idealistic days when he'd expected his work to change the world. These days, he preferred to think about beer...and breasts.

The ones beside him, to be exact.

The green flight suit hugged her slim body. High, pert breasts thrust a subtle invitation increased by the cooling blasts of night wind. Velcro straps cinched at her sides, accenting a hint of hips—

Whoa. Stop. He geared down his thoughts.

The woman who was ready to kick his ass over a simple "little lady" comment would fillet his liver if she could step inside his brain right now.

But the loss of his uniform had stripped away mental inhibitions, as well, leaving his world and expectations as off-kilter as his vertigo-stricken senses. He'd been a boundary pusher in the air, but understood the rules of convention implicit in his officer commission on the ground. He'd always kept protocol in place with female officers.

No such rules applied now, because he wasn't an officer anymore.

"You should be nice to me." He held up a hand. "And before you get your politically correct G-suit in a twist, I'm not implying a damned thing of a sexual nature. Yeah, I know I'm a bit of an ass. Okay, a lot of an ass. But if you'd pay attention, I talk like this to everyone. I'm just curious as to why you're huffy and defensive when it would serve you well to be kissing up. So to speak."

Her shoulders lowered, captain rank on her flight suit glowing luminescent blue in the dashboard lights. "Sorry. Instinct, I guess."

"Been hit on a few too many times?" Idiotic protective instincts fired up, much like the ones that had chewed his hide when he'd been sitting in the bar shooting the breeze with Birddog and the others.

"I've just learned it's better to keep things superficial." Wind-whipped coffee-colored hair around her face in a rare disorder from this overly composed woman. "People at work look hard enough for your vulnerabilities on their own. No need to give out private information for free."

What hints of vulnerabilities could be found in her pristine car, a place more personal than her office? He scooped her beanbag puppy from the drink holder.

"Could you put down the Beanie Baby, please?"

"Your favorite?"

"It's a gift for Craig Wagner's daughter when I go to dinner. I don't want it to look all rucked up when I give it to her."

"Sure. Sorry." He fit the toy basset hound back into the cup holder. "I'll get the kid a new one."

"Don't bother. You didn't do any harm—yet."

He heard her loud and clear. Get his mitts off her stuff and thereby off her. Somehow, he'd stepped too close. "So tell me about this test of yours."

Her white-knuckled fingers loosened around the steering wheel. "What do you want to know?"

"How about start with the basics. Assume I know nothing."

She would think he was an out of touch idiot who needed to review fundamentals. Not that he cared much as long as she didn't throw another one of those sympathetic looks his way like she'd done when he'd talked about not flying anymore.

Yeah, let her do the talking before he shoved his boot in his yap again. Captain Buttercup probably wouldn't even realize how much he could interpret about her core methodology from the way she presented foundation elements. "Talk to me."

And damned if he didn't enjoy the sound of her uptight, precise voice with its hint of huskiness begging to be encouraged.

"Our mission with this project is to improve the stealth element on the Predator unmanned spy drone. It has served the air force well in the past, but we've learned a lot about ways it could perform better, and thus keep more pilots and ground-intelligence forces out of harm's way."

He tried not to think much about his active-duty days, flying bombers then gaining admission to test-pilot school. He'd accepted the possibility of dying in battle or during a test. He'd never considered what to do with himself if he survived.

"Morel?"

"Yeah, I'm with ya, Buttercup." He looked at her and her uniform, her idealistic eyes reminding him of how many years' experience separated them.

And still he wanted Josie Lockworth.

The intensity of that desire blindsided him like a bogey from his six o'clock. Sure he'd been turned on by her at first look, even though she was a prickly priss. But he hadn't expected to get hard over just the thought of skimming aside the hair streaking across her face.

What the hell was up with that?

His head fell back against the rest. The sky beckoned. He closed his eyes. "Keep talking."

He focused on the clipped tones of Josie reciting facts, letting dry data served up with whiskey-warm tones intoxicate hungry senses that ached to fly.

Josie gripped the steering wheel and lost herself in the intoxicating oblivion of routine. Reliable facts would never betray her. "Stealth is comprised of five elements—electro-optical, radio transmissions, visual, acoustics and RF."

Diego folded his hands over his chest, his head still reclined, eyes closed. Late-day beard darkened features already weathered by the sun, wind, years of hard living.

Of loss.

Sympathy hit her. A dangerous emotion. God, she needed to remember her mother's lost career. Josie studied the stretch of road, so straight she could likely drive for hours without looking.

She lifted one finger off the steering wheel. "RF covers the more popular element of eluding radar frequency. The Predator already kicks ass on that one."

A second finger lifted. "Next, the electro-optical tricks the infrared camera and low-light optical trackers. Again, got it licked.

"Third element." Only her thumb and pinky stayed on the wheel along with her other hand. "For the visual with the good old eyeball check, the craft still holds up well."

She waggled her pinky. "Radio transmissions aren't a problem, either, because our data-link control signals are so low power they have a lesser probability of intercept."

Josie wrapped her hand around the steering wheel again. "The Predator's only weakness comes from the fifth element—its acoustics. Enemy listening posts can pick up the propeller motor sounds in low-level flights. But the lower the flight, the better quality on the intel."

"Uh-huh," he grunted, shifting his legs to swing one booted foot over his knee without once opening his eyes, as if she barely warranted his whole attention. "And since much of your mother's work focused on the acoustics of stealth, you decided the Predator is the perfect craft to use for resurrecting her theories."

She didn't answer or even blink for the passing of four telephone poles while pain from her mother's breakdown roared as loudly as the ever-constant desert wind. "Way to lay it all out there on the table."

"Does it bother you to talk about her?"

"The facts are public record. It's not like I can hide from them." She peeled a strand of hair that had stuck to her lip gloss. "Actually, I appreciate your honesty. At least I don't have to wonder if you're whispering behind my back."

"I'm an ass, but I'm a straight-up ass."

She didn't want to like him. But just when she longed to punt his arrogant butt, he surprised her with his self-awareness. "Since I believe in my mother's core concept, yes, if it works, the Predator will be a more efficient asset to the reconnaissance community."

Her methodology was sound. She knew that. She hoped her developmental testing would be equally so—because she could talk higher air force benefits all she wanted, but eventually it wouldn't escape anyone's notice that this was personal for her. The career fall from failure would be far and fatal.

Then there would be nothing left for her but to burrow out in the California desert in one of these geodesic domes, single-wide trailers or old ranch-style houses that infrequently broke the monotony of space and quiet. "What else would you like to know?"

"What will I be looking at when we get to the paperwork?"

"Our first round of testing involved active noise cancellation. For example, if the acoustic signature of the aircraft was a sine wave with a magnitude of one-hundred-ninety decibels at fifty hertz, we would create a sine wave of equal but opposite magnitude to conceal the noise." She glanced over at the leather lug barely moving in the seat next to her. "You used to fly bombers, right?"

He grunted again.

"Basically we employed the same technology that's used in noise-canceling headsets worn by bomber crew members to weed out the engine sound so they can hear each other talking."

The graded road roughened. She downshifted to third gear, her knuckles grazing his knee. Chaps warmed from his body heat launched a shower of tingles up her arm and straight to her breasts. And he didn't even flinch, damn him.

Work. Think work. "Once the active noise was addressed, we moved on to passive ways to decrease sound, such as making the engine vibrate less. Our main source of concern with the Predator has been modifying the propeller. It makes too much noise when the tips break mach. In this stage of the testing, we're improving the flight propeller balancing...."

The road evened out. She reached for the gearshift again, bracing herself for the feel of heated leather against her skin. Still he didn't move.

"Are you asleep?"

Diego turned his head along the rest, lashes lifting to unveil eyes hotter than the leather against his skin. "Was I snoring?"

"No." Her hand clenched.

"Then I wasn't asleep." Straightening, he pointed left to the narrow one-lane road. "Turn here."

She slowed, her car still undulating. The rearview mirror reflected nothing but a cloud of sandy dust kicking up behind them. Out of the pitch night, one of the old ranch-style homes appeared, dark wood scarred by wind and time. The sturdy, functional structure sprawled, surrounded by eucalyptus trees. Sweet perfume rode the wind along with a distant coyote howl.

The front porch stirred with motion, two dogs leaping to life and bolting down the steps. A shaved retriever and a mutt of indeterminate origin scampered in a dangerous dance in front of her car, forcing her to slow.

At a near-crawl pace, she pulled her shuddering Mustang closer to the deserted yard, past patchy brush, cacti, a crappy lawn chair beside what looked to be about an eight-hundred-dollar grill.

She braked to a stop, engine still humming. Kangaroo rats scampered away from the headlights. "Here we are."

"Thanks for the ride." His booted foot slid to the floorboards. "I owe you a new set of shocks and a car wash for this one."

"I might take you up on that, Morel," she offered noncommittally. Safely.

He seemed in no hurry to get out of her car now. The man never hurried, period. Even as that trait annoyed her, she couldn't help but be intrigued by someone so unfettered by life. "How are you going to get back to base?"

He gestured toward the prefabricated metal garage set back from the house. "I have a truck, too."

"And what about your Harley?"

"You could stay over and give me a ride in the morning."

She blinked hard. Twice. Then covered with an overly polite smile. "I don't think so."

"That no-sex-with-workmates rule of yours again?"

Self-preservation was more like it, if just a simple brush against him could burn her. "Perhaps I'm not interested in going to bed with a drunk who snores."

His half smile tucked a dimple into one cheek. "I like you, Lockworth."

Whoa. Like? That was a whole different matter than just sexy leather chaps and lust. "Uh, thanks."

"Not that you're particularly likable."

She scooped the puppy from the drink holder, something soft to ease the sting of echoing old taunts of Josephine the Tattletale Queen. "Charm doesn't seem to be your strong suit, either."

A rusty laugh rolled out in a *lomcevak* tumble. "Exactly what I like about you."

"I'm not following."

"You don't kiss my ass just because once upon a time I flew some pretty missions."

His answer made sense and confused her all at once. "I respect the work you accomplished."

"But not who I am now."

The scent of leather and eucalyptus swirled inside her. She needed to leave. Now. "Who you are doesn't matter to me. How you work does. And I've yet to see any work accomplished to judge."

Draping his elbow on the back of his seat, he gripped the edge of hers with one hand while plucking the dog from her other. "Yeah, I like your take-no-shit attitude. And I like the fact that you're straight up with me. Makes me trust you more and that's a good thing. But honest to God, you need to wash some starch out of your spine."

She bristled, more Josephine-prickly than that cactus patch by his garage. Who the hell did he think he was? And she couldn't afford to say squat back.

He dropped the Beanie Baby back in the cup holder. "I know this mission is important to you, and I'm not diminishing what you do. But even with my feet nailed to the ground like they are, I could wade through your paperwork on this test halfway to snoring. Or half-drunk."

She couldn't stop her Josephine sniff.

"That's right, Buttercup. I'm a rude, washed-up test pilot who drinks too much and doesn't shave enough. And, yeah, I snore, since my eardrums and sinuses blew out on that last flight." He stopped short, his hard weathered face freezing. "Ah, shit. Forget it. I'm outta here."

Diego reached for the door handle. Remorse, empathy and something else she didn't want to examine stirred.

"Wait!" She grabbed his arm.

He could have shaken her off easily. But he stopped, staying in the seat.

"I really didn't mean to come off all judgmental. I haven't walked in your shoes so I've got no room to—"

Diego shushed her with a pointed look down at her hand on his arm.

Her fingers slid away.

He canted closer, hand returning to the back of her seat, a whisper away from her neck. "I meant it when I said I like your straight talk. You can feel free to tell me to go to hell when I get out of line and it won't affect my report."

He grazed one knuckle along the vulnerable curve of her neck, slowly, deliberately, his skin every bit as hot as she'd imagined. "But don't ever, ever flash that damn little pity look my way again. Because if you do, I guarantee I'll be kissing it off your face so thoroughly you won't be able to think about anything except getting naked together. Understand?"

The fire in his skin and eyes dried her mouth until she could only nod.

Silently, he backed away and out of the car. He

slammed the door shut, holding on to the open window for one final shot. "And in case you were wondering, I was definitely hitting on you that time. Next move's yours, Buttercup."

Chapter 5

Josie slammed her condo door.

She could allow herself that much emotional venting while no one was watching without worrying about negative reports and whispers of instability. Flicking on the light, she hooked her key ring on the rack by the door, a long silver mirror with a bin for mail and tiny hooks for keys and stray jewelry.

Now to fill the remaining hours so she would be tired enough to sleep once she fell into bed. Alone. She should probably log on to her computer and see if Tory had e-mailed her back about Shannon's feature.

Josie ignored her reflection and walked deeper into her empty home, clicking on the television and popping in a DVD copy of videos of her mother's old test flights. She had reviewed them all at least a couple dozen times each, and still she watched them over and over again like some people played their favorite albums. Her mother's voice echoed from the speakers, calling directives from the ground to the pilot flying the test prototype. Cockpit views scrolled, mixed with other shots from the ground of the test in flight.

While the voices continued, pictures stared down from the walls, a hodgepodge collection of steel-framed photographs from her Athena Academy days—riding, archery, group shots and individuals spanning years from her first day at thirteen all the way to twelfth grade.

More pictures followed of college graduation, then her air force commissioning so long ago. Finishing college in three years had put her on a fast track in the air force that made for a solitary life now, creating boundaries with people her own age. At least at Athena, she'd been surrounded by overachievers like herself. Her classmate Alex had become a successful forensic scientist with the FBI. Tory was one of the hottest reporters on TV, also working as an intelligence courier for the government. And even after going through a teenage pregnancy, Kayla was already a lieutenant on the police force.

God, she missed her friends. Yet even if she had time to build new friendships, who could she be close to? People her own age worked below her. People at her career stage resented her for being younger.

Diego's invitation to stay the night whispered through her mind. Not wise, being tempted by him.

Chewing orange-tryst gloss off her lips, Josie dropped into the curve of the white sectional sofa. She thumbed through the stacks of large green computer printouts from her mother's testing days. She'd been going through the information after hours for months now—algorithms, configurations and data streams. There was so damned much of it, so many notes in her mother's precise handwriting down the sides documenting every data drop, each sensor measurement. No one this meticulous screwed up, damn it.

Josie dropped the stack back on the glass coffee table. She swung a boot up on the edge and worked free the long black laces. A dog tag winked up from the right boot, a duplicate of the ID around her neck. The second was attached to the nearly indestructible combat boot so if her plane exploded, she could still be quickly identified amid the ashes.

Setting her boots on the floor one thud at a time, she peeled off her socks and wriggled her toes, pink toenails winking up at her. Her mind's eye too easily conjured visions of Diego Morel once lacing and unlacing the same boots, not knowing what life held for him after the mission.

The hunger in his eyes when he'd talked about flying had almost leveled her. The profoundness of his feelings of loss made her question the depth of her calling to the sky.

She'd spent so long focused on clearing her mother's name, she'd never considered life after. Was this what she wanted to do with her remaining years in the air force? Did she even want to stay in, or had she only joined to follow her parents' legacy, since it offered the easiest way to right wrongs for Zoe Lockworth?

Josie sagged back on the sofa. Damn it, and damn Diego Morel. She couldn't afford to doubt herself now. She was an excellent test pilot. She enjoyed the challenge of her job and the honor of wearing the uniform. And she wouldn't allow some man with his hungry eyes to shake her resolve just because maybe she was feeling a little vulnerable tonight.

She unzipped her thigh pocket, reached in, brought out the tiny basset hound Beanie Baby. Craig's daughter would receive the match already wrapped and ready, but this one, the toy Diego had tossed, was for her. Shoving up from the sofa's embrace, she crossed to the wall of shelves. She placed the squishy dog inside the jammed nooks housing her Beanie collection, which kept her company along with the stereo and television.

Popping in a new DVD of tests, she watched static morph into flight images. Backing away, her bare feet padding along the carpet, she assessed the dog's place between a birthday unicorn and camouflage bear her mother had given her. The thought of failing shook her more than any *lomcevak* maneuver ever could.

She had work to do.

Josie scooped up the closest stack of printouts, the familiar sight of her mother's handwriting more than enough motivation to forgo half the night's sleep.

"Hey fella," she called over her shoulder to the basset hound addition on the way to the kitchen. "How about we celebrate your homecoming with some mac and cheese while I check over flight configurations from a couple of decades ago?"

Five days later, Josie cleared security to enter the remote control flight area, two leather seats in front of panels of screens, buttons, dials and checklists. She would fly the aircraft from the pilot's seat, while beside her the sensor operator manned the cameras. A seasoned master sergeant with a mono-brow and over two thousand UAV hours, Don Zeljak had been hand-picked. Zeljak now worked over in the scheduling office when he wasn't flying, which made things wonderfully easy for slotting him on her missions.

"Hey, Captain." Zeljak paused beside her, offering a double-size pack of wintergreen gum while he smacked a piece of his own. "Want some gum?"

Josie started to say no, then reached to take a stick after all. "Thanks, Sergeant. I think I will."

She could use a little nerve soothing with a congressional spy/baby-sitter shadowing her. Diego strutted behind her, biker boots thudding against thin industrial carpet. She didn't have to see him to envision his relaxed tread that screamed of slow, confident sex.

Josie chomped her gum harder.

They'd spent the past days reviewing the old data from her coffee table, tackling it in half the time. True to his word, he hadn't made another move on her. And he'd kept pace with helping her sift through the flight configurations for each of the early missions her mother had overseen. Once she finished up here, she could dig deeper into cross-checking that correct software versions coordinated with the hard drives.

Perhaps he actually could do the job with his eyes half-closed. Apparently, the problem was hers and she needed to get the hell over herself—or over him—pronto. Kinda tough to do with him breathing down her neck 24/7.

Not for the first time, she wondered, could he be testing her? Could he have been trying to set her up? Even though an affair wouldn't be an ethical breach, it might make a positive report of his seem suspect. She really did need to call her sister back to find out what Diana had uncovered about Diego's past. But part of her regretted asking, almost wanting to hear it from him.

She was starting to like him. And yes, like was far more dangerous than lust. She could and would harness her emotions. Work provided the perfect distraction. The challenge, her goal to clear her mother's name, drove her relentlessly.

Josie snagged a tissue and spit out her gum. She wouldn't need any nerve crutches once she slid into the pilot's seat.

The Predator was flown from a remote control cockpit, much like a simulator setup. A pilot manned the controls in one of the seats with the sensor operator beside working the cameras, or the sensor suite, as it was called. But unlike normal Predator flights, the test versions required that another pilot be strapped to the vehicle with a modified second set of controls for override in an emergency if things went to hell.

Things would *not* go wrong. Especially not with Craig strapped on. She'd planned carefully. Conservatively. Because no way would she accept anything but a win.

Each test pushed the craft a little further. First, she'd fired up the engine and taxied the modified Predator along the runway. Next flight, taxi faster and test the brakes, and so on. Today's flight would be the second quick loop in the air around the airfield.

Diego lounged against the partition beside her, every squeak of his leather as he moved reminding her he watched. Waiting for her to screw up?

"So why's Wagner the one strapped on the Predator today and not you?"

Was he an idiot or just checking to see if she was? "As the head tester, sometimes I have to step back. I take turns with Wagner and the other four pilots assigned to my team. I know the craft too well. I'm not the average crew member anymore."

"Good answer." He waved her to her seat. "Don't mind me. I'll just fade into the scenery here."

He stood a better chance at winning the lottery.

She forced her attention back on work while she and the sensor operator ran through preflight data. Today's was a simple circle with the camera running, minimal chance of anything going wrong. DT—developmental test—followed such a scripted plan she could have simply passed over the paperwork with the camera footage and he would have been able to assess the mission. But he studied her through hooded eyes, checking her test discipline and methodology.

She knew how to follow a plan, damn it.

Josie keyed up the radio to talk to Wagner. Flying the modified Predator by remote was a snap—except when somebody was in the saddle. Even though he could counteract any of her control inputs, she still carried a lump in her throat thicker than her father's sticky mac and cheese every time she piloted one of these flights. She'd rather strap her own tush to the rocket any day of the week than have someone else in danger. "Well partner," she called over the radio to Wagner. "You ready to ride this bronco?"

"I would prefer that it not buck me off if you don't

mind," Wagner chided through her headset. "But I am checklist complete and ready to go."

Josie ran through her instruments one last time before the countdown. "Ten seconds to throttle up."

"Copy ten," the saddled-up Wagner shot back.

Josie checked her stopwatch and began counting down. "Five. Four. Three. Two. One. Going throttle up now."

She eased the throttle forward. Since she sat in the remote control seat, there was no kick in the ass like in a T-38 or a U-2 to let her know the engine was running to full power. Wagner would get that punt. Only her instruments showed a steady climb as power increased. "Ready for brake release in three, two, one. Brakes released."

Wagner's laughter rocked through her headset. "Yippee ki yay, mo-fo."

Josie suppressed a laugh of her own, if not her smile. He blasted that corny shout every time, even back in test-pilot school. He was an unabashed goober. And one helluva pilot.

Concentrating on the camera looking out the nose of the Predator, she kept the aircraft on the runway centerline with small inputs to the rudder pedals. "Rotating now."

She eased the stick aft and watched the camera view change from runway and creosote bushes to blue sky. Leveling the Predator off at eight thousand feet, she checked her mission data to ensure the craft steered its simple "circle the patch" profile set for this mission. "Everything looks normal down here. How's it look from there?"

"No problems up here, ma'am." Roaring engines

and feedback competed with the hokey accent he always donned for flight. "Thanks kindly for asking."

"Are we going to do the John Wayne imitation every time you ride that thing?"

"You betcha, and I would suggest that you work on your Annie Oakley voice for when it's your turn."

"Maybe we should change your call sign to Cowboy or Duke."

"Sounds great to me. I'll happily ditch that other awful one y'all hung on me earlier."

"We'll have a keg party soon to make you Cowboy for real." Josie vowed to pick up a miniature ten-gallon hat for Wagner's kid for Christmas to match the one he often wore. She turned to her sensor operator. "How do the sensors look?"

"Everything is nominal here also," Zeljak answered, mono-brow lowering with concentration.

"Roger that, you run through your test cards and let me know if we need to modify the profile."

"Yes ma'am, I'll keep you posted."

Josie cross-checked the instruments, then glanced over to see what the sensor operator had found to use for camera calibration. First he locked his infrared on a truck heading up the highway and insured the automatic tracking function was operational. Josie turned back to her own camera view. Horizon level. She scanned her readouts. Everything was still looking good and nary a peep from her cowboy.

A low whistle from the sensor operator drew her eyes back to his monitors.

"Holy crap." Master Sergeant Zeljak waggled his thick dark brow. "Lookee there."

Josie's fingers clenched around the stick. Things

were skating along so well. Please Lord, don't let them go to hell now, especially with her baby-sitter at her back. "Whatcha got, Sergeant?"

"That SUV." Zeljak nodded to his screens displaying feedback from cameras that could see for miles. "Parked all by its lonesome alongside that range."

Josie frowned. "Nobody drives out there."

"Exactly. I can only think of a couple of reasons somebody would go out there all alone on a lunch break."

She nodded. "Vandalism."

"Or sex." Diego's wry voice echoed from over her shoulder.

Mr. Invisible? Not.

Josie eyed the high-resolution image, camera zooming nearer to reveal…a very familiar red SUV, the color of Mike Bridges's vehicle. Camera angles swooped to show…

A license plate that read 1 Pilot.

Zeljak pulled back on the angle to encompass the whole vehicle again. "Hey, maybe he had car trouble and is walking for help. We should scan up the road—"

On cue, the SUV started rocking.

It was almost funny. Almost. Bridges wasn't doing anything illegal, but what piss-poor judgment on his part.

Morel chuckled low behind her. Craig's laughter blended in from the headset as he rode along.

A grin twitched at the sensor operator's face. "You know, I always wondered what he and that civilian employee from the next building over were doing on those long lunch breaks."

At least now she didn't have to worry about whether or not Bridges was hitting on *her.* He was most definitely otherwise engaged.

Zeljak glanced back at Diego. "Hope he finishes up in time for General Quincy's briefing. It would be a shame if we all have to sit through the whole spiel and the boss doesn't even notice. Maybe we ought to tell Wagner he doesn't need to rush over from his flight after all—"

"Sergeant," Josie interrupted what was fast becoming a situation harmful to Bridges's credibility. "I believe we should stop. The man's entitled to his privacy."

"Hey, they're out in the open on government land. They've waived any right to privacy. Maybe my wife and I ought to try the back-seat gig more often. God knows there's not much privacy around my house with five teenagers and all their friends underfoot." The master sergeant glanced back at Morel. "The boss has some staying power, I'll give him that."

Heat burned her skin from embarrassment and more than a little anger. "Enough. Go look at something else. *Anything* else. Turn the camera forty degrees south. That's an order."

"Yes, ma'am." He clicked through commands, spun dials. "I hear there's a nudist colony out there that your reporter passenger got a special sideshow view of the other day. Maybe we should go check out that."

Heat clawed up her face again. She outranked the guy, but those old sergeants sure had a way of putting a junior officer in his or her place. "Thank you for the reminder, Sergeant, but we can skip that scenic tour today, as well."

"Yes, ma'am."

Camera angles swung away, hangar images growing in size on the screens that were scheduled to show desert. Daily, technology on the camera imagery improved. What they could have done with this in the Middle East. Her U-2 flights could have been even more effective, some missions unnecessary altogether. If only her mother's meticulous research could have been used.

The urge to succeed charged through Josie stronger than ever, patience harder to find of late. But she couldn't let the old impulsive Josie overpower her.

She studied the video footage filling the monitors.

"Stop!" she ordered, narrowing her eyes to better identify the flicker of movement by the hangar. A person.

"Close-up, please."

The figure turned, as if sensing laser eyes on…her. Shannon Conner.

Crap. Josie shot over her shoulder to Diego. "Call the base police. We've got a security breach."

Birddog secured his flight-suit zipper. Tab down. Uniform smooth and crisp in spite of a morning spent out in the California desert wind.

Locking his vehicle, he tucked into the gusts and strode toward the beige building at the Palmdale testing facility. He had important people to see, meetings and briefings to attend. And during every minute he would enjoy the gratification of knowing Josie Lockworth's version of the Predator stealth project was that much closer to self-destruction.

The reporter was now well on her way off the base

with the information he'd planted for her television exposé. Excitement chugged through him. He was so close, details locked and loaded. Grit-laden air itched along his wired nerves.

Morel was proving more vigilant than expected in his investigative role. Damn him, he'd been chosen *because* he was a screwed-up burnout. If Morel began posing too much of a threat with his thoroughness, a few reminders of his past should send the man diving back into a keg of beer.

And Josie Lockworth?

He didn't want to hurt her. Quite the opposite.

Birddog shoved through the door into the narrow corridor toward the auditorium, exchanging salutes. He scanned the women filing into the rows of seats, wondering if he dared risk taking one of them up on the offers that sometimes came his way.

He shouldn't be this damned hungry and unsatisfied, not when he enjoyed regular sex. Except lately sex offered only physical release without satisfaction, as long as the wrong woman writhed beneath him. It was this whole damn project that had him so touchy. He checked his zipper tab again, straightened his flight scarf.

If he could have *her* one time, the woman he really wanted, maybe then she would leave his system and stop haunting his thoughts, tainting his every success because it was never enough without that final victory.

The triumph of possessing her just once.

Chapter 6

Josie packed her flight bag, beyond ready to clear this boring mandatory briefing from General Quincy. Two more minutes and she could return to her office, where Diego waited, sorting through her paperwork unsupervised.

At least she wouldn't be alone with him. She and Craig needed to write up the quick-look report on the morning flight before he could go home to romance his pregnant wife.

And before Josie could dig deeper into what Shannon Conner had been doing at Palmdale—again.

Security police had descended on Shannon, a most satisfying moment even viewed through remote cameras. Too bad it had ended so fast. Shannon had presented an official base pass and wasn't technically in a restricted area. Since a speedy initial scan of her background hadn't produced anything suspicious, they'd escorted her out the front gate, assuming she was nothing more than another scoop-hungry reporter. Not an uncommon occurrence around a government testing facility.

But someone must have vouched for her. Who? The SPs—security police—weren't ponying up the info. Josie had sources of her own via her network of Athena friends.

She snapped her flight bag closed with more force than needed. Making tracks toward the auditorium exit, she nearly slammed into Major Bridges as he slid out of the back row.

"Lockworth, just who I was looking for. How'd today's test flight go?"

Josie didn't dare risk a look at Craig or Master Sergeant Zeljak behind her, even though she could imagine their barely restrained smiles. She kept her eyes plastered on Bridges's face, his dark hair ever so slightly mussed as if from a frantic lover's hands.

How freaking embarrassing. "You'll have my quick-look report by the end of business today, sir. But overall, it was an excellent test run with Wagner strapped in, me flying the stick. The propeller modifications performed above expectations. We'll break for a week while the contractors rewrite the software to optimize the adapted control program, but overall things are moving ahead of schedule. And I can review and update all test data in the interim."

Bridges crossed his arms over his chest. "Actually, you'll be TDY. Thanks to the flu outbreak, we're short a flyer for the Red Flag war game exercises in Nevada. Your down time makes you the perfect candidate to stand in for a few days. And Morel can weed through the backlog of files while we're gone."

TDY? Now? In the middle of her test? Josie shook off shock and frustration. "TDY to Nellis?"

"We take off late tomorrow afternoon. Wagner's following the next day, as well."

Unease prickled. "Sir, I'm really swamped here, especially with Morel on my back." Gulp. Now wasn't that an image to rock her concentration? "Isn't there someone else who could go in my place?"

"Apparently you're healthier than most of the base. You're it, Lockworth, or I would have chosen someone else from the start."

A good soldier knew when to back down. "I should start packing then."

"Who can argue with a free trip to Vegas?"

She wanted to. Leaving her office unattended with a congressional spy underfoot and Shannon Conner somehow gaining free run of hangars made her itchy. Again, it seemed the fates were conspiring against her.

Or someone a little more earthly bound.

What was Bridges thinking, sending her off at such a critical time with a congressional investigation underway? He could tap someone from another base with only minimal extra effort. She didn't like this one damn bit. Not that she had a choice.

She would have to use the TDY time to her advantage by packing up her research notes to go through the same words she'd read a hundred times already in an effort to find out who'd sabotaged Zoe Lockworth's career. And she would damn well rebuild her defenses when it came to Diego Morel and discovering any agendas he might or might not have.

* * *

Josie hurtled through the sky in her T-38, clouds stroking past her clear canopy. Any other time she would enjoy the edgy flying in Red Flag mock war exercises. Right now, she just wanted to get back to her primary mission.

Gripping the stick, she held steady on her speed. Major Bridges flew beside her in a two-ship of T-38s in the faux war. The small jets were pretending to be enemy red-force cruise missiles. She and Bridges would assume a missile profile and flight path to see how far they could penetrate before blue-force defenses halted them.

Josie tucked in tighter on Bridges's wing in fingertip formation. She scanned the horizon with eagle eyes as she knew he was doing in synch, looking for an aggressor squadron F-16 that would act as the launch aircraft for their flight-simulating cruise missiles.

As in all aviation, this was a contest. A challenge.

Josie caught a glint off a canopy out the corner of her eye. Ooh-rah. She'd won a round over her boss in sighting the fighter first.

Victory pulsing, she thumbed her radio on. "Tally ho, Boss. Viper at my two-o'clock about ten miles out."

No doubt, Bridges shouted damn at the loss before keying up his radio to acknowledge her transmission.

"Roger, P.C." He brought the nose of his T-38 up and began a slight turn to intercept the F-16. "All right, spread formation now and joining on the Viper as briefed."

She bumped her throttles and maneuvered abreast of her leader's aircraft. Screaming through the air, the two T-38s in tandem joined up fifty feet off each wing of the F-16. Josie turned her head toward the "Mother Ship," awaiting a hand signal indicating they'd been "missile launched."

Excitement clenched as she focused, winding tighter, ready to spring. Damn straight she could punt Diego Morel and all the questions he raised right out of her head. She'd only needed a reminder of why she enjoyed her job. Maybe she'd spent too much time in an office, missing the exhilaration without realizing it until something—or somebody—came along and shook her snow globe a little.

This should be fun. Flat out, ass-kicking fun. No high-tech fancy terrain following or avoidance systems in these modified trainer planes. Just her hands and brain to keep her from smacking into the desert at five hundred knots.

While she waited for the launch signal, she ran another cross-check of her instruments, read her fuel state just as Bridges's voice barked through the radio. "P.C., fuel state?"

"Damn!" He'd beaten her to the mark this time. She keyed up her microphone and reported, "On the curve with twenty-one-hundred pounds."

Reaching, she pulled her harness tighter in anticipation of the roller-coaster ride ahead. God, she hoped the radar games didn't log a shoot down before she lowered to two hundred feet. She wanted this flight. She needed the electrifying release of full out speed and air and edginess. Testing her mettle and winning.

She trained her eyes on the Viper pilot and squirmed in her seat like a kid ready for recess. "Come on," she muttered. "Come on. Come on, damn it."

The gloved hand of the fighter pilot came up.

Josie inhaled, held her breath. The pilot's arm pumped twice, signaling the start of the surrogate missile mission.

She launched. Speed, adrenaline, all-out thrill punched through her. Starting her anti-G straining maneuver, she rolled inverted, pulling toward the ground. Blood rushed down toward her ass while the G-suit inflated to push the blood back up to her brain.

Roll out.

Roll out.

Training overrode the buzz of increasing dizziness. Two thousand feet. She leveled out above the terrain. The G-suit deflated. Gs diminished. Her breathing regulated back to a normal rhythm. Adrenaline gushed harder and faster than the blood shouting through her veins.

She milked the aircraft down to the two-hundred-foot en route altitude and played tag with the rocks, kissing each one with the ripples of air jettisoning from her engines. Hell, yeah. Bring it on.

She glanced north to check Bridges flying a similar path four miles away. No shoot-down yet. Let the fun continue. Josie scanned ahead, behind, searching for blue-force fighters coming to terminate her "cruise missile."

All was well so far, exhilaration without any seriously hairy crap to scare a year off her life. With so many planes in the air engaging, evading, attacking, accidents were a constant hazard. Bottom line, they would be more effective in real-life scenarios, saving more lives—especially civilians—long-term.

Jogging north to avoid a town, she kept her eyes

peeled. High and ahead she caught sight of contrails streaking the sky. Mountains peaked ahead, leading her into a winding path. She was so damned low she could read the road signs, a green one looming, lettered, The Extraterrestrial Highway.

She chuckled. No flying saucers yet.

The sun blotted. Her aircraft fell into a shadow. "What the hell?"

Her head snapped up. Through her clear canopy, she looked. Not a spaceship, but still a huge aircraft fell out of the sky toward her.

The damn thing was seconds away from landing on top of her plane.

"Sheee-it," she spit as she racked the aircraft into a turn. Hard. Harder. As hard as she could take, tearing away. Putting her belly up to the other aircraft blinded her from seeing how close the intruder was to splattering her into nothingness.

Josie keyed up her radio and yelled, "Knock it off, knock it off, knock it off! Bull's-eye one-ten at thirty."

Red Flag control echoed her knock-it-off call over all frequencies as she rolled her aircraft level and took a long look back at the other aircraft. A dark B-1 Bomber scooted away in the opposite direction with a red-force F-16 climbing. The fighter must have jumped the bomber at high altitude, forcing the bomber into a speed-down to the deck to try and evade.

Which had landed him right in her flight path.

Her pulse hammered in her ear, everything inside her shaking harder than the rattling aircraft after the near miss with the Grim Reaper. She shut down her emotions, called on training to assume command of her hands and focused on getting herself back on terra firma.

"P.C.," Bridges barked over the headset. "Status report. Over."

"All's cool." Thank God. "My hydraulics are reading a little low though. I may have overstressed the plane."

"Roger that. You need to reroute and land, ASAP."

No kidding. But at least she would be landing on her wheels instead of her face. "Copy, Boss, calling in for an emergency landing."

Radio calls and clearance passed in a daze as her brain went on autopilot, her body overrevved. Finally her wheels touched down at Nellis AFB, Bridges right on her tail, landing seconds behind her.

Once she'd parked her plane, unstrapped and removed her helmet, the full extent of what could have happened jolted through her. She'd been in tense situations in test and battle, but never anything that close.

She hauled herself up and out of the cockpit, deplaning down the ladder hung on the side.

Bridges waited at the foot of the steps, helmet tucked under his arm. Sweat plastered his dark hair to his head. "You okay, P.C.?"

"Fine. Just fine." Forcing shaky breaths in and out, she stifled down the vulnerability. "Real kick-ass flying up there today. Fun stuff."

"Well I'm glad *you're* okay. Because I about pissed myself when I saw that bomber coming down on you." Bridges's exclamation offered generous and face-saving balm, reminding her of one of the reasons this guy was such a well-liked leader. "I thought you'd enjoy the break from test regimen, but I sure as shit didn't mean for something like this to happen. You handled it well though. Did our unit proud."

He touched her.

Just a clap on the back. Was it her imagination that it lingered a second too long? That his hand slid away rather than merely lifting off?

God, she hated suspecting her own boss. The guy was seeing someone else, after all. Literally.

She had nothing to go on but that feminine intuition at a time when her emotions were rattly at best. All the same, those shaky instincts said the guy had a radar lock on her. The same sense of attraction she got from Diego. Sheesh, where were the offers when she actually had time for a man in her life?

The old Josie whispered inside her that she never made time. "Thank you, sir. I'm just glad to have landed in one piece."

If she made time, she was now a hundred percent certain it would never be with Bridges. Even if he wasn't her detachment commander, she wasn't much for the type who made lunch dates in a car with one woman and dinner dates with another.

Helmet under his arm, Bridges strode alongside her toward the Suburban waiting to take them to Base Ops. "Hope you don't mind a little advice from someone who's been around the military block longer. Too much work gives you tunnel vision. It's all about balance, recognizing when you've hit the point of diminishing returns and stepping back to air out your brain with some R and R. Speaking as your boss, and I hope a friend, as well, I'm telling you—you're working too hard."

Her spine went rigid. "Is that an official order to take time off? Has my work been anything less than top-notch?"

"Of course not. And we don't want to let it happen. Just a little friendly advice for what it's worth." He nodded toward the Suburban. "But first, we've got one helluva debrief to get through."

"Of course." She followed, working to lower her hackles.

Yet was there merit to Bridges's advice? Some redeeming value in pursuing something recreational outside of work?

She wasn't interested in a relationship with Mike Bridges. But what about Diego Morel? He certainly intrigued her. She was actually even starting to trust him. More than she trusted Bridges, oddly enough.

Again she thought of her friend Rainy's unexplained death, too young. Facing her own death made her dread that lonely condo all the more. And damn it, she did need to unwind before she snapped.

Like her mother had snapped.

Josie swallowed down a fear greater than any she'd faced in the air today. All right. She had a plan to keep her life better balanced. She would start by having a drink after hours with Diego once she returned. Shoot the breeze to discover more about his methodology. Job and fun combined to free up her thoughts. No great risk and it could pay off in a better working relationship.

It wasn't like she was looking for a flaming affair. Right?

God, she had a flaming headache.

Massaging her fingers along her pounding temple, Josie entered the flight-control area, the panel doubling as a simulator for her today. While the area wasn't in use, she would practice recovery from emergencies, then rehearse an upcoming mission.

Her turn in the saddle of the test model Predator the day before with the updated software had been flawless. A good thing, because she'd needed an airtight mission after that near miss at Red Flag.

Thoughts of Red Flag brought her right back to Diego, and her hopes of letting off steam with him. She'd been trying to shoot the breeze more, but now he was all work. Sheesh. Sure she remembered he'd said the next move would be hers, but she could use a little reassurance.

Her head throbbed. Where the hell was everyone?

Technically no one else needed to be around. Personnel still occupied the building even though the workday was nearing an end. There just wasn't anyone in this room. Except her. And Diego.

Josie took her place in the overlarge seat while Diego ambled past and dropped into the vacant sensor operator's chair. Faded jeans stretched tight over black boots and thick muscles. His onyx button-down shirt paid token homage to business wear, sleeves rolled up to reveal arms sprinkled with dark hair.

Damn but leather smelled good on him. "Are you sure you want to sit through this? I'm just running some EPs."

Chicken.

"I got no place else to go, the chair's comfy and the company's…if not pleasant, at least interesting. I think I'll stick around. Hell, I could use the overtime pay. The Harley needs a tune-up."

Yeah, right. He took better care of that bike than most people did their houses. Of course, she'd spent an hour washing and detailing her Mustang the day after dropping him off at his place. Maybe they could shoot the breeze over a can of TurtleWax instead.

"Fine. Just keep yourself over there."

"Yes, ma'am, Captain Buttercup."

"Jerk," she muttered, flattening a traitorous grin as she began to run through the setup routine to convert the control station that flew the Predator into a simulator for practicing procedures.

The controls and displays powered up and froze to a predetermined point in flight. Setting the simulation into motion, she worked her way through emergency after emergency—engine failure, engine fire, sensor overheat, fuel leak.

As each presented, warning lights flashed. Josie recited aloud the necessary recovery actions while her hands flew across the controls. She didn't need to speak the lists, but every recitation imprinted the procedures deeper into her subconscious for that critical moment when she wouldn't have time to think.

Emergency procedures continued to unroll, one after the other. Power surged through her. No hesitation. No mistakes. She was dead-on.

Out-freaking-standing! Take that, Diego "Cruiser" Morel, flight god with a killer bod.

She transitioned to her mission rehearsal and guided the simulated Predator onto the end of the runway, launching a dry run of a flight slated for next week. She clicked through take off actions, lifted the Predator into the air, climbed to nine thousand feet.

Diego angled closer. God he smelled good.

A bold callused hand thrust over her controls.

"Hey!" Frustration fired.

He fiddled with the simulator panel.

"Damn it, Morel!" Frustration upgraded to anger. "What the—"

The visuals on her screen rolled, inverted, started to spin. Anger increased as fast as airspeed on her control panel, but she didn't have time to chew out Diego. Yet. Her hands and feet whipped into action, lowering the nose, applying opposite rudder to control the spin.

Order restored. The landscape leveled. And now she could level Diego Morel, too, for messing with her rehearsal.

She glued her eyes on the screen, hand on the stick. "I don't know what the hell you thought you were doing, but keep your damn hands off my control panel. Next time, I'll break a finger. Got it?"

His silence hung heavy.

"Don't play games with me. And if you were trying to make me screw up, you failed. I recovered from your induced spin. Now back off and let me finish my flight plan."

His eyes seared into her like hot black coals.

"I did recover." So why wasn't he smiling or congratulating her or even taunting her. "What?"

"Nothing."

"Bull. What are you thinking?"

He leaned back, stretching out one booted foot. "Have you considered that there would be a person in the wide-open air straddling the Predator when you recovered from the spin?"

"Of course I have. I think about every pilot I put out there with every flight. I hope like hell the spin doesn't happen, but if it does, he's strapped on and wearing a parachute. He's protected."

Diego nodded, didn't say anything.

And damn but she could still hear his unspoken censure. "What?"

"It's *your* flight. Run the show however you want."

"Damn it, Morel, say whatever it is you're bottling up."

"You executed a perfect spin recovery."

"Thank you." Warmth swelled over a silly little compliment.

He hitched a booted foot up on one threadbare knee. "It was picture-perfect for a conventional aircraft or even an operational Predator. But that pilot strapped to the craft sort of changes things. The book answer may not be what you need."

Prissy Josephine couldn't resist snapping back. "Well, the book answer's there because it's right."

He went silent again.

She sighed. "Okay, what's the other answer?"

"You need to feel the plane."

She snorted. "You're kidding, aren't you?"

He stared back without speaking, confidence, experience and patronizing patience stamped on his rugged face.

Fine. No need to get her G-suit in a twist, as he would say. She would be a fool not to tap into his knowledge base because of pride. She might not agree with that spooky bullshit "feel the plane" mind-set, but it would be awesome to see this man fly.

"Show me."

He hesitated. Hunger simmered so hot in his eyes she almost jerked back to avoid being singed. Just as fast, he doused the look. He gave her a curt nod. She paused the program and swapped places with him in the sensor operator's seat. Diego sank into the pilot's position. His fingers wrapped around the stick.

He reset the aircraft to level flight and punched in the same malfunction code to cause the spin. She scrutinized the nose camera where the world began to tilt, flip, swirl.

His hand gravitated off the stick.

The air damn near hummed around him.

He applied one pump to the opposite rudder before both feet came up off the rudders. The spinning image in the nose camera slowed. The world steadied again.

Diego took back the stick and gently raised the nose to resume normal flight.

Josie struggled to comprehend what her brain told her shouldn't have happened. "What the hell was that?"

"Didn't you ever take up a single-engine prop plane when you were learning to fly?"

"What does that have to do with anything?"

"The Predator is a lot like the Cessna or a Beech Trainer. They aren't made to be manhandled like military airplanes. In fragile aircraft such as those, less is better. Sure you can jerk around the Predator if you're in a crunch. It's tougher than the civilian craft. But why force it if you don't have to? Plus, I'm fairly certain that if your butt was in that saddle, you wouldn't want the nose pointed toward the earth."

She shook her head. "But the regs say—"

"Screw the regs. Sometimes when your ass is up there, in order to know the spin-and-recovery characteristics, you just have to let it go and see what happens."

She was smart. A fact. And a truly smart person

knew when to recognize times others knew more. This was one of those times.

Diego Morel had a rare gift. A deep sadness permeated her. How could she not grieve over what the air force had lost? Even more heartbreaking, what this man had lost.

"Swap seats with me and we can run it again—" He dragged his gaze away from the screen to glance at her.

His eyes read her unguarded thoughts in a heartbeat. Then his gaze heated to metallic black. "Hell, Buttercup, I warned you about the consequences if you threw your damn pity my way again."

His eyes went hard and hungry all at once as he leaned toward her.

Her wait for reassurance was definitely over.

Chapter 7

Stunned stock-still, Josie watched Diego cant closer. She'd looked for reassurance he still wanted to blow off steam together.

But this was more, faster than she'd expected.

Then he stopped short of actually kissing her, his nose so near hers she could feel his warm exhales of coffee-scented breath. Spots danced in front of her eyes much like the light-headedness from pulling Gs.

Oh. Yeah. She should be breathing.

She released pent-up air. "Diego?"

He continued to hold her with his eyes if not his arms. "Did you have fun out there with Bridges at Red Flag?"

His question blindsided her, a rare feat since nothing surprised her anymore, thanks to her careful planning.

Awareness burned over her, inflamed by abstinence. No. Wait. Somehow she knew that even if she'd experienced five incredible orgasms yesterday—ha, she should be so lucky—she would still be turned on by this man.

She swallowed but held her ground. "Lots of hairy flying goes on at Red Flag, but then I imagine you already know the sorts of tight midair situations that can happen there."

He nodded slowly, still close enough for the intimacy of shared body heat that contradicted dry tech talk. "Yeah, I remember those days mighty well."

"A training exercise like that is good though." Her breasts tightened under her sports bra. "It helps me remember what all of this is about, you know?"

"Sure do, Buttercup."

His eyes devoured her lips until she fought the urge to lick them. Lick *him*. Would he like the taste of orange tryst? "What does this have to do with our simulator flight?"

"So, you and Bridges had a fine ol' time then."

And in a flash, she understood the direction of his question. Even as it surprised her, angered her, too, she couldn't deny the surge of desire, because he would only ask for one reason. "There's nothing going on between Bridges and me."

"I didn't ask."

A swell of feminine power smoked through her. "Yes, you did."

Three lazy blinks later, he angled away, a low laugh rumbling an echoing bounce through the small chamber. "There you go again, cutting me no slack."

She sagged back into the leather embrace of her

seat. There would be no kiss after all. "You said you like that about me."

"I do."

Here it was. Her chance to blow off steam with Diego. "I need to pack up soon. I have that dinner with Craig's family."

"Of course. You go on ahead. I'll finish things here."

That was it? He was going to let her walk out?

Decision moment. Launch or not? She opened her mouth, half certain she would walk away from temptation in spite of his encouraging move. "How about you come with me to Craig's?"

Apparently the old impulsive Josie was alive and dancing under her controlled exterior. The more cautious Josephine backpedaled to justify. "The whole test team will be there along with other folks from the base. You'll have a chance to evaluate people in a relaxed setting. Craig's got beer, and his wife always makes enough to feed an army anyhow."

Boots crossed at the ankles, he lounged. "You don't want me in here alone with your precious data."

"Not particularly. But I was also thinking perhaps you didn't want to be alone. And maybe a home-cooked meal might dilute the crankiness in your system."

No flickered through his eyes as he battled her controlling their path. Then faded. "Sure. Sounds like a fine idea. I can get to know Wagner better and eat some real food for a change instead of my own cooking. A good deal all the way around."

"Excellent. Give me a few minutes to run over to the gym and change, then I'll be ready." She leaned to scoop up her flight bag. When she rose, Diego stood, too.

"Hey, Buttercup?" He stared down at her with deep brown eyes full of promise. "I haven't forgotten about that look of yours. You owe me once we're through at Wagner's."

This was more than she'd bargained for, but she reminded herself of the recent midair near miss that all logic said never should have happened. She needed to balance her life before she fell off the edge like her mother.

Josie stared right back. "I'm counting on that."

Anticipation fired through her much like before the pilot pumped his arm for a launch sequence in Red Flag for a kick-ass flight.

A flight that at any minute could turn deadly wrong.

"Damn, Wagner, your wife sure puts out a killer spread of food." Diego hitched up to sit on the deck rail by the tapped pony keg of beer. Outdoor stereo speakers throbbed with *Jimmy Buffett in Concert* for the packed backyard in military housing. "Thanks for letting me crash the party."

"No problem," Wagner called from a few feet away. Wearing a ten-gallon hat, he pushed his toddler on the sprawling wooden swing set. "You're part of our team for a while at least."

"Seems so." Diego nursed his lone mug of beer for the night, determined to keep a clear head. He had plans for Josie Lockworth and he had the distinct feeling he would need full control of his wits to take on that woman.

And damned if he wanted the sensation diluted in any way.

Floodlights flickered on with the setting sun, illuminating the small patch of fenced sandy grass. Josie stood in a cluster of aviators flying their hands through the air. A short jean skirt hung low on her hips, wide black belt resting just above her butt. He figured they'd crossed a line now that made it okay for him to check out her ass, then her long legs all the way down to flip-flops that somehow looked elegant on this woman.

Of course she transformed even combat boots into runway-model material.

Yeah, he sure enjoyed looking at her. She wore a couple of shirts, gray and white layered, both stretchy fabric that clung to her like a second and third skin, stopping shy of the top of her belt. He liked the hint of lace along her scooped neckline and rimming the hem, too. When he kissed her—soon, now that he'd finally gotten the okay from her—he would have easy access to the small of her back, then around front to the flat expanse of her stomach.

Her slim bare arms glided through the air in another fly-talk motion. He remembered well the days of shooting down his wristwatch with his other hand while spending every second on the ground reliving all the missions in the air.

These days, he only relived one mission.

Damn but he needed another beer. He shifted his attention away from the tap and over to Wagner at the swings. "Hey, I read your quick look on your last flight mission. That was some excellent work, my friend. Great after-action evaluation. Not everyone has as much detail in their quick looks."

"Thank you, sir. I like to get out everything I remember as fast as I can, spill it all out of my head while it's fresh before I go on to the next one. A tip I picked up from Josie. That woman has attention to detail down to a fine art. Nothing but the best is going to come from this test."

Protectiveness pulsed from Wagner. For a moment Diego wondered if maybe…but he believed Josie. To her, Wagner was a friend. And a damned fine source of information about a certain Buttercup currently executing a flat spin with her left hand. "Aren't you two TPS classmates?"

"Yep. That we were." He shoved the airplane-shaped swing, his drowsy little girl drooping sideways in the contained cockpit seat.

"What's her story? Anybody make a run at her?"

Diego knew he wasn't a great prize, and he figured if a woman could put up with his faults he could put up with hers. But he absolutely would not share. Finding his wife with another man had damn near exploded his head, even though he'd known their relationship was on the skids after the accident. When he wasn't her officer-and-a-gentleman flyboy anymore.

"A run at her?" Wagner's brow creased.

"You know the…boy-girl thing. While you were in test-pilot school, did some guy with a Harley run over her Pomeranian or something? Because sometimes she sure acts like it might have been me."

And other times not, like back in the simulator when she was more than open to a lip-lock with him.

Wagner's brow smoothed, his eyes turning speculative. He gave the swing with the sleeping toddler a final push and joined Diego at the deck railing.

The younger man leaned toward the tap and re-filled his mug, foam rising, the barley scent moistening the dry desert air. "Don't feel special. She treats most men like that."

"And the ones she doesn't treat that way?"

"Are a lot less dusty. Usually shave more often than holidays and funerals. The type to roll around on the floor with kids rather than roll around on the hood of a car with a bar bimbo. No offense."

"None taken." Diego studied the lounging flyer through narrowed eyes. The pilot's plaid shorts, polo shirt and deck shoes screamed straight-laced all-American. Wagner even had a spatula sticking out of his back pocket. "So you're saying she goes for guys more like you."

Wagner extended his arms with good-natured arrogance. "Can you blame her? Check me out. Am I a catch or what?"

Diego laughed along, then took a drag off his mug. "So? Did you and she ever hook up, before the wife?"

"Dude, I've been married since I was twenty." His eyes skated over to the pregnant woman waddling toward Josie with a bag of chips. Wagner's gaze held and warmed on his wife.

Or on Josie?

"So does that mean no?"

Wagner's humor evaporated faster than water on parched ground. Apparently Captain All-American had a temper. "In my world, that definitely means no. I love my wife. We've got a kid to bring up and another on the way in three months."

Diego raised his hands in surrender. "My apologies, Wagner. I'm an ill-mannered son of a bitch who just insulted the man supplying my beer."

Wagner's anger dissipated as quickly as it flared. "I'll accept the apology, for me and for Josie, too. You're just lucky you made that comment to me and

not her. She'd have gutted you. Even if I weren't totally gone on my wife, Josie's sense of rights and
wrongs are clear-cut."

"Sounds like you know her pretty well."

"She's a damn good friend. She put in a positive
word for me for this job so my wife could be near family with the second kid on the way. Josie remembers
who her friends are."

"And it doesn't put a burr up your ass to be working for someone your own age?"

Wagner set his mug on the railing slowly as if working through a ten-count calming. "Hey, I know you've
gotta ask these questions because it's your job. But
you've read her file. She earned what she got. And that
file doesn't tell you the most important part. She never
stabbed anyone in the back to get there."

"Are you trying to sell me on her?" The guy didn't
seem to realize how hooked he already was. Diego
hefted his mug to his mouth again.

"I just think she gets a bad rap sometimes from
people who are jealous of her connections."

Diego paused mid-swallow. "Connections?"

"Her grandfather, the old CIA director."

Pieces came together in his head. "Joseph Lockworth."

How had he missed the name? Even though the
guy had retired years ago, the link should have clicked.
And did any of this have something to do with a small-
time program coming under congressional oversight?
His dormant instincts itched.

Wagner drained his beer, swiping the foam from his
upper lip. "Then there's all that mess with her mother's
career and breakdown. Hell, Josie feels like she's got

a thing or two to prove. She works herself into the ground. She doesn't take much time for play. None, actually."

The younger man leaned to refill his mug, silence echoing until his words permeated. The guy was giving him advice about Josie easily when Diego had expected to pry it free.

Well, hell. The dude was giving his consent in a pseudo-brother kind of way. Diego thumbed the moisture on his mug. He would lock up his sisters rather than let any of them near an ass like him.

Yet already a plan had formed in his mind. He wasn't the kind of guy a woman like Josie Lockworth brought home to Daddy, but he sure-shooting knew exactly what kind of play she would appreciate. "Thanks for the advice."

"You're welcome." Wagner straightened. His easygoing face made a quick shift into a hard mix of protective brother and warrior. "Just treat her right or you're a dead man."

What a to-die-for night.

Stepping onto Craig's front porch, Josie inhaled perfect night air at the end of the longest evening she could ever remember. But overall, productive. Lifestyle Balancing Act 101, going good so far.

She scanned the cars lining the street, searching for a looming Harley while shrugging into her leather flight jacket. The party had been awesome—except for being hours too long while Diego's eyes followed her wherever she walked.

Finally she could leave without seeming rude. Funny how she'd never minded staying to clean up in the past rather than return to her condo. Tonight, she couldn't whip those dishes into the dishwasher fast enough. Only the sight of a poor pregnant woman's swollen feet had kept her there, out of guilt.

Then Diego had offered up his thanks to the host and hostess, tossing Josie one last heated look before striding out the front door. She'd been no less than ten steps behind him.

So where was he?

A car cruised down the street, headlights sweeping the area to reveal…Diego leaning against the front quarter panel of her Mustang. Waiting.

For her.

She took her time descending the steps, enjoying the anticipation, the thrill, the challenge this man posed. She thumbed the unlock button on her key chain. "So you like my V-eight engine?"

"I just might at that." Boots crossed at the ankles, he smoothed a hand along the hood like a tender lover. "The question is, did you buy it for the looks or the horsepower?"

"I'm not about the looks, Morel."

"Damn lucky for me." That wicked grin of his brought vivid reminders of his promise of a kiss to make her forget everything else. "Wanna compare engines?"

"What did you have in mind?"

"Climb into your car and follow me." Without waiting for an answer, he shoved away from her Mustang and headed for his Harley.

More surprises. Already she tingled in anticipation.

Revving the bike, he waited for her again until she turned the key and lowered the car top for an open-air ride. He peeled away from the curb, taillights glowing in the night, through base housing, out the front gate. She kept him in the crossed beams of her headlights, his broad back in leather offering a perfect pacing target.

For twenty minutes, maybe thirty, even forty, she lost track and just followed. The wind in her hair aired out stresses she hadn't realized existed. Deeper and deeper into the desert they drove. Smooth paved roads gave way to pocked asphalt, then graded dirt ways.

He pulled off onto the dusty shoulder, pointing his bike toward a dried-up lake bed. She stopped alongside. "What's the plan now?"

His gaze flicked to the wide-open lake bed, then back to her. His bike gave another growl. "Ready to see whose engine's better?"

A challenge.

Oh, yeah.

Ultimately, in a long race, no car could match a motorcycle, but maybe in this short stretch, if she lunged out a second ahead of him... Either way, it would be fun to let the engine loose.

She smiled back, her hand sliding surreptitiously to the gearshift. Without blinking, their eyes held. Tension snapped while engines idled in wait for the signal to—

Go!

In lightning synchronicity, she released the clutch and nailed the gas. The Mustang sprang forward onto the hard-packed desert. Sand spewed from her tires in a puff behind her, barely visible in her rearview mirror.

She tore her eyes from the reflection. Diego wasn't there anyway. She could feel him, hear him keeping up beside. His single beam and her double striped ahead, providing minimal warning of rocks and pot-holes.

Forty. Sixty. Ninety miles per hour.

God, this was dangerous as hell and so damned incredible. She hadn't felt like this since horseback-riding lessons as a kid, tearing across the countryside with the wind in her hair, power unleashed to eat up the ground. Diego called to a side of her she'd been suppressing since her mother's breakdown nearly twenty years ago.

She wanted to believe what he'd said about learning to trust her instincts as well as facts. She needed to think this sudden impulsive yearning to open up and feel would somehow lead her to answers about all those questions about the past. That she wasn't just being selfish. Reckless. Plain stupid.

Her hands tightened around the wheel. Her heart raced faster than her car. Adrenaline sheeted through her veins like the wind tearing at her hair from the open-air ride.

Topless.

She grinned just remembering his audacity. Then her body tightened in response. The screaming gusts whipped inside her jacket in brazen caresses that left her hungering for the touch of a man, of *this* man riding alongside her. Equal, without giving ground. A man who, even if she inched ahead, wouldn't diminish but would instead applaud her.

And challenge her all over again.

The stretch of flat land grew shorter, the gentle roll of dunes and rock drawing closer. Closer still, marking an end too soon.

She sped past the border of the dried-up lake bed. Nailed her brakes. Spun out in a cloud of sand and dust and stimulation.

The dust settled around her. An image of Diego straddling his Harley emerged from the night-lit cloud.

Who had won?

She wasn't sure.

For the first time she could ever remember, she didn't care.

The time had arrived to stop or go forward with Diego Morel. The part of her that never backed down from a challenge insisted she face him. The wise book-worm told her that if she left the car, he would kiss her. Maybe more.

And she would like it.

Temperatures dropped in the night, but not nearly enough to cool her overheated flesh. She almost hoped he would leave her no choice, that he would swing his Harley in front of her car in some bold move. She would have to stay. She could laugh and even snap at him a lit-tle.

Instead, he swept off his helmet but stayed on the motorcycle. In spite of his "promise" of a kiss to wipe away whatever sympathetic look she'd slipped up to toss his way, he would still leave the final choice to her.

Desert winds were never gentle, especially not now as the unrelenting currents streaked Diego's dark hair behind him. Leather and muscle. Her warrior spirit recognized his. Elemental. Raw.

Arousing.

A wise woman would throw her car into reverse and haul back across that dried-up lake bed faster than the first race. There were so many reasons she shouldn't get involved with any man—this man—right now, if ever. But the old *Josie* stirred within her, daring, double daring and most persuasively reminding *Josephine* of an empty condo with nothing but pictures and Beanie Babies for company.

She reached for her gearshift. Her fingers curled around the stick and held. Diego's eyes flickered with disappointment, a maelstrom of emotion from this stark man.

Decision made, Josie turned off the car.

Chapter 8

Josie threw open the door of her car, enjoying the slow smile that slid over Diego's face. There was no mistaking his sexual intent.

Standing, she steadied her legs and determination. With the thrill of their night ride still buzzing through her like the wine she never drank, she craved more.

More than just a drink and shooting the breeze.

She leaned against her door while he walked toward her. The wind roared almost as loud as the pounding of her heart in her ears. She was a woman of calculated, safe risks in the air and on the ground. There was nothing safe about the man stalking toward her.

He stopped in front of her, inches away. A touch away.

Her hands fisted against the car behind her. "Thank you for an incredible ride."

"You're welcome." He hooked his thumbs in his back pockets, drawing the black button-down taut across his chest as he stroked her with his eyes if not his hands. His mouth. "I hope you'll find the one to come as incredible."

She shivered, her breasts tingling, tightening from far more than the chill of a November desert night. "Mighty confident there, aren't you, Cruiser?"

He stared down at her for one long blink, neither advancing nor backing away. "Do I have reason not to be?"

She let her hands slip from behind her back, fall to rest on his shirt and toy with the top button. "I'd say things are looking good for you at the moment, but you could always work to tip the odds in your favor."

"Worried I'll say something asinine and ruin the mood?" He planted both hands beside her on the car in a touchless embrace.

"It's always a possibility."

"Guess that will just keep us both on edge." He angled closer until their torsos met, hip to hip.

"Edgy's good." Unable to stop a subtle rock of her hips against his, she gazed into the molten heat of eyes gleaming in the dark.

"Good?"

"Better than good." Her words trailed off in a whisper.

"Damn straight." He skimmed his mouth over hers, gentle brushes at odds with the rasp of his late-day beard.

Once. Twice. Again, until finally she slid her hands up and around the back of his neck, into hair surprisingly soft. "You're far more patient than I am."

Josie arched up on her toes as she urged his head down. His open mouth met hers, hot and hungry. He explored her mouth, along her teeth, inviting her into him.

Yes.

"Touch me," she demanded.

His hands answered her. He cradled her head in one broad palm while his fingers stroked back the shoulder of her jacket before skimming along her side to her hip.

He growled into her mouth and guided her closer against…oh, my…he really did want her. Now. At least as much as she wanted him.

She was nearing thirty, damn it, and at the moment, she couldn't imagine living another day celibate. She wasn't a virgin, but her experiences had been few and far between—only two actually, one in college, one after she'd finished the intense pilot training.

Each time had been carefully thought out after knowing both men for months. The relationships had been satisfying. But nothing that made her want to throw away caution for the risk of more.

Diego Morel was a huge risk in so many ways, one she had to have. She could handle it. He'd proved over the past couple of weeks that he could do his job well. And she trusted her own paperwork trail to protect her.

Oh, God, was she really analyzing data in the middle of the hottest kiss ever? She seriously needed to get a life. "Your place or mine? It's about as far a drive in either direction. Maybe we could race again?"

"What about here?"

"Here? Now?" The now part was definitely appealing.

"Why not here?"

Her inexperience was showing at a time when she wanted to dazzle this beyond-dazzling man. "It's not that I need a closed bedroom door."

His head dropped back. He dragged in air. "Damn. I'm sorry. Not thinking. You deserve better than rolling around on the hood of a car."

"That image sounds pretty good to me. But—"

"No need to justify." He tipped his head forward to stare into her eyes again, his smile almost managing to lighten the tense cut of his jaw. "We'll find a bed with sheets to mess up."

"Honestly, it's just…"

"What?" He smoothed back a strand of her wind-snarled hair, tangled from his hands, as well.

"That whole camera swoop of Bridges's SUV kinda gives me the creeps."

He tensed, scanned the air. "Anyone flying tonight?"

"Not that I know of."

"A moot point since we have a date with sheets." He tugged her jacket back onto her shoulders. "Yours are probably prettier than mine. We'll enjoy the hell out of another race back. More anticipation."

She was already primed to explode as it was. So why wasn't she climbing into her car?

"Josie?"

A coyote howled in the silence before she finally forced the truth out between gritted teeth. "I'm just pissed at myself."

"Well, I guess that's a change from your being pissed at me."

She tried to smile. Failed.

"Okay, what's got your G-suit in a twist?" He gentled his demand by caressing his thumbs along her jawline. "Spill it, because I'm not interested in anything but your full attention right now."

She hesitated, out of habit and yes, the very real fear that this man would think she was a paranoid nutcase.

"Josie?" he insisted, and for some reason she wanted to trust him.

She had no idea why, only that impulsive Josie was clearly in control over her more practical Josephine ways at the moment. "I really do like the idea of being wild and uninhibited out here together. And I hate that it won't happen because I can't shake the creepy feeling that someone's watching me. Okay?"

He stilled against her. Already-honed muscles hardened to a sheet of steel in his wolflike wariness. "Right now? You feel like someone's watching us now?"

"I'm sure it's because I'm spending so much time peeping with reconnaissance cameras, I've started assuming everyone can see. Totally paranoid, I know. And if you tell anyone I said it, I'll vow you're lying."

"Your instincts say someone's watching us now?" he repeated as if to insure her exact perception.

She hesitated, searching his eyes until she was certain he wasn't looking at her like she was a nutcase. "Yes. Even though we're in the middle of nowhere without a tree or hill in sight for anyone to hide behind, I feel like somebody's watching us."

He didn't argue, merely nodded, all passion gone from his face and replaced by pure lethal drive. "Get in the car. Go straight to your place, since at least it's in a populated area. Mine's too remote. I'll be behind you the whole way."

"Diego?" She'd wanted him to believe her, but his quick insistence rattled her. She almost didn't recognize this man barking orders at her, a strange contradiction of military authority packaged in a rough biker body. "I just wanted us to slow down and head home. I don't honestly think there's someone right here threateningly close—"

"We'll talk when we get to your place. Time to go. Now," he ordered.

She grappled behind her for the door handle. Diego Morel might not be wearing his uniform these days, didn't even carry the commission any longer, but there was no denying that this man was still a warrior.

And he sensed danger, as well.

Ever aware of the danger of discovery, Birddog adjusted camera angles on the Predator's remote control screens. Working both the pilot and sensor operator jobs was challenging, but doable with some autopilot settings. A hazardous risk? Maybe. But the payoff would be rich.

And the thrill made it all worthwhile. Besides, he wouldn't be caught. Hadn't he proved his invincibility over the years?

Officially, there weren't any flights tonight. But Josephine Lockworth didn't know everything that went on around here. He had a few connections of his own to log unofficial flight time on a regular, unmodified Predator that didn't require a test rider on the craft.

He'd simply disguised the request as an interest in keeping skills honed on projects in his testing world. In reality? He wanted to test a little idea he had in mind for an upcoming mission.

He'd hoped the near miss at Red Flag would shake her focus, since siccing Shannon Conner on her hadn't. But no luck. He'd been certain the adjusted coordinates at Red Flag would go undetected in the fog of practice war fighting, and he'd been correct. He'd been equally certain she would survive. Again, correct. But he had also expected her to doubt her instincts, and therefore falter on her next Predator ride.

Wrong. She'd come back stronger than ever, grabbing hold of her life.

Or rather, grabbing hold of Diego Morel.

Birddog watched the two trails of dust puffing behind the Mustang and Harley as they tore back across the dried-up lake bed.

He could get a better look if he didn't have to man both crew positions. But something was better than nothing. She was looking over her shoulder far too often these days, double-checking her work. Listening to Morel.

Now their out-of-control necking session left him with no doubts. They'd teamed up. He could see that well enough. Morel was supposed to have been so riddled with resentment over Josie Lockworth living his dream that he would screw up and offer an easy conduit for disinformation. Instead, this woman somehow seemed to be bringing the old Diego Morel back to life.

If women had any clue how much influence they had over a man, how much power they wielded, the male species could well be doomed. Hell, wasn't his life even now being shaped by one rejection?

Birddog swiped dust from the screen, then from beside the keyboard. Didn't anyone clean this place? The damn dust and dirt were everywhere.

He forced his hands to still. It would never be clean enough anyway, since *she* never seemed to notice and appreciate his attention to detail.

The bitter gall of being tossed over for another man, an unworthy man, roiled bile up his throat. He swallowed down the burn. Who knew what the hell drove women to pick such obvious losers—men never destined for greatness because they were weak when it came to women.

He wasn't weak. He'd lost the opportunity once, but wouldn't fail again.

No more time for wondering. Time to act.

Inaction was about to kill her.

Josie steered her car into her parking lot. Thank God, their hour-long ride back was finally finished. The whole way, Diego had kept his bike centered neatly behind her Mustang, but there had never been a sign of anyone following them. Her sense of being watched faded with every mile.

Other gut feelings, however, were still at full roar…and were damn glad they were approaching her condominium complex, where they could find a bed. A wall, floor, sofa, hell, even a table, would work, too, as long as they were minus some clothes.

She scanned her parking lot, which was filled with cars but quiet. Logical for this late at night. Lines of two-story stucco town houses stretched, lights glowing from only a few windows. The last of her jangling instincts quieted. For now at least.

Josie flung open her car door. Diego had her by the arm, hauling her toward her condo, barely leaving her time to grab her bag from the seat. Hand on her back, he shuttled her deeper into the condo complex along the curvy sidewalk.

"Diego?" Her flip-flops slapped the walkway. "I really think we're okay now. We're safely home and I'm already starting to laugh at myself a little for getting wigged out—"

"I'm almost certain someone was also watching you a couple of weeks ago."

Her feet slowed. "Then it hasn't been my imagination all this time."

Shooting her an exasperated look, he tugged her along. "You've wondered about someone watching you before tonight in the desert? Why the hell didn't you say something sooner?"

"It's not like I'm getting creepy calls or letters. It's just a feeling that I thought had more to do with my project being under such scrutiny." She paused. "Hey, wait. You said you knew someone was watching me?"

"Back at the Wing and a Prayer, the first day we met."

"But I thought *you* were the one watching me there. You thumped on my roof right after I got that being-watched intuition."

"Great. You thought I was a stalker perv."

"Apparently I got over that impression fast, since I'm here with you now." Likely to be much closer.

"I came to your car because I thought someone was watching. Even though I never saw anyone, I was mighty certain. At the time, I figured it was some drunk looking to take advantage. But now with you having the same sense—more than once—that's too much to put down to coincidence."

"You didn't need a ride that night."

He shrugged.

"Why didn't you tell me then so I wouldn't have to worry that I'm losing my freaking mind?"

"I thought it was just someone looking to hit on you. I didn't have reason to believe otherwise."

She scrunched her toes in her flip-flops and started walking again. "I can take care of myself, you know."

"Yeah, I hear ya, Buttercup. But sometimes it doesn't hurt to have a little help on your side to tip the scales. I just don't want anything to happen to you."

Stopping in at the corner unit in front of a silver gray door with stained-glass stars inset, she reached into her purse and pulled out her keys. "Sorry for being an ingrate when you were just worried about me."

"There you go again, being all fair and genuine." Backing her under the safety of the porch overhang, he tucked a strand of hair behind her ear. "I didn't know people like you still existed. I figured they would have all been gobbled up by the Big Bad Wolf a long time ago."

"Is that a proposition to gobble me, Mr. Wolf?" She gripped his shirtfront, yanking him closer.

"I believe it could be. How will you protect yourself?"

"I do have some serious martial arts training."

Angling her hips closer to his, he grinned. "Wanna mosey inside and wrestle?"

She smiled back. "I'm a black belt."

"And I'm a street fighter. Should be fun."

"It could get messy." She tugged the leather band from his hair.

"I fight dirty, as big bad wolves are known to do."
He flattened her against the door.

She plowed her fingers through his hair. No teasing brushes of mouths and tongues this time. She went after what she wanted. Took it. Demanded more.

Her fingers tangled in his hair while her other hand scaled along his back, lower to guide him against the cradle of her hips.

He mumbled against her mouth, "Give me your keys."

"My keys?" She held up both empty hands. "Oh, uh, I thought I had them. I must have dropped them when I—"

Damned if her face didn't heat.

"When you put your hands in my hair? Or on my ass?"

Josie swatted him. "The keys are probably on the sidewalk or in the bushes somewhere."

She leaned just as he scooped the key ring from between his boots. He began to straighten. She didn't.

"Hey, Buttercup? You okay there?"

She was still staring at the dim glow streaking through the stained-glass inset on her door, casting shadows on the walkway. Her brain tried to push reason through the passionate fog. "I didn't leave the light on inside."

"Are you sure?"

"I'm sure. I always turn off the lights."

Someone had broken into her apartment. Might still be inside. Even as her fingers dialed 9-1-1, she wouldn't wait idly by, allowing the intruder the opportunity to sneak back out. And she knew without question there was no way in hell Diego would stand by while she tackled this alone.

Black belt and street fighter, they were going inside together.

Chapter 9

Diego could actually see Josie's muscles bunch in preparation for whatever threat waited inside her condo. Undoubtedly, she could put up one helluva fight. But with his instincts still on high alert and testosterone in overload...

Well, hell. He just couldn't bring himself to let her take the lead. Now he had to figure a way to maneuver her into staying outside the condo and out of the intruder's path. She could chew him out later.

And he didn't doubt that she would.

"Is there a back entrance?" he asked low.

She nodded. "With a fence around the patio about five feet high. And a balcony on the second floor off of my bedroom."

"No need for either of us to go in. Just kick the door wide. Loud. Most likely whoever it is will make a dash out and we can tackle him."

"Works for me."

"You watch the front. I'll take the back entrance."

"Since he's most likely to leave out the back?"

So much for maneuvering her any-damn-where. "Hey, I'm a guy. I don't care how capable you are. The protector syndrome comes with the testosterone for us men. You're lucky if I don't lock you in your car until this is done."

Josie rolled her eyes. "And you're lucky I don't have time to argue. Take the back exit, Thor."

He knew how to accept a win gracefully.

Without a retort, Diego tucked around the side of the corner unit and stopped behind one of the trees planted for decoration and watered endlessly to survive in an environment not meant to support shallow-root life-forms.

Of course, wasn't he as out of place with Josie?

Mind on the moment, Thor, he mentally thumped himself.

From this vantage point, he could keep his eyes on Josie at the front and the patio out the back. She slid the key into the lock, turned. Click. Click. He tensed.

She flung the door wide with a crash. Then flattened herself to the stucco wall beside the portal.

Waited. And waited. For nothing. Not a sound drifted from the condo. Maybe the intruder had already left. He debated how much longer to wait.

A shuffle sounded from inside. "Josie?" a female voice called. "Is that you?"

Josie's shoulders sagged as she all but deflated against tan stucco.

What the hell? Diego eased from behind the tree.

Spinning into the open doorway, Josie propped her hands on her waist, one hip jutting too damned enticingly. "Holy crap, Diehard. You're lucky we didn't kill you."

"You could have *tried*." A woman, mid-twenties maybe, scuffed toward the door in holey sleep socks with a bowl of macaroni and cheese cradled in her hand.

Diego assessed her as a possible threat in spite of Josie's—warm?—welcome. Medium height. It was tough to gauge her build or muscle tone buried under layers of baggy black sweats at least a size too big. Cheese sauce drips stained her left shoulder and the insignia on her top—a lightning bolt slashing through a red-and-gold crest.

Her short blond waves were swept back from her face with a wide green sweatband. Most women he knew would have run screaming in the other direction if faced with a man while wearing slouch clothes. Yet her oblivion gave her an appeal most women wouldn't understand.

There was potential under those sweats. *Waaay* under those sweats. Not that he was interested in looking, beyond making sure she wasn't out to hurt Josie. He had his hands more than full with a certain mouthy test pilot.

Diego ambled up to the two women exchanging hugs with a hint of awkwardness, as if out of practice. Watching them both so close, the family connection clicked as he spied their common ground. "Moxie."

"Huh?" Josie and Diehard answered in sync.

"You two don't look a thing alike, other than your eyes and similar height, but I could tell you're sisters by the attitude alone."

"No kidding?" Diehard shuffled back inside, Diego and Josie following. "I take after Dad, she takes after—"

"Our crazy mother." Josie slammed and locked the door.

"That's not what I meant."

Tension washed from Josie's spine. "I know. Sorry for snapping. Just one of those hot buttons, I guess."

Diego filed away the cryptic statement along with all the rest of the surprise personal info about Josie to process later. When his body wasn't testosterone fogged to Thor level.

He thrust out his hand. "Diego Morel."

The woman's eyes widened in recognition before she took his hand and shook. "Diana Lockworth, and it's an honor to meet you, sir."

Sir. Diego winced. "Thanks. But if you start telling me about how you studied my work 'back in the day' I'll have to kick your ass."

"Like I said before." Diana hitched her hands on her hips in more of that sisterhood-inherited moxie. "You could try."

Josie stepped alongside Diego, close, oddly so in a way she'd never done before. Damned if she wasn't claiming her man.

Testosterone levels rose. Thor-overload alert.

Diana simply laughed, turning to mosey into the great room. "Sheathe the claws, Josie, I'm not into poaching."

Diego winked down at Josie. "Does that make me a piece of meat or a carcass?"

Josie scowled.

Diana jerked a thumb in his direction. "I like him."

Hooking her hand through the crook of his arm, Josie stared up at him, scowl long gone and replaced by pure sensual hunger. "Me, too."

Need hammered through him like…well, like Thor's hammer. And there wasn't a chance in hell of relief tonight, thanks to Josie's surprise company. He needed an about-face away from temptation. And all told, the night had still been damned incredible. "I'm going to head out so you two can visit."

Diana gestured with her mac-and-cheese spoon. "Give me twenty bucks and I'll do the good little sister disappearing act with a movie and some jujubes."

"No," Diego insisted, "really, it's okay. I need to feed my dogs."

Josie followed him toward the door, calling back to her sister. "Hold on a minute and I'll be right back."

"Take your time. I've got a pot of mac and cheese calling my name for seconds." Diana disappeared into the kitchen with a *shoosh-shoosh* of her slipper socks along the tile floor.

Josie stepped into his arms. "I'm sorry things didn't work out for us tonight."

"Did you have a good time?"

"Yes."

"Then they worked out just fine." He met her kiss halfway. Ah, hell. He groaned against her lips. "How long is she in town?"

"I don't know," she whispered with a hint of regret. "I wasn't expecting her at all."

"I'll be at the Wing and a Prayer tomorrow night if you want to bring your sister along."

"Such a romantic date, my sister and a bar."

At least he didn't have to wonder about her picking up men in bars like his ex-wife used to do the minute his plane took off. "I'm meeting with a subcontractor who's pioneering new technology in propeller propulsion. None of which has been made public yet."

A purr vibrated up her throat. "Better than roses for this girl any day of the week."

"That's what I figured." His arms convulsed around her. His lingering physical regret over having to leave was at least somewhat appeased by relief that her intruder had only been her sister. "Be careful. Keep your eyes open and don't doubt your instincts for a second."

He issued the warning. There was nothing more he could do tonight. Yet his instincts were cranking again with impending doom, the sense that a death spiral was imminent and all the skill in the world wouldn't pull him out alive.

Wouldn't save her.

Damn, but he needed some perspective back. He grazed a final kiss over her lips, the last taste of Josie and orange he dared allow himself if he wanted to make it out her door without flattening her against the wall.

Closing the door after Diego, Josie sagged back flat against the hall wall. Silver picture frames rattled.

By the time Josie cancelled the 9-1-1 call, Diana emerged from the kitchen with two bowls of pasta and a smug smile. "Looks like maybe you don't need this after all."

"Think again." Josie arched away from the wall, her voice not much steadier than her knees, and snagged the second bowl from her sister.

How strange to have Diana here, since they rarely talked, much less visited. With her super-spy intel officer skills, Diana certainly hadn't needed to use the key Josie had given her—a token gesture at reaching out.

Navigating Diana's prickly nature was tricky enough long-distance. She would have to tread warily if she wanted to get through this visit without a huff-fest. And more than she would have thought, Josie wanted to reclaim some neutral ground between them. They'd lost so much time together because of dodging land mines in discussing their mother's breakdown.

Diana plopped cross legged onto the leather couch. Her oversize sweatsuit draped around her like a bunched black blanket. "Guess my timing really sucked then."

"It's okay," Josie rushed to add before Diana hopped out the front door. Josie dropped onto the white sofa beside her sister and flung off her flip-flops. "I'm probably not ready for him anyway."

"That intense, is he?"

"More so." She swung her legs to the side and tucked a pillow to her stomach. Josie thumped the stack of computer printouts on her coffee table absently. Thank God, she'd made copies in case someone genuinely *had* broken into her apartment.

The pieces of information were starting to shuffle in her head more and more each day. Back in her mother's testing days, computer data had still had a mystique. Far more had to be accepted on faith when it came to software.

The best she could do was cross-check the software versions notated with updated, current knowledge perceptions. All was accurate, each version the same. Yet for some reason the hard drive on her mother's program had been replaced frequently. Sure, parts were swapped out, but why so often? Probably nothing. Or could be everything.

"Are you seeing him again?"

Diana's question pulled her back to the present—to thoughts of Diego. Damn it, she should have been thinking about work tonight, not sex. How was a person supposed to balance both sides of life?

Hell if she knew. "Tomorrow night, at the Wing and a Prayer."

"A bar? You?" Diana's brows shot toward the headband holding back her mop of wavy blond hair. "But I thought you never drank. The whole Josie-never-loses-control-like-Mom mentality."

Josie bit her tongue. Hard. How like her sister to toss the big pink elephant out there in the middle of the floor and then get pissed if someone pointed it out.

"It's a business meeting." Subject-change time. She swatted her sister with a throw pillow. "It's great to see you, but what brings you out this way?"

"I had the day off with nothing better to do and frequent-flyer miles to burn." Diana flicked at the cheese sauce crusted on the front of her faded sweatsuit, then shrugged like the attitude-queen teen she'd once been not so long ago. "I guess Rainy's death has made us all think a little more about what's important. So, after I heard your voice on the phone, I decided maybe we could visit in person."

Josie winced over how close she'd come to e-mailing instead. "I'm glad you're here."

"No big thing," Diana garbled through a spoonful of mac and cheese.

Rainy's death had been officially labeled an accident—falling asleep at the wheel. But too many facts didn't add up, and the Cassandras had all been digging for answers, Kayla in particular. As if Kayla didn't already have a full plate as a single mother with a full-time job on the police force.

Josie's eyes tracked to the bookshelf full of Beanie Babies, the collection started by her mother. With Rainy's death still weighing heavily, Josie couldn't help but think about time being precious. Precarious. And sometimes tragically limited.

Her hand fell to rest on the stack of printouts. "Speaking of Rainy, did you ever find out anything more about that assassin—Cipher—who died last month?"

"There's nothing much in the official channels to add to Kayla's investigation. Doesn't help either that dead men don't talk, and Samantha sure put the Cipher six feet under."

A damned shame, information-wise, but their Athena comrade hadn't been left with a choice when it came to saving her own sister. Josie could see herself making exactly the same choice.

"So there's not even a lead to pass on?"

"No leads? I didn't say that." Diana's hazel eyes glinted with mischief. "Just that info from official channels is sparse. But I have my sources and I can hack almost anything out of a computer."

"And what do your sources say?"

"This guy was somehow affiliated with an obscure government lab numbered thirty-three. Something to do with an experiment, not a person. That's all I could find before I hit a massive firewall. This must be hot info for someone like me to have trouble cracking it. I'll forward you what I have once I get home."

Josie eased back, unwilling to damage the tenuous connection they were reestablishing. "I'll call Kayla this weekend so she can add the puzzle piece. However the hell it fits."

Josie sagged into the giving softness of the sofa and spooned macaroni into her mouth. Her endorphins shouted a huge thank-you for the much-needed boost. Thinking about Rainy's senseless death made her weary to her toes.

Diana stabbed her pasta into mush. "While I'm relaying the fruits of my cyber labor here, would you like a verbal summary of my other report before I leave in the morning? Or would you rather have an official printout once I get back?"

"Your other report?"

"On your guy Diego."

Her sister had gone above and beyond for her. She wanted to cry—which would probably send Diana into heart failure.

Now, how would she tell her sister she didn't want the report after all, since wouldn't he just be pissed at the invasion? Two weeks ago she wouldn't have cared. Two weeks ago he hadn't put his tongue in her mouth. "Uh, I'm not sure I need it anymore."

Diana's spoon paused mid-lift. "You made me work my computer geekdom magic into overtime for nothing?"

"I'm sorry." And God, she really was, for so many things when it came to her sister. "But I wasn't involved with him when I asked you to look. Now it seems…"

"Dishonest? Like something that might piss him off too much to go horizontal with you?"

Totally. And more. "I want to hear about it from him."

"Ooh!" Diana waved the spoon at Josie. "You've got it bad, sister."

"No. It's not like that." And if it was, she didn't want it to be. "We're attracted to each other. No doubt. But long-term? We'd combust." Too true.

"Then why not let me pass over the scoop on him?"

"Because he likes that I'm honest with him."

"Do you think he's playing you?" This prickly, blunt—smart—sister of hers never pulled punches.

"Why would he?"

"You tell me?"

She didn't even want to go there in her mind, where whispers of the abandoned kid still echoed, no matter how hard she tried to pretend she didn't care what the hell her father did. "Quit with the intelligence-officer interrogation crap, little sister."

"*Excuuuse* me for helping." Diana slouched back on the sofa in a mass of wrinkled fabric and surly sulk.

Contrition chomped hard. "I'm sorry. I'm being a bitch. It's not your fault this guy messes with my focus. Is there anything you found out that I need to know? Is he involved in anything illegal?"

"No." Diana's slouch eased to mere flounce level. "He's pushed it a few times with speeding tickets— *excessive* speed. There was also one near miss at a 'drunk and disorderly' in a bar right after his accident, but that's about it."

"Is there any reason for me to worry about him being sent in by the oversight committee? Any reason to suspect he's on the take? Or has some hidden agenda?"

"Not that I could I find."

If her computer-whiz sister couldn't find it, it didn't exist. Her ability to squeeze information from the cyber waves even made the military uncomfortable at times. Right now, it brought Josie nothing but relief. Diego might have shaken her focus, but he wasn't a threat to her project. She hadn't screwed up.

So far.

Josie stirred her pasta. "Does he have bizarre habits like communing with outer-space creatures or collecting toenail clippings?"

Her mouth twitched. "Absolutely not."

"Well then, as long as he doesn't have a wife tucked away at home, there's nothing else I need to know."

Silence echoed. Diana shoved an overlarge bite in her mouth and made a major production of chewing.

Josie's spoon never made it to her mouth. "Ohmigod. Please say he isn't married."

"He isn't married," she answered with too much precision.

"Really?" Her spoon clanked against gray stoneware. "Or are you just saying that because I told you to?"

Diana's gaze met and held without faltering. "I promise the guy is completely single and currently unattached to anyone else."

Josie stared back, searched, found honesty. Her arms turned limp with relief, her bowl dropping to rest on the pillow in her lap. "And I know for sure he's straight." She could still all but feel the imprint of his rock-solid arousal. "*Very* straight. So I guess I'm set then. I'm sorry to have put you to work for nothing."

"I'm glad you asked."

"Thank you…for looking and for coming here."

"I appreciated the call." Eyes so like her own skated to the carpet. "It's strange how our parents worked through everything and we still get pissed over it."

"I was thinking the same thing recently."

Diana studied the carpet as if it held some kind of mystery in its silvery expanse. "So we'll agree not to talk about who's right and who's wrong?"

"Probably a smart idea." Josie spooned macaroni up to her mouth, suddenly in need of the oblivion of starchy comfort more than ever. Cheese saturated her taste buds. "Hey, this isn't too bad, Diehard."

"I've had plenty of practice lately, thanks to my sporadic love life. Thus my free weekend to visit my sister." She rested her empty bowl on the coffee table. "So why did the two of you freak out so much over my being here?"

Josie opened her mouth to catch her sister up-to-date on the bizarre sense of being watched. She could use her sister's military intelligence insights.

Except she was about to leap out of her skin with nervous energy and frustrated cravings that had nothing to do with starch. "First, let me throw on some sweats. We can hit the gym and talk it over there. It's open twenty-four hours a day and I really need to work off energy."

Diana's smile turned dry. "Why do I get the feeling I'm about to be pounded by my big sister?"

"Don't try those mind-game tricks you intel officers study." Josie swung her feet to the carpet and stood. "You hold your own just fine."

"Hey, I'm using whatever weapons I've got in my arsenal to lower your defenses."

"Fine." She tossed over her shoulder on her way to the staircase. "But it won't work any more than that boo-boo lip garbage you used to toss my way when you didn't want to clean our room."

"But that *did* work.

"Argh. You're right." Starting up the steps, she held up her hand. "Forget the boo-boo lip, though, because I'm not looking."

Eyes watched her.

Josie's instincts didn't scream tonight as they had the evening before in the desert with Diego. Rather they whispered, stroking her reason with a sinister insistence.

Outside the Wing and a Prayer, she tugged on the hem of her brown leather flight jacket. Even worn with jeans, the coat still gave her an extra sense of armor and invincibility.

Parking-lot lights hummed. Damn it, why couldn't Diana have stayed on another day rather than leaving on the first flight out in the morning? Then she wouldn't be out here alone.

And their sister time had been some of the most fun they'd shared since… God, she couldn't even remember when.

She wouldn't have minded the reassurance of a second person walking alongside, affirming the spidery sensation. Or even to laugh at her silliness.

Only a few more steps and she would be inside the bar. Diego knew to expect her. And she could handle a mugger.

She hoped for just a mugger.

Her tennis shoes smacked gravel. If the recurring creeped-out feeling could be trusted, stalker was more probable. She'd heard and heeded Diego's warning by tucking a 9mm in the jean bag slung over her shoulder, had even parked under a light. She wasn't stupid or reckless. But she felt more like a paranoid nut than ever, packing a weapon against an imagined threat.

She reached for the knob just as the door swung open. Music, laughter and the clank of glasses blasted outside, red light flowing over her.

"Josie!" Mike Bridges blocked the entrance with his body and smile. Red light and noise faded as the door shooshed shut on its receding arm. "I didn't expect to see you here tonight."

"Diego's meeting with a subcontractor who's apparently right on the edge of a breakthrough with propeller technology."

"Come to think of it, I did see him inside."

"I should go on in. Diego's waiting for me to join them."

"Mixing work with play? Excellent." He gripped her elbow to guide her away from a large group streaming outside. "You're almost relaxing—and still keeping your project ahead of schedule."

"Thank you, sir." She inched her elbow free, although at least with Bridges around she wouldn't have to worry about creepy eyes. "I heard what you said at Red Flag and am taking it to heart."

"I'm glad. Your work's top-notch. But since you're already talking business, there are a couple of things I'd like you to bring up in conversation." He sidestepped another couple leaving. "Let's move out of the way over here for a minute so I can catch you up to speed."

She hesitated.

"We can talk in the bar, but then the guy Morel's meeting with will know I tipped you off."

Valid point. And the parking lot was well lit. If he'd wanted to hit on her, there had been ample opportunity in Vegas. Nodding, she followed him away from the entrance, past a row of cars until he stopped by his looming SUV.

"Okay, sir, what did you need to tell me?"

"Mike."

Her gaze jerked back to him. "Pardon me?"

"I'm not that much older than you, younger than Morel, in fact." He leaned one hip against the quarter panel, far more casual than any business chat. "When we're out of the office, it's fine to call me Mike."

Damn. Damn. Damn! She'd really wanted to be wrong about Bridges. Panic bubbled, even a little fear, but she refused to let it overtake her.

A calm head and plenty of distance would take care of this. "No, I can't. And it's time for me to join the others."

She started past him.

"I really wish you would reconsider." He circled in front of her, bracing one hand on the SUV, trapping her, blocking out the light and lot as he stepped closer.

Too close to be mistaken for anything but sexual intent.

Her throat closed. He had her back to the wall, professionally and personally.

But damned if she was going down without a fight.

Chapter 10

Where the hell was Josie?

From his chair at the small round table, Diego searched the bar for about the thousandth time. Easily he could envision her backing away from him. The woman was more than a little bristly about relationships.

Relationship? *Sex.* It was about sex, hard-driving lust.

Ah, shit.

Who was he kidding? Josie Lockworth had crawled right up under his skin like a burr he didn't particularly need in his life but couldn't avoid. He more than suspected she felt the same way about getting involved. So yeah, he could envision her standing him up in a heartbeat.

But he could not imagine her being a no-show for

meeting a subcontractor with scoop on her project. Without question, Josie Lockworth lived for her work. Something he understood, since he'd been there himself, once upon another lifetime ago.

Then why wasn't she here? Scooting aside his untasted beer, Diego scanned the bar again for her silky brown hair in the crowd of bobbing heads. All those unwanted warning instincts twitched to life again. He shot from his chair, cutting off the subcontractor midramble.

"Hold that thought, Pete. I need to make a quick phone call." Sprinting toward the door, Diego shouted to the waitress to add any more drinks to his tab.

Outside and away from the noise, he fished his cell from inside his leather jacket and punched in her number with impatient fingers while he searched the parking lot. The phone rang. And rang.

Her voice mail picked up at the exact moment he spotted her Mustang spotlighted in a fluorescent circle. The car was empty.

His brain burned.

"Josie?" he called in a voice deep and full of authority. With luck, his approaching presence would stop any possible threat, like the night in this same lot when he'd sensed someone watching her.

No answer, just the distant rumble of cars echoed from the highway leading out of this middle-of-nowhere bar. He strode deeper into the parking lot, muscles bunched.

And then he heard it—just a rustle, a slight whimper two car rows over.

"Josie," he called again, calmly, in defiance of his slamming heart and feet picking up speed along gravel.

He rounded yet another row of vehicles, visibility dimmer without a light nearby. His eyes adjusted, saw—Josie and Bridges against the bastard's SUV.

Both bodies blended into one without enough room to slide so much as a military reprimand between them.

Blood pounded to his brain, clouded his vision, until all he could see was his ex in too damn near the same position outside a bar with a guy from his squadron. The final showdown had ended their marriage—the day he'd gotten shit-faced drunk because he was officially out of the air force.

Diego inhaled deep into his belly to clear the crimson haze. She wasn't his ex-wife Stephanie. Josie might not want him, either, but she sure as hell cared about her job enough not to risk it for a quick grope with Bridges.

Bridges was hitting on her against her will, pressing her too flat against the car for her to move. An entirely different red fog fired through now.

Diego forced a casual lounge against a truck bumper and let his voice stop the action. If this turned into a fight, he intended to have Josie at least a few inches away from the man.

"Bridges, the way I see this you're about a tonsil tickle away from a court martial."

Diego's voice cut the air with a lazy—and damn welcome—authority.

Disgust churning her gut, Josie took advantage of Bridges's momentary shock and shoved her way clear of him. She scooched along the car, under the bastard's arm and away, straightening her shirt and leather flight jacket with shaking hands. "Diego, am I ever glad to—"

"Well hell, Morel." An angry vein pulsed at Bridges's temple, making lie of his easygoing smile. "You're interrupting something that's none of your business. Head back inside the bar."

Diego shifted to look at her. "Is that what you want, Josie?"

"No! No." Her shaking voice steadied. "Of course it's not." It was all she could do not to hurl on the gravel.

Bridges raked his fingers through his mussed dark hair. "Fair enough. If the lady wants to go, by all means she can go. Nothing's happening here against anyone's will. Just two adults getting carried away by the moonlight. Luckily, nobody but you saw a thing. Right, pal?"

And with that came the implication that Josie couldn't file a complaint because there were no witnesses to anything beyond a kiss that had probably appeared mutual since Bridges had flattened her to the car.

She'd shoved at his chest repeatedly—without budging him. She could have taken him completely out. But that would have risked an article 15 for hitting a senior officer. Definitely damned unfair for him to ignore the very rules that kept her from delivering a much-deserved pummeling. So she'd been forced to resort to simple shoving and waiting for him to move just an inch so she could slide away.

Her jaw worked in frustration. "I hear and understand. But you'd better understand this, *sir,*" she delivered the surly salutation with lengthy disgust. "If you ever lay so much as one finger on me again, I'll make sure your career ends in the fastest crash and burn you can imagine. And I won't care if mine ends, as well."

She scraped her hand slowly, roughly across her mouth.

The major continued, "You don't want to do anything rash. There are already enough questions going around about you after your rescue stunt a few months ago for that friend. Then there's your mother's history and that near miss at Red Flag. Even if you make it through an investigation, do you really want yet another dark cloud of doubt following you for the rest of your career because of a simple misunderstanding?"

Stepping in front of Josie, Diego stared Bridges down. "Thing is, I don't care much about my career these days. So there are no constraints on what I may or may not do."

Bridges held up his hands in surrender. "Hey, back down, pal. I thought the lady was interested. I misread the signs. Not the smartest moment in my life, but nobody was hurt."

No one hurt? The guy was nuts. Sure she'd had a momentary attraction to him once, but she'd never, never said one word or acted on it. She wanted to confront him here and now on words that smacked of that clichéd "she asked for it" bullshit.

But now wasn't the time. She knew that, and would plan her next move carefully. When she didn't want to gut-punch the man.

Diego continued his deliberate look, not moving. Finally Bridges shrugged, smiled again and slid into his SUV. Gravel spit from the guy's retreat. Josie sagged back against a truck bumper.

This was so unfair.

She didn't consider herself one to shake her fist at the moon and bemoan her fate. But the horrible, flat-out injustice of Bridges's come-on enraged her. She'd said no. *Emphatically.* Right before Bridges had plastered his smarmy lips onto hers.

She wanted justice now, but knew she would have to be patient and follow the channels in place.

First thing Monday after her Predator flight, she would find a senior officer she trusted. She would be calmer, more rational and articulate after a breather. She would then make an official signed, dated, sealed Memo of Record about the incident for that officer to keep, detailing everything that had happened with Bridges. That would lay the groundwork for establishing a pattern of behavior. If anything ever arose from him again in regards to her or anyone else—and she prayed to God it wouldn't—her statement would be opened. She would take great pleasure in slapping it down on Bridges.

Meanwhile, she definitely had some swelling anger to vent.

Knowing that Diego was an undeserving target didn't stop words guaranteed to halt him in his tracks. "I can't believe you threatened him. I can fight my own battles. I do have a plan for dealing with this."

"Excuse me." Leaning against the hood of a Ford F-250, he hooked his boot heel on the bumper. "I thought you didn't want to play tonsil hockey with him."

"I don't." She shuddered.

Diego's words registered. He really believed she wasn't at fault in spite of Bridges's adolescent posturing. There Diego went again, being fair and deflating her anger. She wanted the chance to get all-out mad and stomp.

She needed a good fight.

Apparently she wasn't going to get one from Diego. "Thank you for not assuming I invited that crap from Bridges."

"Oh, I did actually—for about four red-fog seconds. And then I managed to think."

"You realized I really want you."

"I realized you wouldn't jeopardize your career with such a stupid risk."

Well now wasn't it just swell that he hadn't assumed she would turn Bridges away because she was already involved with another man? The hardheaded biker jerk standing a foot away was lounging against that truck so casually she wanted to knock his boot back onto the ground.

Maybe she would get her fight after all. "Good God, Diego, I was ready to sleep with you less than twenty-four hours ago. No way would I turn around and crawl all over some other guy. I thought you knew me better than that."

"Know you?" He shook his head, hair grazing shoulders encased in black leather as dark as the night and his eyes. "Not really. We only met a couple of weeks ago. It's not like we have some relationship going."

His words slapped her with the implication that she was only after sex with him. Something that, sure, she'd told herself. But somehow the words sounded ugly coming out of his mouth.

"Screw you, Morel." And screw this whole damn evening.

Men. More colorful, uncomplimentary terms came to mind.

Already she could see a punching bag at the gym with some specific male faces on it. She stomped away, mad at Bridges, Diego, herself and, hey, why not toss in some frustration with her dad and global warming while she was at it?

"Hold up." Diego stopped her with a hand to her arm without moving away from the truck. "I'm a rude son of a bitch."

"Is that an apology?" She sure couldn't tell from his stony face.

"Yeah, I guess it is."

"Well, thanks." She shrugged off his arm. "But I'm not accepting it. I've taken enough crap off men for one night, thank you very much. Do you have any idea how frustrated, upset, flat-out pissed I am right now?"

Anger glinted in Diego's eyes. He folded his arms over his chest, stretching leather taut across his shoulders. "No one can understand exactly what another person has been through."

"That's right!" She shot back in his face, too close, too tempting.

Her anger was misdirected and she knew it. None of this was Diego's fault. He'd never been anything other than straight up with her. Even super cyber sleuth Diana couldn't find anything on the guy. So he must be trustworthy on at least some level.

She angled around Diego and slumped beside him against the truck. "God, I couldn't even rack the guy's family jewels to get out of that for fear of being brought up on charges of assaulting a senior officer.

That comes with a far harsher penalty than if Bridges ended up accusing me of being the one to instigate the lip-lock. What the hell was he thinking?"

"Some people don't think when it comes to sex."

"It's just so damned wrong that he would use his position of authority this way."

"I wish I'd come looking for you sooner."

"I wish Bridges had gone somewhere else to drink tonight." Although she suspected that would have only delayed exactly the same situation. She shivered beneath the warmth of her flight jacket. "I had to wait and hope for a moment to break away before things got out of control and I was left with no choice but to deck him."

Josie gasped in gulps of chilly night air that did little to ease her tightening lungs. "I need to hit something and you're making yourself too easy a target. I gotta get out of here."

She spun away and toward the bar, where the subcontractor was hopefully still waiting.

"Bridges is going to start trying to cover his ass."

Diego's low words rode the ever-constant desert wind, stopping her more effectively than his grip a moment ago.

She turned to face him again. "Excuse me?"

"I've seen his type before. He's going to make a preemptive strike."

How could Diego stay so calm when she could barely understand English through her disillusionment? "What the hell are you talking about?"

"He's going to start dropping subtle hints that you've been hitting on him."

She shook her head. "He wants this to go away as much as I do."

"His ego's bruised and his ego is definitely tied into the size of his airplane, and thereby his career. He's going to be gunning for you now. You need to strike first if you want to protect your test project…and *your* career."

"I will. After my flight Monday, I'm going to write up an official Memo of Record. If he tries this again with anyone, there *will* be a paper trail to nail him."

"Good. Excellent move and completely warranted. But why stop there?"

"You think I should file an official complaint now?" She returned to slump against the truck beside him. "Even though it's just my word against his? That won't accomplish anything without corroboration."

He turned his head to stare down at her. "That isn't what I meant by preemptive strike."

"Excuse me for not taking Devious One-oh-one when I was in college. What do you suggest?"

Reaching, he gripped her chin in two fingers, tipping her face up to his. "Make it clear to everyone that you're involved with someone else so Bridges knows he'll look like a fool if he says you were hitting on him."

Oh, my.

Desire tangled with frustration and anger, dangerous emotions to mix with passion. But then, her feelings for Diego had never been gentle or pretty. And kissing him sure beat hitting a punching bag.

A car door slammed in the silence stretching between them. The bar door opened, people exiting. "Well then, Diego, I guess there's no better time than the present."

Catapulting into the plan with the force of too-many

fired-up emotions inside her, Josie pressed her lips to his.

Ah. Yes. Just as good as she remembered. How could that be when she'd been certain she couldn't have experienced anything this mind tingling?

His mouth opened beneath hers. A growl swelled from him into her as each bold, insistent, possessive swipe of his tongue bathed away the bitter taste of Bridges's betrayal.

Losing faith hurt. She should have developed calluses over the years, but instead each broken trust slashed deeper than the last. Too many foundations of her world had been shaken, starting with a child's certainty that Mama would always care for her and Daddy could fix anything.

She'd thought at least she could believe in the credo of duty, honor and service she'd found in her air force commission. Bridges had made a lie of that. And damn him for tainting something so many were willing to die for.

God, she didn't want to think anymore, just lose herself in sensation, Diego's hand sliding up to the side of her breast to erase memories of the press of Bridges's body against hers. His kiss deepened until she could have sworn she saw stars. Bright sparks shimmered behind her eyes once, again, flashing brighter like—

A camera.

Sparks turned to icy shards of premonition. Josie tore herself away from Diego.

Shannon Conner stood a few feet away with her camera and a smug smile.

Chapter 11

Josie blinked to clear her vision, if not her anger over Shannon Conner's latest backstabbing attack. No question, Shannon was gunning for more than photos to use as backdrops in some docudrama.

Well, she would be going away empty-handed.

Josie strode forward, anger lifting with the wind to swirl around her. "What the hell are you doing here, Shannon?"

"Searching for a story." Shannon held up her camera. "And it looks like I found one. These still shots will make fabulous insets during the rest of my video footage of Athena grads."

Josie snorted. "A few pictures of me making out with my boyfriend? How's that network-worthy news?"

Shannon zipped her camera case, swishing her no-doubt processed blond hair over her shoulder. "He's working with a congressional oversight committee looking into your test."

How did a television reporter know that? Suddenly a helluva lot more was going on here than she'd originally thought.

"Big freaking deal," Josie forged ahead. "There's absolutely nothing in the regs that says I can't see him if I want to. And if you learned nothing else about me, you know I don't break rules."

"Then you shouldn't have a problem with me including a few of these pictures in my little piece on Athena Academy graduates. I got a really flattering shot of you with his hand plastered on your breast."

"I've had a crappy day, Conner." Josie issued a final warning. "You really don't want to mess with me."

"Well, here's a newsflash for you. I've had a crappy lifetime. Athena grads like you and Alex Forsythe never understood what it was like to scrap for everything, to make my own opportunities." Her lip curled. "You with your CIA granddaddy and Alex with her family fortunes. But this story will show you all for what you are and finally launch *me*."

"Any grief that's come your way, you've brought on yourself. If your own stupid jealousy hadn't led you to set me up on that bogus stealing charge, you might have actually graduated from Athena."

"Bullshit." Shannon leaned forward as if to spit the word out of her painted mouth with all the venom she could muster. Her veneer peeled away in layers, revealing a mighty damn pathetic resentment beneath. "Right from the start, you elitists in the Cassandra group had your clique and all the privileges that went along with your collective family influences. I didn't stand a chance at being number one."

Josie's feet planted. She wasn't backing down. "You just don't get it. It was about the whole group succeeding. You could have been a part of that. But you're right on one thing. Athena Academy women do stick together. Just like you said during our desert flight about us being there for Kayla when she had her baby girl. Support and friendship helps you get ahead a helluva lot faster than going it alone." Her shoulders sagged with a sigh. "When are you going to let go of this vendetta?"

"When you and your coattail-riding friends are washed up."

"And how does taking cheesy clinch shots of me improve your chances for respect?"

"I call this news, hon."

"God, Shannon." Josie swung her jean sack purse to the ground. There was no other way. Shannon Conner was seconds away from eating gravel. "It's so damn sad to see someone as smart as you turn out to be such a pathetic loser."

Diego smelled blood in the air.

He assessed the two women. They seemed evenly matched height wise. But the blond cupcake had a mean edge to her. That one wouldn't fight fair. Still, his money was on Josie pulling out a win if the fur started flying.

He figured since there weren't any senior-officer issues here and the parking lot was pretty much abandoned, he would step back and let Josie have her outlet by handling this one on her own. And heaven help that soon-to-be-pounded reporter.

Shannon launched, swinging her precious camera bag like a medieval spiked mace toward Josie's head. Diego's muscles bunched. Before he could move, Josie's arm shot up. She snagged the camera strap, taking only a glancing blow to the shoulder from the bag. She spun, leg raised, the flat of her tennis shoe catapulting Shannon backward.

The reporter scrambled, swiped her feet to knock Josie's legs, toppled her off balance. The two women rolled, each seeking dominance. Cupcake had a few moves of her own that attested to martial arts knowledge.

Another time, he might have fallen victim to that male tendency to get fired up by a catfight, especially one he knew Josie would win in spite of Cupcake's training. But there was no thrill in this for him tonight, with fury still storming over Bridges's stunt.

Josie slammed Shannon onto her stomach, kneed her in the back and twisted her arm behind her. She wrenched the camera-case strap from the reporter's tight grip and tossed it to Diego. "Get rid of the film. I may want people to know about us, but not this way."

He totally agreed with Josie on that.

"Can do." Diego popped the camera and exposed the roll with one gratifying jerk.

"Jesus, Josephine." Shannon spit grit from her mouth, her cheek still pressed to gravel. "It's not like the two of you are Brad Pitt and Jennifer Aniston, for crying out loud."

Still, Josie didn't let go. A battlefield sheen he recognized well from his past slicked her eyes.

"Hey, Josie?" Diego squatted beside her. "Are you with me here? We need to haul out of the parking lot before somebody calls the cops."

Her eyes blinked clear. "Oh, right."

Diego angled his head into Shannon's line of sight. "And don't even think about pressing charges, because I will testify very honestly that you threw the first punch. You can be sure those charges will be reversed right back around on you."

Diego dropped the camera case in front of her.

Hefting Josie gently by the arm, he passed her purse to her. Shannon snatched her bag and scurried off to her car.

Josie stood silently until Shannon's nondescript blue rental left the lot, before turning back to Diego.

"Thank you for not interfering," she said with all the formal precision of a stranger.

"You had the fight covered."

"Such as it was." She flicked dirt off her leather flight jacket and picked at the split in the knee of her jeans. "She wasn't much of an opponent for somebody in need of a good tension-relieving workout."

"Wanna wrestle with me after all?" he offered, only half-joking.

Josie didn't even smile, just stared up at him with cold anger—and a hint of hurt. "We only met a couple of weeks ago, remember. You don't even know me."

"Okay. No wrestling." Disappointment stabbed. Too much.

She made a big production out of dusting the rest of her clothes, her black jeans, adjusting her belt buckle, in control and so distant. "Is the invitation still open to speak with your contractor friend even though I'm no longer on the market for a wrestling partner?"

He was insulted that she would even have to ask.

But then the male species hadn't done a lot to redeem themselves in her eyes over the past hour. His ex-wife and Mike Bridges would sure make a helluva pair.

"Of course the invitation is still open. He's inside waiting for us."

She nodded, lips tight as she strode toward the bar. "Then let's get to work. I'll eat off your French fry plate a few times and that should go a long way for starting the couple gossip without Shannon's pictures."

Diego opened the bar door, voices and music swelling out. "One sampler platter from the bar menu, coming up."

He'd learned something valuable tonight that didn't bode well for him. Josie Lockworth carried a grudge.

Man, Diego Morel pissed her off.

Josie stretched along her living-room sofa, head propped on the armrest. She tossed a Beanie Baby up again and again and again, working out the ache in her shoulder from the glancing blow of Shannon's camera case.

Pitch. Catch. Pitch. Catch. Her military bear. Up in the air. Kinda like her future.

She snatched the Beanie bear mid-plummet and plopped it on the coffee table. Leaning over the arm of the sofa, she hefted her flight bag up and open. She fished out the latest stack of data and dropped it into her lap.

Thud.

Great.

And she was only halfway through the stuff.

Josie shuffled aside the pages upon pages of data streams that were already blurring together and tugged free an old scheduling logbook instead. Musty pages crinkled as she turned them for...*yawn*...she glanced at the clock.

Five hours.

What a way to spend a Sunday afternoon. She scrubbed a hand over her eyes, turned the page, reading dates for TDYs to bases in Florida, New Mexico, Ohio, back to New Mexico.

Josie slammed the book closed. She didn't even know what she was looking for. Maybe her mother really had screwed up. But if she had, was there faulty logic lurking in this test, as well?

Damn it all, she'd gone over everything in her current day procedures. Diego hadn't found fault either. Must be that mess with Bridges that had her doubting herself. Come Monday, once she filed the Memo of Record, she would feel better, more proactive and in control of her life. Instead of feeling lonely and frustrated on a Sunday afternoon with nothing to do but play catch with a toy.

Her feet twitched with the need to act. Maybe there was something she could do now. Diana had e-mailed the requested information on the Cipher early this morning. Did her sister never sleep?

She could forward it to Kayla for the investigation into Rainy's death. Or she could call. Hadn't she been trying to reach out and connect with something more than cyber waves?

Tossing the Beanie bear to the coffee table, Josie snagged her cordless phone from beside the stacks of papers. She keyed through until she found the stored number and hit dial.

The phone rang once, twice...until by the fourth ring she was about ready to give up.

"Hello?" a gasping voice interrupted the ringing, background noise of computer games and a television cartoon pulsing through.

"Kayla? Josie here. Hope I'm not catching you at a bad time. I can call back later."

"Josie! Great to hear from you. And there's never a peaceful moment anyhow. I have a daughter. Remember? I'm just trying to restore order to the house before we start a new week. Jeez, I welcome the excuse to sit with a soda for a few minutes." Bleeps and music from the computer game grew louder in the background as Kayla yelled away from the phone. "Jazz, turn that down! I'm trying to talk, sweetie."

The noise level lowered from deafening to a dull roar. "Okay," Kayla exhaled a long breath. "I'm here now. Sorry to sound so scattered. What's going on with you?"

Josie couldn't imagine Kayla anything but mega-organized and intense. A single mother, she juggled solo parenthood and a high-pressure job on the Athens, Arizona, police force with seeming ease.

Which brought Josie right back to the reason for her call. "I wanted to let you know I'm e-mailing some new scoop for you that may or may not have something to do with Rainy."

"Once I get the youngun' off to bed tonight, I'll log into the secure lines." The pop and fizz of a can opening crackled. "Where did you find the information?"

"My source would prefer to remain anonymous."

A low laugh wafted through the lines. "Did your computer geek source enjoy her mac and cheese while she turned over the information?"

"Damn, you're good." Josie tried to laugh along, but

this weekend had sucked the life right out of her and her chuckle came off like more of a strangled squawk.

"Are you okay?" Concern coated Kayla's solemn tones.

Innate defensiveness rose at any mention of possible depression or, heaven forbid, instability. "Of course I'm okay. Talking about Rainy just makes me a little blue. Normal blue though, understand what I mean?"

"Completely." A pause stretched with the sound of Kayla changing the phone to the other ear. "And there's really nothing else going on?"

"Just some crap at work." She scooped the bear up again and started tossing higher and higher. "My boss thinks it's okay to hit on me." The tumbling toy deflected off her hand to the floor.

"Oh my God. Did you kick his tail?"

"And get thrown into Leavenworth?" She angled off the couch to snag the poor bear from his crash landing on the gray carpet. "I don't think so. I warned him not to come near me again. I'm also going to make a sealed Memo of Record tomorrow after my flight to back up my story in case there's a second incident. But beyond that, without more proof—or his admission— there's not much else I can effectively do."

"Sounds like you're following procedure and doing what needs to be done. You hang in there, now."

She smoothed and redistributed the uneven lumps in the tiny beanbag after its fall. "It just sucks seeing someone you admired turn out to be so—"

"Scummy?" Kayla offered between slurping sips of soda.

"Pretty much sums up Mike Bridges."

Silence filled the phone lines. Kayla always had been good about listening with a sympathetic ear, but Kayla's silence grew more thunderous than the bleeping computer game blaring in the background—way beyond sympathetic attention.

"Kayla? Are you still there?" Josie asked even though she could still hear Jazz's computer game.

"Yeah, I'm here." Her voice shook then leveled. "I was just pouring Jazz some juice."

"Mom," Jazz's voice floated through. "Did you just say juice? Can I have some?"

But hadn't Kayla just said…

It didn't take a rocket scientist to figure out her friend was lying to cover an awkward silence. "Kayla? What's going on?"

More quiet screamed through, followed by a heavy sigh. "Hold on. Let me shut the door so Jazz doesn't overhear." Footsteps and a click sounded before one more deep breath vibrated through. "Do you remember how we used to admire all those lieutenants in uniform when they came to town? Well, I was actually involved with one."

Oh, God, this couldn't be going where she thought.

"Mike Bridges is my daughter's father."

Holy crap. She hadn't seen that one coming.

Josie dropped the Beanie Baby onto her lap. She'd known the guy Kayla had been seeing was named Mike, but she'd never imaged… "You're serious? But you were a teenager when Jasmine was born. He was an adult. A commissioned officer in the air f—"

"Stop," Kayla commanded, her near whisper carrying an indisputable authority that would halt criminals in their tracks. "I was young, easily dazzled and God knows he had charm."

Josie clenched the phone. She couldn't deny Kayla's words. Hell, even as an adult, she'd almost been snowed by Bridges. And the man must have some good points if he'd managed to charm serious Kayla for any length of time. "God, Kayla, I'm sorry."

"Don't be. I'm over him. He didn't want to get married, and quite frankly after the way he acted when I told him about the unexpected pregnancy, I wasn't so sure I wanted him anymore, either. I mean it that I'm over him. It was just strange hearing his name out of the blue like that."

Bravado on Kayla's part? Or truth? Either way, Josie knew proud and serious Kayla would never admit a lingering hurt.

"It's not a big secret *per se*. We just don't want to advertise the fact and get Jazz worked up. He makes his child-support payments like clockwork. I'm not too proud to take what my child deserves. But he isn't a part of her life or mine. Mike and I decided it was better that he stay away completely rather than break Jazz's heart by not being a good father."

"And you let him live?" Josie would have kicked his butt for abandoning a child. An image of Jazz's sweet little face flashed to mind, those wide hazel eyes that— holy cow—the child had inherited from her father.

Josie's fist clenched around the toy in her lap. Her desire to pummel Bridges now far outstripped anything she'd felt earlier. And she'd been mighty darn mad at the man earlier.

Kayla continued, "It's his loss, missing out on this

incredible little girl. She's the best thing that ever happened to me."

Contrition nipped. Firing up her friend wouldn't make the situation better. "You're right. I'm sorry for saying the wrong thing."

"Don't even worry about it. I've had years to come to peace with this."

"You're amazing." Josie wished she had Kayla's calm.

"I'm glad somebody thinks so." Blips and music swelled in the background again, Kayla returning to her normal life. "Oops, I think Jazz is trying to hint at me to get off the phone. It's been great talking to you, but I promised I would join her for a computer game of Roller Coaster Sim."

"Take care."

"You, too, friend. I'll be looking for the files after the youngun' here goes to sleep tonight. G'bye now."

"Bye." Josie turned off the cordless phone and replaced it on the coffee table, draping the cammo bear on top. Her eyes skipped over to the shelves full of other Beanie creatures crammed into every nook in a rainbow splash of color.

Quiet blanketed her condo, the silence even thicker now in contrast to Kayla's full and noisy life. And how pathetic that she was sitting here feeling sorry for herself when Kayla had yanked her life back together after a tough start with the teenage pregnancy. Kayla had overcome so much to be a successful cop already on the fast track.

Josie gave herself a mental thump. Time to quit whining and be honest. She was totally pissed at Mike Bridges and was transferring that to Diego. Oh, her biker boyfriend had been a butthead, no doubt. Yet not so much in comparison to her boss.

Yeah, she was a prickly, tattletale grudge holder, all a product of that nagging, deep-seated sense of fair play. But she wanted to forgive Diego. If only he would offer her bruised pride some salve first.

Standing outside the control room on Monday, Josie watched Diego Morel stride up the empty hallway. Jeans and black leather had never looked so good.

Her temper had cooled somewhat. But the Josephine inside her still cringed over what Diego had said about their kiss in the desert being a meaningless encounter. Words hurt. More than punches as far as she was concerned.

After being the target of so much gossip over the years, she should have been immune to hateful barbs. But somehow the verbal slap from Diego stung her in a way Bridges never could. Although currently Bridges was high up on her dirt list.

She should have been strapping on to the Predator for today's morning test flight. Instead that bastard boss of hers had ordered a crew change in some macho, message-sending power play. She would fly the remote control instead, while Craig Wagner rode in the saddle for this exciting-as-hell mission, taking the modified aircraft to a higher altitude.

Thanks bunches, Boss.

Kayla's revelation about Mike Bridges only added more tinder to her fiery anger. He didn't deserve her respect. And once this mission was complete, she would take great pleasure in filing that Memo of Record.

Diego drew closer in the solitary corridor, his dark hair pulled back today. Her fingers itched to tug it free.

Biker boots thudded down the thin industrial carpet in a swagger that somehow kept a hint of the military precision. He halted beside her, one shoulder to the wall. "I owe you an apology."

Yes, he did. But in spite of her wish for ego balm, she was now starting to wonder if she could afford to accept it. "You already gave me one back in the parking lot this weekend."

"One that you rejected. I was there, too, and yeah it was a half-assed apology that didn't deserve to be taken seriously."

"We do agree on something then."

A dry smile kicked up one side of his face before it faded again. "I was in a crappy mood because of things that had nothing to do with you. I owe you a real apology. Whether you want to accept it or not is up to you. But I'm still damn well going to say my piece."

Ah, hell. He was going to be reasonable, something Josephine would never be able to resist.

Still, the ever-fair Josephine said, "Go on."

"I was wrong to make the 'couple of weeks' crack, and I was wrong to insinuate you would hop from my bed to his—"

"Insinuate?"

His half smile returned, dug deeper into his face. "You're not going to make this easy for me, are you, Buttercup?"

"Nope."

"I don't know everything about you, but I do know you better than that. And I like what I know enough that I—" he paused, skimmed a hand up to smooth along her French-braided hair "—really want to know more, which is why all of this torqued me off until I went into Thor mode."

"You were jealous." Her breakfast flipped in her stomach.

Diego bit out a curse. "Yeah, I guess you could put it that way if it helps."

"It shouldn't. And somehow it does anyway."

He hadn't gone violent with his jealousy the way some guys might have. Just been a jerk.

Hands jammed in his pockets, he studied the top of his boot scuffing the carpet. "My, uh, ex, wasn't exactly the faithful type. That doesn't excuse what I said, but maybe at least you'll understand where I was coming from."

An ex? Jealousy sure was an ugly emotion. Josie forgave him a little more. Practical Josephine, however, wanted to know more about this ex of his. "Your ex-wife?"

"Stephanie. We were married for five years, during which time she plowed her way through every available guy in town the minute I went TDY."

"That bitch." She wondered why she hadn't thought to ask him about an ex in his past. Hadn't Diana hinted Diego had been married? "What she did was inexcusable. You deserved better than that."

Diego shrugged. "Well, I was an ass…and an idiot. I didn't believe what my buds tried to tell me until I saw it with my own eyes—her in a bar parking lot on the hood of a car with her dress hiked up around her hips. She was quite clear on the fact it was totally consensual."

Seeing her plastered against the side of Bridges's car would have been a hellish replay for him. "How long ago did this happen?"

"Nearly three years ago."

Which would have been shortly after his recovery from the accident. The bitch had left him because he couldn't fly. Josie knew it with a certainty that fired her righteous indignation over the injustice of it all. He'd lost so much in a short time.

Josephine gave up the fight against forgiveness.

He continued to study the tops of his dusty boots. "I would have sworn it didn't bother me anymore. I got most of my anger out during the six months I was too damn afraid to have sex for fear she'd brought some disease back to our bed. Once the last round of lab results came back, I got rip-roaring drunk and—"

"I get the picture." Or rather, didn't want that picture anywhere near her head. Yeah, jealousy bit the big one.

He shifted his focus from the floor to Josie, eyes direct, hard and still more than a hint angry. "When I saw the two of you, I went a little nuts again. Not your fault and I apologize."

Yet even with all that baggage, he'd helped her and been fair in not assuming she would welcome Bridges. Diego had anticipated Bridges's next move, even offered to help her. In light of what she'd learned about Bridges from Kayla, how could she not admire Diego's grassroots honesty and integrity?

She touched his arm lightly. "You're forgiven."

"That easily?" His muscles tensed under her fingers.

"Oh, somehow I don't think it was all that easy."

He sketched his knuckles across her cheekbone. "You're too good, Josie Lockworth."

A few days ago she would have invited him to help her be bad, then. But while she'd forgiven him, she wasn't ready to hop into bed with the guy. Before, it had been about sex. Now the whole relationship had somehow become more complicated by his personal revelation.

Her hand fell away from his arm. "Let's hope I'm more than good when it comes to flying this aircraft. Time to roll, Morel."

Josie settled behind the controls in the windowless room, preflight complete. After today's mission there wouldn't be any question for the oversight committee but that her test project was fast on its way to being an unqualified success. Furthermore, her unspoken fears that maybe, just maybe, her mother had been wrong would be laid to rest.

Would that send Diego out of her life? Or only out of her work world, since he did live in the area? An hour wasn't that far, although it had been far enough to keep their paths from crossing in the past.

She needed to shuffle questions aside. None of it mattered if she didn't get through this flight. Thanks to Mike "Small-minded" Bridges, she was stuck with this last-minute change. She knew the mission inside out, due to the practice runs she'd made to insure the plan was pristine for Craig to pilot from the remote-control booth. Frustration over being on the ground today churned anew.

Josie adjusted the fit of her headset earpieces, then

the small boom mike by her mouth. "Cowboy, how's your mojo today?"

"This filly is ready to go, P.C." Craig Wagner's voice flowed through loud and strong. Enthusiastic. Pumped to fly. "Say, could we change the call sign of the control box to Bunkhouse to go with my new name here? I kinda like the whole cowboy theme."

"I'll think about it." His enthusiasm was infectious, darn him. She settled deeper into her seat. "Ready for power?"

"Roger, ready for power out here."

Josie flipped switches, ran further checklists with the sensor operator, Don Zeljak. Displays and gauges hummed to life.

When her pilot-view camera on the nose of the craft materialized, the screen filled with a man in a Stetson on top of his headset. Afternoon rays sheened the image.

Laughing, she keyed up her radio. "Cowboy, you may be getting a little too into character."

"Gotta have fun with this." The pilot struck a six-gun-drawing pose with a vast desert backdrop. "We may be the last of the cowboys out here."

"Roger that." And the sooner they got this mission complete, the sooner she could breathe easy again. "Now put on your helmet. Ready for engine start whenever you are."

"Copy, give me a few minutes to change headgear and strap into the saddle." He disappeared from view, minutes passing. "Okeydoke, P.C., all set to go."

Josie called back, "Prop clear?"

"Roger. Prop clear."

Josie flipped the starter and advanced the throttle.

Her engine instruments began a steady climb until all indications entered green bands. "All indications good here. How're you doing up there, Cowboy?"

"Systems nominal. Feels like this baby is ready to slip the surly bonds."

Josie switched radio frequencies. "Palmdale ground, Pred two-zero, spot seven, ready to taxi."

"Copy Pred two-zero, altimeter is three-zero-zero-one. Winds are from the north at ten knots. Cleared to taxi to runway twenty-five. Hold short of the active. Cleared local area VFR."

Josie repeated back the required information to the ground controller in the tower responsible for deconflicting aircraft on the ground. The Predator proceeded to taxi toward the runway, holding at the hammerhead. "Palmdale Tower, Pred two-zero ready for take off."

Finally the tower responded, "Pred two-zero, cleared for take off. Altimeter three-zero-zero-one. Cleared test profile altitudes."

Advancing the throttles, Josie guided the aircraft around and onto the runway. "Ready to ride, Cowboy?"

"You bet. Put the spurs to her."

Josie swept her instruments one last time, then ran the throttles up to the stops. The aircraft advanced, sped, the front camera providing a straight-ahead view. She tapped the rudder pedals a touch here and there to stay centerline, ever aware of Craig, strapped into the saddle seat, out in the open.

At rotation speed, she gently raised the nose, her camera switching from desert to sky. She set her climb angle and began instrument cross-checks while Master Sergeant Zeljak smoothly did the same. Zeljak was a great old guy with solid test knowledge honed in the early days of stealth. He had hands to trust.

The test profile had a planned level-off at three thousand feet for final checkout of the new instrumentation before climbing to the nine-thousand-foot test altitude. Once she leveled at three thousand feet, she allowed herself an exhale of relief. Most accidents happened at take off and landing. She eyed the screen full of sky. Clouds puffed past.

God, she wanted to be there. No matter what doubts she may have had lately about her profession and future, she did love to fly. She knew if she turned to Diego, she would find his gaze glued to the screen image, hunger in his eyes.

The sky image swooped upward, fast, steep. What the hell? She glanced down at her hand, doing exactly what she told it to on the stick, a slow and steady climb. Not this screaming ascent that had taken over.

A scan of the instruments showed the aircraft climbing at too high an angle. Her throat closed. She called on training to override niggling panic. She pushed the throttle all the way forward and lowered the nose.

Nothing happened.

All right. No sweat. That's why they had secondary override controls on the craft to abort the flight and bring the Predator home. Craig would have some piloting fun now and the craft wouldn't go crashing into anywhere dangerous, risking lives on the ground. "Cowboy, assume control of the craft. My controls have malfunctioned."

A single crackle over the headset echoed before, "Roger. Taking control."

Craig's heavy exhales echoed over the radio waves. Josie kept her gaze locked on the dials, the climbing altitude. Too steep. *Hurry. Hurry. Hurry, Craig.*

"Crap, P.C.," Wagner barked. "Mine aren't working either."

No freaking way. This shouldn't happen. Didn't happen.

Screw calm. She shouted into the headset, "Get the hell off that thing. Now!"

"I'm fixing to, P.C." Panic lent a shake to his tone.

Heavy breaths huffed through the audio waves while Josie scrambled to regain control of the Predator. She felt Diego at her back, leaning, watching. Even the seasoned sensor operator beside her tensed. She jammed code after code into the system and nothing changed.

Memories sledgehammered her brain of being a little girl on the edge of the runway, so proud of her mama's work, then seeing it all explode into a ball of flames. She could still smell burning flesh.

Her breakfast revolted upward. She swallowed it down through sheer will alone.

"Diego," she snapped without looking up. "If you have any ideas, speak."

"Bailing out's the right call," he answered, fast, clipped. "No question. There's nothing else. The whole computer system's crashing."

Airspeed bled from the craft. Dials fluctuated.

The Predator stalled.

Her heart pounded denial in her ears. The aircraft rolled over, lurching into an inverted spin toward the ground. Her screen, as well as the sensor operator's multiple screens, all showed variations of the same image.

Tumbling sky.

Oh, God. "Cowboy, did you get off?" *Please, please be long gone with your parachute inflated.*

No answer came but the roar of winds and whisper of her prayers.

Her hands sped over the controls as if she could force her will into the malfunctioning equipment. She stared, riveted by the spinning camera image. Then at the altimeter.

The screen went blank.

Chapter 12

Whomp. The explosion rocked the ground, rattling the walls and up through her boots.

Josie tore off her headset, blasting out of her chair on the way to the door. Already she could hear firetruck sirens screaming outside.

She started a nonstop prayer chant.

Diego jammed open doors ahead of her so she could continue to run unfettered down the hall, around corners. She accepted now that she would see flames, a crashed craft, but none of that mattered as long as she also saw a parachute drifting down.

Panting, she dashed through the last door out onto the runway.

Black smoke bloomed from the cracked desert about a hundred yards from the cement's end. Fire trucks, security police, an ambulance all raced across the packed earth. She scanned the horizon for the speck that would prove Craig had made it off in time, even looked behind her, praying that for once her eagle eyes were wrong.

She flagged a military Suburban and crawled inside, Diego still less than a second behind her. The door slammed behind him as the tires squealed against pavement.

Diego's hand dropped onto her shoulder. She shrugged off his hand and comfort, because, if she took it she would have to step into that next realization and into a reality she wasn't ready to accept.

For some absurd reason, she kept thinking Craig couldn't be dead. There hadn't been time to have his new call-sign naming ceremony so he could officially be called "Cowboy" instead of "Opie" from *The Andy Griffith Show,* a reference to his clean-cut looks.

Sirens and wind swirled through her brain. She kept searching the sky through the window and found...

Nothing.

Boom.

The first reverberation of the twenty-one-gun salute vibrated from Diego's feet, up his spine and through his memory. Seven gunmen, firing three times in tribute to a fallen comrade in arms.

Captain Craig Wagner's funeral mirrored the one Diego had attended three years ago. Back then, he'd left the hospital against orders, stumbled into his uniform and somehow managed to stand unwavering while they buried his wingman.

Today, Diego wore the uniform again, hand still snapped to his forehead for the twenty-one-gun salute.

His uniform fit looser, but he'd resurrected the precise creases for the pants. Shine for the shoes. Alignment for his rows of ribbons.

Wind skimmed his hair along the sides beneath his hat, hair freshly shorn to regulation out of respect for the funeral, for the uniform. For the man being buried.

Boom.

Now, as then, planes roared overhead, flying the missing-man formation, signifying that one of their own had been lost. Through it all, Josie stood tall in her military precision and pressed blue uniform. Dry-eyed. Stoic. He'd expected as much. The emotional crash would come later. Hard. Fast. And unrecoverable even years later.

The crowd was packed with uniformed service members. Wagner's death sent far-reaching shock waves through the air force testing community. Every one of them almost certainly imagined themselves strapped to that aircraft, unable to cut loose in time to parachute.

Even General Quincy had attended. Diego refused to look over at Mike Bridges. None of them needed extra crap messing with their heads right now.

Diego knew there wasn't a way to get over carrying the weight of another person's death on your shoulders. Nothing could replace what a widow and her children had lost.

Boom.

Flanked by her parents, Wagner's wife clutched a folded flag to her chest above her pregnant belly, a flag that had minutes prior draped her husband's coffin. A toddler girl gripped her mother's dress in one fist and a basset hound Beanie Baby in the other.

Lowering his salute, Diego adjusted his hat. That other funeral washed over him again, threatening vertigo on the ground. But that was in his past. This was about Josie's present. He'd patched his wounds alone.

He would make damned sure Josie didn't have to do the same.

Josie dropped into the front seat of her car. Alone. Oh, she knew Diego was only steps behind her, but she couldn't face all the emotions that knotted whenever she spoke to him. Her control frayed by the second. How odd to feel so numb yet fragile all at once—an alien emotion for a woman used to fighting the world head-on.

She'd felt his presence throughout the afternoon, looming there quietly behind her. Yet somehow that support made her eyes burn and she would *not* crumble.

Although she had almost lost it when he'd walked into the church. Seeing Diego in his full dress uniform with his stacks of hard-earned ribbons—and, oh, God, his beautiful hair gone—somehow that had broken her heart all over again. She barely recognized him, had in fact almost scanned right over him at first. *Everything* was different, and she wanted more than anything to rewind a few days.

Four, to be exact.

Eyes on her rearview mirror, she watched him close in on her Mustang while a few desert trees rustled overhead. Even his walk now fine-tuned that military essence he'd never totally lost. The even steps clipped with more exactness as if the shined shoes had retrained his feet.

She gripped her steering wheel in white-knuckled fists. "Diego? Thank you for being here, but I can't talk to you today."

"Well, fine then," he drawled, and at least sounded like himself inside that crisp uniform. "We won't talk, but you're not driving. Slide on over."

Hadn't she made herself clear? Could this man be so dense? Or was she? Heaven knows she had been in a fog, running on fumes and autopilot since realizing Craig hadn't made it off the Predator. Her Predator. The ride *she* should have taken to test the modifications she'd ordered. Had her insistence on proving her mother right cost Craig his life? Oh, God, she was going to be sick.

Pressing her hand to her stomach, Josie worked down bile again. She wouldn't dishonor her fallen friend by puking in the cemetery.

Who was she kidding? Diego was right. She wasn't in any shape to drive.

She dared a look up at him, his face all strong angles that somehow seemed older and even harder without the wild hair. "You really don't want to talk? You just want to see me home?"

He swung wide her door. "I've been wanting to drive this car since you gave my Harley a run for its money across that dried-up lake bed. Now move on over."

"What about your bike? You can't leave it." She offered up a token last effort at arguing even though her heart wasn't in it.

"I left it at the base chapel and caught a ride here. It's safe there."

He'd planned to go with her from the start.

His thoughtfulness and concern flicked warmth along the iciness inside her. She shifted her legs out of the car. No way could she scoot over to the passenger seat in her pencil-straight uniform skirt, especially not when her every move felt like swimming through peanut butter.

She circled the hood while Diego took off his uniform jacket. He folded the coat in half lengthwise and draped it on the backseat then unhooked the tie from his starched shirt, transforming the service dress uniform into regular blues.

Gravel crunched under her military, low-heeled pumps all the way to the passenger side. She removed her own jacket and placed it on top of his in back, a somehow intimate mingling that brought an unwelcome shiver.

Josie settled into the embrace of the leather bucket seat. How strange that her senses were so in tune to the sound of cars lining to leave, the rustle of wind in the cemetery trees. The sickening smell of graveside flowers. The urge to hurl.

And yet she couldn't "feel" a thing.

"That'll come later," Diego said from behind the wheel, tucking on sunglasses and apparently reading her mind.

"What?"

"The letdown, the rush of emotions," he answered as he pulled out onto the road. "You're numb now. Be grateful and hang on to it for a while longer to give your body a chance to rest."

Rest. That sounded good. She slid on her own sunglasses and tipped her head back against the seat. Elbow hooked out the open window, she let the wind and miles blur into the fog. She had no idea how long she drifted before she jolted awake.

She straightened, looked, found her exit passing—
"That was my turnoff."

"We're going to my place."

Irritation feathered through the fog. "I'm not much in the mood for sex."

He glanced over, her face reflected in his sunglasses. "Who's offering? Because I'm sure as hell not in the mood, either."

"Oh."

He shifted front again. "I thought you might not want to be alone in your condo."

Of course he could read her mind about this. How could she have forgotten what had happened to him three years ago? The man had most definitely walked this walk. The past few days must have been hell for him.

And in that realization, she linked with him enough to relax at least a little. "You're right. Thank you—again."

He lowered the top as he cleared the city out onto the open roads where Joshua trees led to his remote home. The wind felt good ripping at the constraints of her French braid, swirling inside her to stir words she would have sworn earlier that she didn't want to say. "I thought I understood how my mother must have felt when the crash in her project killed a pilot. I was so damned wrong to assume anything."

"There's no way to know it unless you live it."

"It's enough to make a person crazy." Understanding her mother brought a fresh wave of pain.

"Yes, it is." His bass drawl resonated long beyond the simple statement.

She abandoned mindless desert sight-seeing and glanced back at him. "How did *you* stay sane?"

"What makes you think I'm sane?" He peered over the top of his sunglasses, eyes again the barely civilized Diego she knew.

"Fair enough." Who knew what sane was anymore? She picked at the hem of her uniform, snapping a thread free. "How do you keep going then?"

Telephone poles whipped past again and again before his chest rose with an inhale. "I'm still trying to figure that one out. And somehow, while I'm trying, the years continue to pass."

She nodded. What he said made sense.

But for now, she would settle for getting through the night.

Stuck in the sleepy fog of being half awake and half asleep, Josie batted at the tickle on her face. She snuggled deeper under the covers, not sure why she didn't want to wake up, but certain if she considered it overlong she would be sorry.

The tickle—furry—continued against her cheek and grew more persistent, followed by a wet nudge to her chin. She pried her eyes open and stared straight into the translucent blue eyes of the ugliest dog ever. The mix of mutt and wolf left the animal with spiky fur and mismatched features that would have scared the hell out of most people.

Somehow she found it endearing.

Josie sagged back onto her pillow in Diego's bed, where she'd slept alone except for the two dogs keeping her company. She turned to look at the empty pillow beside her. Not even an imprint marred the plain white pillowcase. Definitely alone.

Memories steamed into her brain of the crash, funeral, ride home with Diego. She'd been so zombielike yesterday she hadn't even argued about staying with him.

Scooching up to sit, she wrapped an arm around the dog's neck, the god-awful, ugly brown blanket pooling around her waist. "Morning, puppy. Which one are you again? Bogey or Bandit?"

At the sound of the last name, the shaved retriever at the foot of the bed lifted its head. She vaguely recalled Diego introducing her on his way to showing her the shower and tossing her a T-shirt for sleep. Thank God he'd left her alone in his sparsely furnished bedroom after that.

Where was he now? She didn't know and wasn't ready to find out until sleep cleared from her head.

She nuzzled Bogey. "Thanks for keeping me company, fellas. You're definitely more snuggly than those tiny Beanie Babies."

Her muscles hadn't ached this much since she'd started martial arts training at Athena Academy. After meeting the mat about twenty times, she'd decided she didn't like that much and had set about determining how to be the best.

Right now, she felt pretty much rock bottom again.

The first couple of days following Craig's accident had been filled with data gathering…and collecting evidence from the crash site. Her empty stomach rolled.

The actual investigation would likely take months, but the initial finding had been "total system failure." Cause? Her modifications to the system were incompatible with the aircraft.

Everyone assured her this sort of thing simply happened. Proposed new projects failed more often than they succeeded. Albeit not always with a casualty. But that was just a horrible reality of military testing, a risk they all understood and a mistake any of them could have logged.

As if that made her feel better.

Meanwhile, she'd been ordered to take a long weekend and encouraged to apply for personal leave beyond that. Just be on hand to answer questions for the accident review board's investigation. And once she returned, she would likely be assigned a new test project.

The knots in her shoulders doubled. She needed to work off tension, punch something or somebody. Or at least run a few miles. Maybe Diego would run with her. There was certainly plenty of wide-open space out here where he lived. Of course she didn't even know if he worked out, but he certainly appeared more than fit.

There was so much she didn't know about him, and there were few hints in this desert-rat home of his. Only that he cared next to nothing about decor, yet invested obscene amounts in electronics and his grill.

And he had pets. There was something sweet about a guy who loved animals.

She scratched behind the wolf-looking one's ear. The shaved retriever nudged her other hand for equal time and attention while she woke up. On the bedside table rested gym shorts with a drawstring and a fresh T-shirt. He would have stood inches away from her to set down the clothes while she slept. Had he watched her? She shook off the image and hustled her butt out of bed to get dressed.

Baggy clothes on, she couldn't avoid Diego or the day any longer. "Come on, puppies." She snapped her fingers. "You probably need to be let out or something."

Like she knew anything about pets. A woman who'd grown up in a boarding school and now didn't risk attachment with anything more than toys. Small ones at that.

The animals leaped off the bed one thud after the other. Doggy nails clicked on the hardwood floor as she entered the sprawling great room. The spacious room sported a butt-ugly burnt-orange sofa, a wide-screen TV and no Diego, just a rumpled blanket and pillow on the couch. This pillow definitely bore the deep imprint of a head.

She glanced down at the two dogs swinging up alongside her like good wingmen. "Where's the big guy? Huh? Where's Diego?"

Bogey sprinted for the door and scratched.

"Okay, so I guessed right on the going-out thing. Hang on."

She swung open the door, but still no Diego, just her car parked in the middle of a dusty yard without any real driveway. Bogey loped toward the garage, hesitated, looked back, tongue lolling.

"Ah," she sighed, understanding. "He's out here."

She followed barefoot, but the dog didn't dart into the open garage as she expected. Instead, he circled around back and plopped down in front of a wooden windowless hut.

She tapped on the door. "Diego?"

No answer.

She twisted the knob slowly. Not locked. It gave. She opened to find what looked to be a dressing area in a tiny cedar-wood room. A bench with a stack of towels lined one wall, hooks on the opposing wall. Diego's jeans dangled, a hint of boxers peeking from behind them. Straight ahead she saw another door, which unless she missed her guess, led to a sauna.

Holy barrel roll, Batman. He was in there naked.

Again she glanced at Diego's clothes, envisioning him in nothing more than a towel—if even that. All the frustration and pain and tension she'd wanted to run out with him suddenly found a new outlet. It felt damned good to be in control of something right now.

After a quick trip back to the house for her purse and some hopefully soon-to-be-needed birth control, Josie whipped the T-shirt over her head.

Chapter 13

Head back against the cedar wall, Diego stretched out his legs on the planked bench. A stark bulb overhead illuminated the two benches, which met to form an L in the rectangular room. The other two walls held the stove and door.

Dipping a ladle into the bowl beside him, he scooped and flung more water onto the stones. Steam hissed into the air and blanketed him. Sweat slicked his skin after only fifteen minutes. He swiped a towel across his face, then tossed it across one thigh. Still he couldn't shake the hell of imagining Josie lost in that ball of flames at the crash.

He'd intended to sweat out his frustrations in his sauna. Instead emotions were boomeranging right back around on him, leaving him more than a little raw. Probably for the best that he'd left Josie sleeping.

He hadn't wanted to risk waking her. Soon enough she would come back to life, her brain as well as her body. And when she did, she would arrive at the same conclusion he had right around midnight.

Wagner's accident wasn't so accidental.

"Diego?" Josie's voice called through the thick wood door as if he'd conjured her from the steam. "I assume that's you in there."

Damn. He'd thought for sure she would sleep for at least another hour. "Yeah, it's me."

"Are you up for company?"

Just the sound of her voice threatened to have him "up" for something else entirely. She didn't need him coming on to her any more than she needed to discuss Wagner's crash just yet.

He adjusted the towel more strategically over his lap. "You're welcome to join me—" understatement "—but be warned, this is a clothing-optional locale and I'm definitely on the optional side right now."

"I'm counting on it."

No mistaking the intent in that one. Surprise stilled him.

The door swung wide and, holy crap, he couldn't breathe, much less move. Josie stood silhouetted, wearing nothing but a fluffy white towel. Long legs stretched, ending in bare feet with painted toenails. He wouldn't have pegged her for pink polish, but the splash of soft color somehow enhanced her strength and allure all the more.

His eyes worked their way back up to where her hand clasped the towel's knot between her creamy breasts. Farther up he looked to the curve of the neck he had dreams of burying his face against once he buried himself even deeper into her.

Dangerous thoughts for a man with only the piss-poor cover of a hand towel over his lap.

He met her gaze straight on and found her eyes no less tempting than the rest of her. Determination, hunger, need exuded from her as if the steam had already begun to take its cleansing effect. Much like after her encounter with Bridges, Josie seemed to need an outlet.

Although he doubted she was looking to kick his tail the way she had Shannon Conner's.

Still, he couldn't afford to misstep here. She'd have to make herself totally clear before he would put so much as a finger on her. He hitched his knee up to shield what was rapidly becoming an uncomfortable erection.

Josie's fingers closed around the condom she'd retrieved from her bag. One look at Diego's towel and she knew without question.

They would be using the condom soon.

"Have a seat." He gestured to the empty bench.

She padded across the planked floor, stopping beside him until her towel brushed his arm. "I was hoping I could sit here with you."

"You're more than welcome to sit anywhere you want. But be warned you're hot and I'm not unaffected. Doesn't mean I'll do anything about it unless you want me to. But I'm a guy and you're damned near naked. And hell, you could be wearing a potato sack and I'd still get hard when *you* walked into the room."

Sweat trickled down her neck between her breasts, soaking into the towel. "Thank you. Now are you finished?"

"Just so we're clear that you're calling the shots."

"If I'm calling the shots, then I want to be on this side with you."

"Fair enough." Diego swung his feet down.

She couldn't resist the temptation to step between his legs rather than dropping to the bench beside him.

He kept his hands on his knees, while each pointer finger stroked up into her towel. "I assume you're up on your sauna protocol. If you're not a frequent user, then you'll want to limit your time to fifteen minutes."

"I use the sauna at the base gym after daily workouts. I'm fine in here for an hour. The question is, can you last that long?"

One hand still clutching her towel, she extended her arm over him, fist closed. Her fingers unfurled. The condom package plopped onto his thigh. She couldn't be much clearer than that.

Still he didn't move forward. "I guess I don't need to ask if you've thought about this."

"I thought about it all the way back into the house to get the birth control once I realized you were in here, and then during every return step with the condom in my hand. I want this." Her knuckles whitened around the knot in her towel. "I want you."

The last words were torn from her with a reluctance he no doubt wouldn't miss. But damn it, surely he would understand. Alone might be lonely, but in many ways it was so much safer.

Leaning, he ladled more water onto the stones, the cloud swelling forward over them. He straightened to face her again. "Then I reckon I'm lucky that you made the trip back to the house, because I don't have a thing on me right now."

"Lucky *us*." She dropped the towel.

He swallowed hard, eyes raking her body, lingering on her breasts. "Definitely lucky *me*."

Reaching around, he palmed her back to bring her closer, her breasts level with his face and her tightened dusky nipples the perfect targets for his free hand.

The sparks that danced behind her eyes had nothing to do with the heat of the sauna or the stark lightbulb above and everything to do with the electrifying caress of Diego's fingers teasing her breasts.

She'd been right to join him. Already the rest of the world began to recede behind the passion hazing her vision. And through the red, she saw Diego watching her while his fingers tugged tantalizing magic on one nipple.

Diego raised his hand and she almost whimpered, until he brought it to her mouth, sliding a finger between her lips. She sucked deeply, fully enjoying the taste of him and looking forward to more.

He withdrew slowly, deliberately and returned his tutored attention to her breast again. "I've wanted to do this since the first time you walked toward me all full of fight and challenge."

His damp finger traced lazy circles around a bead so taut she almost cried out, felt certain she would before he was through with her. "And what else did you think about doing to me? Because I want it all."

His growl answered a second before he angled forward muttering, "I like a woman who knows what she wants."

Josie nudged aside thoughts of his ex and other women he'd known and focused on the here and now. While he stroked her left breast, he lowered his mouth to her right. His tongue laved and his fingers toyed and her skin burned, her legs threatening to fold.

Sweat trickled down her neck, trailing along her over-sensitized skin. Whether the heat came from the sauna or Diego's sheer magnetism she didn't know or care at the moment.

She just needed more.

Hitching one knee then the other onto the bench, she straddled his lap. She cupped his face in her palms and brought his mouth up to hers. "Well, I most definitely want you. Here. Now. For as long as you can last."

"A challenge?"

"If you dare."

"Oh, I would dare more than you could imagine, Buttercup."

Wildness lurked in his eyes and for the first time since she'd seen him in his uniform with the military regulation haircut, she recognized him. She saw the Diego she knew, the man who called to every suppressed impulsive yearning.

"Try me."

He cupped her head and met her mouth in a raw fervor of tongues, teeth, sweat, lust and something more she didn't want to think about because thinking was dangerous. She wanted to feel. Experience.

Forget.

Finally she could kiss him without reservation, confident the passion he inspired would have an outlet this time. She wouldn't go home frustrated, yearning and alone.

She explored with her tongue, wanting to learn all she could about this man on a fundamental level. She stroked down the corded length of his arms, farther, one hand flicking aside the towel as quickly as her other found the steely length of him. Inching closer, she worked him against her damp folds, the heat and hardness rubbing a silken friction against her straining bundle of nerves.

He seemed to understand her need for control over at least some part of her life right now. And although that practical side of her insisted Diego could turn the tables in a heartbeat, somehow she knew she could turn them right back around on him. Ultimately, the thrilling power play would stretch pleasure tighter for both of them.

Perspiration glided between her shoulder blades just as it dotted his thighs. The sound of him sagging back against the wall thrilled her, led her to continue until he gripped her hand and smacked the condom into her palm.

She sheathed him with excruciating precision before lowering herself onto him, slowly, pausing at the first thick pressure of entrance. Holding back. Sustaining that precipice moment between before and after.

Before knowing the complete feel of him.

After taking him inside her.

He stared back at her with eyes shifting from brown to opaque black. His hands stayed gentle on her hips, but his jaw flexed, clenched. Cords of restraint bulged along his neck. A pulse throbbed in his temple. The rapid beat mirrored her own pounding in her ears.

Her nails dug into his shoulders as she steadied herself, lower. Lower still, *yes,* as her body adjusted and sighed its acceptance of him. She sank against the hard expanse of his chest, slick skin melding to her.

Sweat dripped down her brow, into her eyes, and he kissed it away. Thank heaven, for once her brain managed to shut up and allow her impulses to assume control. She moved. He groaned. Her body clenched in response, squeezed and milked him.

"Enough," he grunted, lifting and setting her onto the cottony softness of her towel. Before she could breathe or question, he knelt in front of her and draped her legs over his shoulders, her slippery skin siding against his corded expanse.

Her head fell back with a *thunk,* hair snagging on the knotty cedar wall as she sank into deeper sensation, the warmth of his circling tongue, the rasp of his whiskers along the insides of her thighs. Sensation. So much. Almost too much when she wanted this to last.

As if he heard her thoughts, he drew away, lowering her flat on her back. He thrust into her in a stretching sweep. Her feet traced up the backs of his legs higher, wrapping her legs around him higher still to open herself for a deeper connection.

With rational thought gone, the floodgates on her emotions ripped free. A roaring mass liberated inside her—all the hope of clearing her mother's name, the agony of Craig's death, even her own loneliness, a loneliness banished by the excitement of night races with the uninhibited man over her.

Everything lashed through her in a storm of passion and feeling that left her clawing down Diego's back for anchor. He answered her with firmer thrusts that sent reason deeper into hiding. Hell, and why not? This howling hurricane of need scared her a little.

But it excited her more.

She threaded her fingers through the scant hair

along his head and again mourned the loss. She would have liked to see that hair hanging from his face as he stretched over her.

Would she ever experience that vision with him? Thoughts of the future threatened to chill her in spite of the rising temperatures in the small confines of their heated haven.

She nipped him, tasted the salt on his skin. He pumped harder, faster in piston time with her racing pulse. Her nips turned fiercer, each reddening spot soothed with a frenzied kiss.

"Don't hold back," he ordered, demanded.

Challenged.

How she thrived on challenge even as her mind protested against the total surrender of her body only seconds away.

Gasping, she inhaled and savored the scent of cedar and *them* mingling in the steamy air. Her body stretched tight within, dizziness gripping her with a G-force sensation of the blood leaving her head to rush downward. If she had to crash and burn in this surrender, damn it, she wasn't going alone.

She glided her hands down his sweat-slicked back to cup the crest of his butt and urge him closer while her hips writhed against him in just the right position to bring—

Sparks exploded behind her eyes in a shower of sensation riding the waves of her release and scream. Restraint ripped away, leaving her free-falling into a pulsing plummet of wind echoing with Diego's growling shout of completion.

Her arms flung wide as if to find hold or balance as she arched up to wrest every last imploding shimmer that brought her the welcome oblivion she'd sought. One hand slapped the varnished wooden wall. The other grasped air until finally she glided back to earth again.

She couldn't breathe. She thought maybe the gasping sensation came from the heat or the weight of Diego pressing against her chest. But then he levered off her and the constricting heaviness remained, swelled, pushing all the pain of the past four days and maybe even longer than that up to sting her eyes. She wanted to curl away and hide, embarrassed and overwhelmed and too damn exposed.

Wordlessly Diego scooped her up onto his lap and held her naked body against his while, finally, she cried.

Chapter 14

An hour later, Josie stood flush against Diego in the outside shower stall and tried to hang on to the buzz of incredible sex a while longer before they returned to the house. Soon enough they would have to get dressed and start the day. Not that she was in a hurry by any stretch.

Because that would mean meeting his eyes.

Steam filled the small cubicle, spiraling up into the morning sky through the open top. Eucalyptus and cedar scents hung in the damp air—two new erotic smells she would always associate with this man.

Leaning back against the planked wall, he tugged her closer, running his hands along her back. Slowly emotions returned to her spent body.

Embarrassment for starters.

Not about the sex. Although he likely wouldn't be

going around shirtless for a few days until the marks on his back faded. But after the sex…

Her tears had nearly blasted her apart. She wasn't a gentle crier. Probably because she didn't allow herself much practice.

Instead, she was all red eyes, mucus, shakes and words flooding out in choking bursts. She'd babbled about memories of Craig's humor from test-pilot days, shuffling to her ache for Craig's children, which had led too easily to more tears and ramblings about her friend Kayla and precious little Jazz who had a father, after all, in Bridges. A father alive and well and totally uninvolved.

Then she'd cried over being a bad friend in telling him about Kayla and Bridges.

Now she stood silent, still and abashed in his arms. The shower poured over them to the cement floor, swirling down the drain and rinsing away so much more than perspiration. She wasn't totally steady. But she was better, which meant she would be on her own again soon.

Shouldn't that be what she wanted? God knows Diego didn't seem particularly interested in cleaning up his own act to the extent of letting a woman into his life long-term. She would expect him to paint his walls, throw away his ugly couch. Rejoin the human race. And now she understood just how difficult that could be.

She skimmed her fingers up his neck, tracing to his ears and pressing her fingers into the sensual pulse point. "Your beautiful hair."

"It grows fast."

She angled back, surprised. "So you're planning to let it grow again?"

"Of course. Why would you think otherwise?"

"The uniform looked so surprisingly right on you yesterday." Her fingers continued to toy with his hairline. "I know in my head you wore it before and have even seen some photos of you from the past. But it wasn't real to me...not until I saw you in it."

"That part of my life still doesn't seem real to me, either. Sometimes...ah, hell." He cupped her hips and rocked against her. "Screw discussing that. Let's talk about the part where you got to see me *out* of that uniform."

She grazed her hand over him, pausing and curving to cup his weight. "You sure can be a hoo-hah sometimes."

"A hoo-hah?"

She caressed, stroking until he stirred in her hand. "That's what I said, Morel."

"Hey wait." Water clung to lids fast going sleepy, as if he struggled to stay alert even while she worked to distract him. "At the bar that first night, you whispered hoo-hah under your breath and vowed it was your own private cheer. When all the time it's really your name for a—"

"Oops." Laughing, she stroked up the growing length of him. "Busted."

He gripped her chin and eyed her with mock shock. "You actually called me a d—"

Josie covered his mouth with her free hand. "I did." She slid both of her hands over his wet chest. "But I changed my mind about you later."

"Well, I would hope so since we're currently standing naked together in my shower."

"Actually, you changed that impression for me."

"Would that have been when I raced you across the desert?"

"Partly."

"And the other part?" He swept her hair back from her face, gathering it into a wet twist.

"When you made my sister smile." A similar smile warmed her now. "She doesn't do that very often around me anymore."

"I thought you were jealous. My ex sure as hell always was even when I never once gave her cause." His grip tightened on her hair. "Every time I returned from a TDY, she searched my bags, certain she'd find some feminine contraband to prove I was screwing around on her. Later, I realized maybe she was hoping to find something to justify her own actions."

Apparently they all had their ghosts to work through and she'd been selfishly focusing on her own.

"Jealous?" she repeated, determined to do something for him after all he'd done for her. Reassurance wasn't much, but it was about all she had right now. "Not really. I trusted that I had your undivided attention."

"That you do." He dropped his chin to the top of her head while the water and rising sun beat down on them. "So why doesn't your sister smile around you very much?"

Her head landed against his shoulder again. Hiding? Yeah. "Since things fell apart with Mom, well, everything changed. We didn't lose just one parent. We lost both."

"I thought your father was still alive."

"Oh, he is. But he pretty much checked out when she did, just in a different fashion. He hired a nanny and buried himself in work. Once we were old enough, he shipped us off to Arizona to Athena Academy. I shouldn't complain really, since Diana went even younger than I did."

"I thought you liked it there."

"I did, actually. It was like an all-girl Harry Potter kind of school environment and camaraderie—without the wands and three-headed dogs, of course." She grinned, caught up in her memories. "The opportunities there were incredible. By the time I graduated from high school, I spoke three languages, aced my college entrance boards. I can outshoot, outrace, outride just about anyone—"

She stared down at the swirling water. "I'm rambling again. Suffice it to say, the whole Athena Academy experience taught me more than I would have learned anywhere else, opened doors and gave me lifelong friends who'll never let me down. There's a bond with all of us I'm not sure I can adequately explain."

"I'm sure your grandfather was proud to see you attend, since he was instrumental in starting the place. Maybe your dad had an instinct about the whole thing, family legacy fulfilled and all."

"Maybe," she answered vaguely, then tickled her toe along the top of his bare foot. "Enough about me. Your turn again. What about your folks?"

"Alive and kicking in Mississippi."

"Were they military, too?"

"God, no. My parents are good, working-class, small-town Mississippi folk. Dad owns an auto hobby shop that specializes in rebuilding bikes, which is where I learned to appreciate a finely tuned engine.

Mom runs a day care out of the house—although half of the kids are my nieces and nephews."

"Sounds noisy, normal and wonderful."

"They are."

She stared at his chest, drawing lazy circles through the whorls of hair. "I can see you racing your bike along the railroad tracks, shooting tin cans with your pals and all the while planning how you were going to head out. Do I have it right?"

"Close enough. No one tried to hold me back. Hell, I was their damned hometown hero." His sigh steamed through her wet hair. "Makes going back mighty awkward now."

"So you don't go?" She knew, even though he didn't answer. "I've been ignoring messages on my voice mail from my mother since the accident hit the news."

"She's worried about you."

Josie nodded, avoiding his eyes. "Are you?"

"Am I what?"

"Worried about me?" After her big weep-fest, she wouldn't blame him, the main reason she didn't indulge in tears. The last thing she needed was to give people more ammo to suspect she was losing it.

Especially now.

He cupped her chin and lifted, looking down with steady, no-bullshit eyes. "I'm sorry you're hurting. I understand that hurt. But bottom line? No. I'm not worried about you. You're strong. You'll make it through this and come out even stronger."

And he was right. She knew it. She was just relieved he knew it, too.

"Enough talk." He shifted to press her against the

wooden wall, water beating his back. "I have other ideas for how to spend our time this weekend."

Damn straight. Monday would come soon enough. "So show me, Cruiser."

Her legs slid up his and around his waist and she was more than glad to delve back into their common ground for a while longer. Because, yes, she would be strong again soon. And strong meant alone.

Birddog wanted to walk away from the office window overlooking the flight line, but the scorched patch of desert cordoned off for investigation held him mesmerized.

Absently he scratched a nail against a fleck on the window. Things weren't supposed to have happened this way. He'd planned carefully. Craig Wagner had been a damned good pilot and an asset to the air force. Not a wave-making, stubborn pain in the neck like Josie Lockworth.

He'd only wanted the test to fail to put her in place. He'd intended there to be a simple in-flight emergency that would stall the program for Josie and perhaps give Diego Morel a few nightmares about his own final, fatal project.

Instead, someone had died. Not that it could be traced to him. He hoped. While he liked to consider himself invincible, he couldn't afford to leave anything more to chance. No more warnings. And no more mistakes.

She would have to be stopped.

Dirt from the window and this whole damn mess itched along skin that he couldn't seem to get clean enough. Tearing himself away from the view, he spun back to the office and into the bathroom to wash his hands again before settling behind the looming desk. He jerked open the bottom desk drawer and pulled out his two vices. A bottle of Scotch and a small snapshot taken on the desert base flight line.

He poured himself a shot, bolted it back and refilled again. Fire flamed down his throat and into his gut, blazing almost as hot as the ones whipping through him after just one look at the picture. Long legs and brown hair radiated a blaze she never saw fit to share with him, someone worthy of her.

He'd let Josie live at Red Flag. A mistake. He considered taking care of things quick and simple. He had contacts after all. During his time as head of the acquisitions team selling old F-16s to Malaysia, he'd been appointed a bodyguard, a man he'd later found had L.A. mob connections. Those came in handy on occasion.

A simple call on his cell phone would take care of it. Birddog swept a tissue along the rim of his glass and considered the option of a quick hit—then decided to place that alternative in reserve. Better to exhaust other options first. Why risk another fatal accident with an investigation into Wagner's crash already underway?

Still she had to be kept out of the office. Once she returned to work, she would no doubt be prodding for answers with the help of that washed-up desert rat she'd been seeing.

Birddog bolted back another shot of liquor, alcohol sanitizing gritty anger from thoughts of women attracted to unworthy men. He was damn near certain he'd covered his tracks, but Josie Lockworth would turn this into some kind of personal quest.

He definitely needed her otherwise occupied.

Flipping through his Rolodex, Birddog stopped at the Cs. Conner, Shannon.

The number and purpose both branding his brain, Birddog slammed the Rolodex back and dialed.

Slamming her car door, Josie started toward the standard military-shade brown building that housed her office. Only a few minutes more and she would be back on the right path for restoring order.

First, she would file the Memo of Record about Bridges's come-on. Second, return all the data print-outs from her mother's test. That hurt. But she had to focus on Craig's accident now or she wouldn't even be working at all. Maybe the answers to the past waited in the present.

The never-ceasing grit-filled wind tore at her flight suit and braided hair. She clapped her hand to her hat and ducked into the gusts toward the entrance.

She hated that so much time had passed since the incident, but she hadn't been able to focus on anything except Craig's crash. Aside from the near-debilitating grief, there had been practical concerns at work. Questions. Investigations. She'd been running flat-footed for nearly a week.

Except for the mind-blowing weekend of sex with Diego.

He would probably be pissed when he realized she'd slipped out of his bed without waking him. But since the project was on hold, his role with the con-gressional oversight committee had ended anyway.

And even as she recited the logical reason for him not to accompany her, she knew she was avoiding the truth. She needed to face this alone, and she couldn't think with him around. The temptation to lean on him was too great. Hearing him snore had tugged at something deep inside her, more than an impulsive Josephine longing. Knowing that his obnoxious and kind of endearing snore came from his accident squeezed at her heart.

So, yeah, she'd run like hell.

Guilt tweaked. She *had* left him a note, damn it. It wasn't as if she intended to cut him off altogether. Just keep him out of her workplace for a while. And maybe sketch a few boundaries against more probing questions in the shower that left her feeling naked in a way that had nothing to do with discarded clothes.

Was it even possible to segment herself into clean delineations of practical Josephine at work and impulsive Josie with Diego? She would have to, starting now.

Josie yanked open the door, mind already on the stacks of files to review, aerial footage to scrutinize, people to question. Deeper into the building she charged, the walls closing around her to swallow her back into the routine world she understood.

The door to Bridges's office swung open. His desk loomed behind him with stacks of what she suspected were copies of the same files she would be searching in a few minutes.

She smoothed her face into what she hoped was an emotionless mask. She didn't want to gift him with any hint of her intent about the memo.

Josie saluted without stopping. "Good morning, sir."

"I didn't expect to see you back so soon, Captain."

Bridges returned the salute. "You were given extra time to regain your balance for a reason."

And let the investigation into her test crash go on without her supervision? Uh-uh. "I would prefer to keep busy."

She didn't trust him not to pull another stunt while she was gone. Did he perhaps feel even the least bit guilty over his scheduling change? As much as she wanted to think she could have saved the craft in flight, chances were she would have died instead.

Except she wouldn't have left behind a spouse and a child. She couldn't even bear to think about that other baby who would never see its father, or she would be a mess all over again.

She almost couldn't contain her hatred for Mike Bridges, loathing made all the worse by the fact she didn't detect the least hint of culpability on his handsome features. Just an odd blankness, as if he didn't want her reading him at all.

What was he covering?

The sooner she started searching for answers, the sooner she would be able to prove whether Bridges had been responsible for more than a schedule change. "Well, I need to get to my office."

She started to turn.

"Oh, Captain?"

"Yes, sir?"

"It's fortuitous that you came in. It actually saved me a call. General Quincy wants to see you."

A meeting with the general? Her skin burned with foreboding. Maybe she'd gleaned some of Diego's feel-the-plane instincts after all, because she couldn't escape the sense that she was headed for a crash and burn.

Chapter 15

Josie stood outside the office and listened to the general's aide announce her. Her mind raced through the million things General Quincy could want to discuss with her. Some positive, like maybe they'd already traced the problem in Craig's flight and it was a tragic accident but not her fault so all would proceed on schedule now.

Fat chance.

Other more reasonable options loomed darkly. That somehow in spite of all her careful planning, she'd screwed up and Craig's death was truly and completely her fault.

She braced herself and entered. The general oversaw squadrons and detachments at a number of bases, and this office was simply the one he used while in town. Minimal extras lent a spartan air, just a big desk, a few chairs, a computer—and of course, flags.

Major General John Quincy filled the leather chair with his presence more than size, a fit man in his fifties with a full head of blond hair fading to gray. He wasn't known for his enlightened views on women in the military, but at least there had never been so much as a whisper of him ever hitting on a female service member. All encounters with him at formal military functions showed an apparently happily married man with twins nearly her age.

She didn't completely trust him to look out for her welfare in the workplace, but at least she didn't have to worry about him grabbing her ass.

Josie snapped her salute. "Captain Lockworth reporting as ordered, sir."

"At ease, Captain." He returned the salute then steepled his fingers under his chin.

Her arm lowered but still she stood, meeting his eyes now. "Yes, sir."

"I'm sorry to have to call this meeting so close to the events with Captain Wagner. But a situation has arisen that involves you."

"In what way, sir?"

"I'll let these pictures speak for themselves."

He opened a file and tossed down an array of five photos—all of her kissing Mike Bridges. Her leaning forward as if to deepen the kiss with the scum-sucking bastard, when she knew damn well she'd only been leaning to shove past him without kneeing him in the balls. Even though she knew the events had unfolded in a disgusting case of Bridges breaking protocol, the pictures seemed to suggest something different.

Only years of military training kept her rigid stance

from crumbling. Her fingers itched to snatch the pictures from his desk and shred them. Shannon must have snapped shots of her with Bridges before catching her with Diego, probably a whole roll of film that she'd neatly stashed somewhere besides her camera bag.

Why hadn't she seen a flash? Could her anger have been that blinding? No matter how it had happened, the pictures were there and somehow Shannon had captured angles that made Josie seem the aggressor.

General Quincy scooted the photos into a single stack. "As you know, a certain television correspondent has been working on a special about Athena Academy graduates, showing whether or not the grant money funding the all-girl's prep school is paying off. A sort of 'where are they now' focus."

Where was she now? From the picture on top it appeared she was working Bridges toward a hotel romp. Who would have thought disgust could look so much like passion?

She forced herself to listen rather than shout in her own defense. She needed to stay calm and logical.

"I've already met with Major Bridges to question him. He says you expressed an interest in him the first day you met."

Damn Bridges and his quibbling. She may have glanced at him before she knew his rank and position. But she'd never once made a move toward him.

Josie kept her head high, much preferable to staring at herself in compromising photos that brought the disgust of that encounter roiling through her again. "The photos and Major Bridges are lying. He came on to me, sir. I was on my way in today to file a Memo of Record to begin documenting a pattern of behavior."

"But you haven't already done so?"

Frustration and the first hints of fear smoked through her. "No, sir. There hasn't been time with Captain Wagner's crash."

"I see." The general rocked back in the office chair. "Do you have any evidence or witnesses in your defense?"

"Diego Morel walked into the event in question, sir. He knows what really happened."

Already the general was shaking his head. "A jealous boyfriend? I'm afraid you'll have to do better than that. Of course he believes the other man was at fault. That isn't going to help you, Captain. I would advise you to stop talking now and contact a lawyer."

Fear mushroomed into a toxic cloud inside her. She would rather face combat than this. "A lawyer?"

"Yes, you can make the call here or once you're confined to quarters."

"Quarters? Excuse me, sir, but I'm not following." Confinement to quarters was extreme for a charge like this, which expanded her fear. But she had no recourse to argue his decision.

"Captain," the general said slowly, as if to a dense child, "this is a court-martial offense and charges have been filed. As much as I would like for it to go away for the good of the air force, this—" he shook the stack of photos "—makes a quiet resolution impossible. You are being confined until the mess is settled. If you lived on base, we could keep you under guard there. But you don't. So you will be held in the Visiting Officer's Quarters over at Edwards Air Force Base. Much better than a prison cell, don't you agree?"

As though she had a choice. Cold realization hit her with leaden force. "Will I be allowed visitors?"

"Of course."

Did she even want Diego around right now? No. Definitely not. She'd be in his lap naked and crying again in a heartbeat.

Unacceptable.

But she would need help given the extreme measures already in the works by confining her. She would start with contacting her Athena network to find…something, *anything* to make this right.

She kept her shoulders squared, military posture intact even as the world around her tumbled out of control.

"Captain."

"Yes, sir?" She forced herself to focus through the dizzying haze.

He relaxed forward on his elbows signifying an us-against-them shift to the meeting she couldn't afford to trust. "Fraternization rules are important, but I understand human nature. I've been around for many years and battles. My guess is that very likely there will be a deal put on the table."

She knew better than to think a deal would leave her unscathed. "And what kind of deal might that be, sir?"

"You'll probably be offered the chance to resign your commission in exchange for all charges being dropped."

Denial howled through her. A few weeks ago she hadn't been certain about staying in the air force after the test project wrapped up, and now she couldn't imagine leaving. What a bittersweet way to find out how much the uniform meant to her. "Not an option for me, sir. I'm innocent."

"Captain, pressures have been intense for you lately."

A spidery tingle started over her as she sensed his logical direction.

"Take this time to level out and plan your life so family patterns don't repeat themselves. Choose wisely, Captain. There are plenty of other ways to serve your country. None of which will be possible if you're in prison or have a dishonorable discharge hanging over you."

He reached to press the buzzer on his phone and the door opened again. Footsteps sounded behind her just before two SPs—Security Police—fanned to her sides.

The general stood and returned their salutes. "Escort Captain Lockworth home to collect some personal belongings before you see her to the VOQ."

Military training assumed command and she functioned, registering her own automatic reactions, a salute, a precisely executed pivot toward the door with her escorts ever present.

Josie shuddered even imagining how her parents would feel about this and the old wounds it might open for her mother. As frustrated as she was with her father sometimes, she *had* tried to demand as little as possible from them given their own difficult times.

She couldn't think about that now. She had to get her butt out of this sling. Fast. With every second wasted, the trail grew colder on how that flight had gone wrong.

Now more than ever she believed someone was

gunning for her. Personally. If the crash wasn't accidental, then Craig's death proved they didn't care who went down, as well.

She stepped outside, mid-morning sun blinding her until she slipped her aviator glasses in place. She couldn't escape the crushing weight of her own flaws. She'd been so focused on losing Craig, on the defeat of her program, she'd all but forgotten about the incident with Bridges. And that brief lapse in defenses had been too costly.

No more emotional weakness.

She climbed into the back of the SPs vehicle, the demoralizing moment making her all the more determined.

Pressure?

Hell, yes, she was under pressure, and she was learning something about herself. She thrived on pressure because damn it all, that was just challenge in another form.

She tugged out her cell phone and her e-mailer. She needed to get in touch with a lawyer. Athena grad Selena Shaw Jones, with her law degree and current position as a CIA legal attaché, would recommend the best. Diana would need to know, too, so she could troubleshoot with their parents.

Josie considered calling Diego, after all—the man she'd run from, leaving just a paltry note. But the reasons for stepping back from him still applied. Besides, this was her mess, not his. If she called, he would come. And help. And then she would lean at a time she needed to hold strong more than ever.

Josie gripped her cell phone and called her sister.

Straddling his humming Harley, Diego scanned the desert road stretching out of the testing facility. If he had his timing right, he should be seeing a certain vehicle come his way any minute now.

Thanks to the heads-up from Diana Lockworth.

Josie would be pissed as hell when she discovered her sister had sold her out. But Diana had been scared spitless of what would happen to Josie in the hours it would take Diana to get on a plane and head back to California.

In Diana's own words, Josie would never put herself first, and right now somebody needed to. She trusted that he would do what was best for her sister.

Diana was right.

He didn't give a shit about rules and fighting fair, and he sensed that perhaps Diana Lockworth might skirt a few rules herself on occasion. Their rebel kindred spirits recognized each other and together they would make sure people like Josie, pure of spirit and intent, were protected.

He figured he had two options for straightening this out—take on Mike Bridges or Shannon Conner. The decision cost him less than a quarter of a brain cell.

Bridges was the weaker of the two.

Diego gave the idling Harley another pulse of gas, the hum, rev and growl echoing the one inside him, anticipating Bridges emerging into view.

And if not? Diego kept one foot planted on the ground, the other on the bike. Well, he was a patient man when it came to righting the wrong done to Josie. Yeah, he was torqued with her for walking out while he slept, but the emotion definitely took a back burner to dealing with Bridges.

An SUV peeked into view, drawing closer, clearer

on the road empty but for the SUV and his own Harley. It was him. Bridges. Diego revved his engine, waited for just the right moment to—

Swing his Harley out into the middle of the road.

Diego roared his way out, cranked into a turn, sliding, forcing the SUV to swerve onto the shoulder. Sand spewed from Bridges's tires. The vehicle jerked to a halt.

The door flung open. Bridges stepped out in a cloud of sand and fury. Aviator glasses did little to hide his anger. "What the hell was that about? I almost killed you, you crazy son of a bitch."

Diego swung off his bike. "I wanted to make sure we had a chance to talk without interruptions." He advanced toward the uniformed man with slow, deliberate steps. "And I didn't trust that a weasely bastard like you wouldn't whimper for help on base or back at your place when we have our *talk* about what you did to Josie."

"Whoa, hold on there." Bridges held up two hands. "You don't want to make this any worse for your girlfriend than it already is."

"No." Sun had baked the sand into a hard, cracked surface, pretty much like his anger. "Things are going to be just fine for her once I tear you apart."

"Kill me and everything's better?" Bravado starched up the man's noodle spine now that the shock had worn off. He strutted forward.

"It would be for me. But that's not what I'm talking about. You're going down one way or another. I'm only giving you a chance to set this right so it goes easier on Josie."

"How big of you. But you can pound the hell out

of me and it won't change my story. You went through the same POW survival camp training I did. I'm not impressed with your fists or your mind games."

"No mind games." Diego stood his ground, watching Bridges strut and posture—and fidget. He had the guy on the run. "Facts. See, I figured pretty quick that you've probably got a history with this sort of thing."

A flicker of unease whispered across Bridges's face before his cocky assurance slid into place again like a shield. "You don't have jack-shit on me."

"That's where you're wrong. You seem to have forgotten Josie's sister works military intel for the army. That lady can wring things out of the system you would think were impossible to squeeze free," Diego continued with a slow-blink stare, studying for the right moment to break the man. "If there's a whisper on you anywhere—on file, in print, even so much as a suggestive e-mail, she'll find it. If that's not enough for you, think on this name for a minute. Kayla Ryan."

Shields slid away to reveal pure wariness. Everyone had a weak spot, and apparently Kayla was his. Bridges stayed silent. Smart man.

"She was a teenager when you seduced her, you bastard. There's no denying it since your daughter's DNA and age proves you did it. You've managed to keep it quiet with your timely child-support payments and damned good luck that the woman didn't decide to skewer you. I won't be so generous."

"You'll be hurting Kayla and Jasmine."

Like Josie wasn't already hurting? He refused to feel guilt over this man's mistakes. "You scum. You don't even know they call her Jazz."

"Jazz?" Remorse flickered, fast, but there. "Damn

it, leave my kid out of this. Josie would never go for dragging Kayla through this."

"Josie won't have a choice. I'll do damned near anything before I let her lose her commission, much less go to jail."

"She won't forgive you for interfering."

A lone car hummed in the distance, neared, passed by.

"Then that's the way it will have to be, Bridges. But make no mistake, I'm going to pull apart your reputation layer by layer. Once Josie's side becomes public, then with Kayla's story, as well, there will be enough questions to start people talking. Maybe even give other folks confidence to speak up. Now, if you don't have more skeletons in your closet—"

"Fine, damn it," Bridges spit out, muscles bunching and jumping under his flight suit. "Just leave Kayla and Jasmi—" He paused, frowned. "Jazz. Leave them out of this."

Possibly the guy really did care what happened to them. Maybe he had a human bone in his body after all. Diego wrestled with the surprise revelation. But then scumbags weren't always clear-cut evil. Still, even knowing there was some good buried deep— way down deep—wouldn't stop Diego from delivering one last message.

"Hey, Bridges?" Diego advanced, slowly, stalking.

"Yeah?"

Diego jabbed his fist up into the bastard's gut. Bridges grunted, doubled over, stumbling back against his SUV. Diego pressed his forearm over the gasping man's neck.

"How does it feel to be pinned against this car? Not

so great, huh?" He flexed his arm a few millimeters deeper into the guy's Adam's apple. "And by the way, that was from Josie, the punch you deserved from her in the parking lot. If you ever hurt her again, I swear I *will* kill you."

She was free.

Sitting in the passenger seat of her car, Josie hitched her elbow in the open window and let the wind swirl around her. Her head was still reeling from the shock of being detained then released all by the end of the workday.

And somehow Diego was in the middle of it, because when word came through to let her go, he'd been waiting by her Mustang shortly before sunset. Now he filled the driver's side, unspeaking as he guided the car toward her condo. She hadn't even bothered arguing. Even if she'd been able to grab hold of her tilting world, the fierce gleam in Diego's eyes would have stopped her.

Was the anger directed at her for leaving him? Or at the situation with Bridges? Regardless, Diego was in some feral territory she was wise enough to steer clear of.

After that horrifying meeting with General Quincy, the SPs had escorted her to her condo to pick up clothes and other necessities. She'd packed her belongings and barely made it back to the VOQ before the whole mess simply disappeared.

Quincy had arrived at the VOQ with an apology and release. Apparently Mike Bridges had cleared up the "misunderstanding." Quincy would do his best to see that the television feature never aired—probably easier now that the reporter had been discredited for her incorrect information.

How damned ironic.

When it was her ass on the line, the show ran. But when Bridges was at fault, suddenly everything went away. All this injustice could really start to give a girl a complex.

All the same, she owed Diego. She'd walked out on him—had it only been that morning?—hadn't even bothered to call him and still he'd been there for her. She didn't doubt for a minute that somehow he was at the heart of her release. Even as much as she'd wanted to save her own hide, she wouldn't be an ungrateful brat.

"I don't know what you did to make all of that go away for me, but thank you."

"No problem." His eyes stayed hidden behind the shades, his jaw taunt.

"Did my sister contact you?"

"Yes."

She pressed her lips tight to keep from calling her sister an insulting name she would later regret, because Diana had only been concerned. She counted telephone poles whipping past to calm herself.

Seventy-nine later, it hadn't helped.

Why couldn't Diana have just looked up the questions on Bridges like she'd asked? There had to be dirt on the guy that wouldn't bring Kayla into the picture.

Kayla.

Mortifying heat tingled. She'd told Diego all about Kayla and Jazz while crying her eyes out in the sauna. "Diego, what did you do?"

"I threatened him." Diego downshifted gears with

deceptive calm, muscles flexing under faded denim as he slowed. "Then I gave him the punch you should have been able to deliver."

"And he crumbled that easily? I'm not buying it."

Diego turned into her condo complex. "Guys like him are basically cowards. I brought up your sister's amazing ability to find any dirt in the guy's past, not just in formal records but unofficial channels, as well. You had even asked her to do just that. You set this in motion by calling her."

Had she subconsciously known Diana would call him? She chewed her bottom lip, which was devoid of orange tryst today.

He cut the engine. "Confronted with that, just as you undoubtedly expected, Bridges folded. My guess is he'll cut his losses and take the offer of an assignment out of here."

She crossed her arms over her chest. "Great. He gets to move while I was threatened with a court martial."

Once the roof was secured, Diego turned off the engine and opened his door. "Unfair without a doubt. At this point, I think Quincy wants it all to go away, too."

He rounded the car while she sat. He raised a brow and waited. But she couldn't go into her apartment with him because they would have sex. She wouldn't be able to resist him. If she'd thought her emotions were vulnerable before, she'd been stripped of a fresh layer today. She didn't want to be that close to him. And she definitely didn't want to cry again.

Diego hitched his boot on the running board beside her. "What the hell's wrong now?"

"I'm pissed because I have no control over what's

going on around me. Bridges set me up. You take him out. Now I can't even tell you to get on your bike and go home because you drove me in my car."

"Buttercup." He hooked one arm on the edge of the roof and leaned inside, filling the doorway. "You really don't want to mess with me today. You may have forgotten this, but I woke up in an empty bed because somebody's too much of a coward to face the morning after. I don't consider myself Mr. Sensitive by any damn stretch of the imagination. But common courtesy applies when two people exchange body fluids."

She studied her bootlaces. "I didn't leave you stranded. You had your truck."

"Don't even insult me by pretending that's what I'm talking about. Or hey, wait, maybe I should get you a pen and paper so you can write it all down in another note to leave me while I'm asleep." Anger leaked into his curt tones.

She understood well the tendency to hide pain behind anger. She looked up at him. "I'm sorry."

"No. You're not."

"What?" So much for feeling sorry for him. "Now I don't get control over my life *or* my own feelings?"

"Do you even know what your feelings are?"

He had her there.

"I didn't think so." Inches of crackling air separated their faces. "I'm a big boy. I can get my own ass home. But if you want me to leave, have the guts to tell me to my face," he challenged.

"Leave."

"Fine." He pivoted on his boot heel.

Ah, hell. This guy really did level her defenses. She slid out of the car. "Diego?"

He looked back over his shoulder. Josie's hand shot out, gripped his fringed jacket.

And yanked his head down to hers for a hard and deliberate kiss.

Chapter 16

Birddog resisted the urge to ram the car ahead and shout at other drivers passing him on the desert highway. All of which would make him look insane.

And he wasn't.

He had faultless control of his senses. He checked his speedometer. Perfect.

The fact that he could manage at all through the howling outrage over Josie Lockworth's release attested to his sanity. That he hadn't strangled Diego Morel with his bare hands for interfering said much about his strength of will.

He only needed a drive to clear his head and remove himself from the temptation to wreak havoc in his office. Mile after mile away from the base, he talked through his options.

He wasn't speaking to himself or hearing voices.

Hell, no. Just reasoning aloud to test how things sounded.

His skin burned raw where he scratched away dust, and he forced both hands onto the wheel. His foot twitched heavier on the accelerator. Sandy landscape blurred in his side window.

Something had to be done soon.

Why couldn't Josie Lockworth have crawled into a hole after the crash like her mother had done years ago? After all, the present mirrored the past so cleanly with the accident and death of a co-worker, he'd thought surely the daughter's reaction would follow the mother's.

Things didn't have to get this complicated. He'd only needed Josie out of the way long enough to plug in his own test theories. They would work as well if not better than hers. He could finally get the credit he deserved.

And show *her* his worth.

Now Josie had messed every damn thing up by wriggling out of the net so quickly. There was little time for him to cover his tracks and start the new path—unless she was completely out of the picture.

Reaching an empty stretch of desert, he roared off the road, skidding to a stop in a tidal wave of sand. He bolted out of the car, slamming the door, his long-bottled howl begging to be set free. The primal scream tore up from his throat until he gasped for air.

Last echoes fading, he bent to grasp his knees. No question about it, Josie Lockworth would have to die. That bastard Morel, too. Birddog straightened, resolve set, in control and already reaching for his cell phone.

One call to his old bodyguard outside of L.A. would set the contingency plan in motion within an hour.

* * *

Fingers digging into Diego's shoulders for balance, Josie wished it were as easy to brace herself against the storm of emotions pummeling her. Her world was a jumbled mess. Work and personal. Past and present. Her days of controlled emotions and careful planning hadn't gained her jack.

The logical part of her brain told her she should get hold of herself and think. But at the moment, with her mouth plastered to Diego's, her hand tunneling under his leather jacket, she couldn't come up with a single reason why she should stop.

What else did she have to lose?

She'd been so sure she was stronger than her mother, that if she never lost control, if she dotted every *i* and crossed every *t*, things would work. How damned arrogant.

Her mother had been meticulous. Her mother had most likely been right, too. Hell, her mother had even known how to maintain a steady relationship with someone other than a pile of tiny stuffed critters.

She'd tried to stay in control and her life had fallen apart anyway. Why not take what she wanted? And right now, she wanted to get inside her condo and get naked with Diego.

Without breaking their kiss, he kicked the car door closed and backed toward Josie's condo. Their feet tangled, her combat boots with his biker leathers, yet somehow they managed to make it to her front door without landing on their butts.

"Key," he grunted against her lips.

Devouring his mouth, she flattened her foot on the wall beside him while she fished in her calf pocket. He wrapped his fingers around her thigh and brought their bodies closer—nowhere near close enough, with so many clothes between them. All the pent-up emotions of the day bellowed inside her, and apparently she'd found a matching frenzy in him.

Her mouth nipped an urgent path down his neck while he jerked the keys from her hand and jammed the correct one home into the lock. They stumbled into the entry hall and again he kicked the door closed, blocking out the world and problems.

He pivoted her against the wall, anchoring them both before they truly did fall on their butts. She should probably call his behavior Thor material. But all she could think of at the moment was how damned awesome it was to be with a man who didn't care if she carried a big knife or if she flew jets. Diego gave as good as he got and she respected that in him.

He braced both forearms to the spackled wall. "Are you sure you want this?"

"Yes. Yes," she panted, clawing at his jacket. "I want this, *you*, now. Here, or I would have flipped you onto the cement back in the parking lot."

"So you're sure? We could go upstairs to your bedroom for slow and thorough—"

"We'll do slow and thorough later. After."

"Fair enough." He jerked down her flight-suit zipper. She shimmied her arms out and raised them over her head in an unmistakable invitation. He gripped the edge of her black T-shirt, sweeping it up and off to reveal her sports bra, which he sent sailing, as well.

Her frantic hands tore at his belt. "Birth control." She worked fly buttons free. "Do you have it or do we go to my bedroom after all?"

"Wallet," he barked as his hands rose to cup her breasts, teasing tight nipples between his fingers. "Back pocket."

Sighing, she sagged into his touch for two breathless seconds before regaining her balance. She abandoned his fly and reached behind to tug his wallet and smack it onto his palm. With determined hands she opened his pants, reached into his boxers and found...

Yeah, he was more than ready.

He whipped out the condom, ripped it open and rolled it down while she whispered her impatience against his neck. The scent of leather clung to him, drifting up and spiraling through her. A swift sweep sent her flight suit and panties down. Could he be any hotter? Could she get any hotter?

And then he plunged inside her. Hotter still.

He filled her again and again while she rocked her response, moaned her pleasure, called out her assent with a ramble of *yes, yes, yes.*

Pictures rattled against the wall alongside them in an echoing tattoo setting a pace, encouraging, louder. One silver frame slid and crashed to the floor. Glass shattered. Not that she bothered to look since the sight of Diego fighting back his release with gritted teeth held her, aroused her as much as his thrusts.

Then her eyes refused to stay open. Her breath hitched. She was close. So close, so soon. So incredible.

Crying out, she arched against him, taut and moaning for...she didn't know how long the sensation pulsed. Until finally Diego's growl of completion against her ear launched a final soaring release. No other word for it.

Slumping against the spackled wall, she couldn't avoid the truth any longer. Cool and logical was no longer an option.

Five minutes—or was it five hours?—later, Josie hooked her arms around Diego's neck to keep from crumpling to the ground. Her fingers glided along the bristly, shorn hair at his nape. She didn't want to think about the emotional meltdowns that seemed to follow sex with Diego. She certainly wouldn't indulge in one now.

Not even twenty-four hours ago, she'd been certain she needed distance from Diego and yet here they were again, open and vulnerable to each other after another explosive encounter. Maybe she needed to ride the wave of this passion. Nothing could be this intense forever. It would have to crest and disperse eventually. They would move on. At just the thought, a sadness pooled deep inside her.

Diego's chest expanded with a breath, muscle pressing against her sex-sensitive breasts before he hefted himself away and zipped his pants. She angled from the wall to right her clothes, but he dipped, swinging her up into his arms.

Josie gripped his shoulders for balance. "Going back into Thor mode are you?"

"Thor?" Diego sidestepped the shattered glass from the picture frame. "Not even close or I'd have pitched you over my shoulder instead."

"All right, then more of a Rhett Butler deal. But be warned, I'm not the Scarlett O'Hara type."

"Rhett?" He snorted and tossed her onto the sofa, her legs draped over the arm with her flight suit still tangled around her ankles. "In case you didn't notice, I'm not hero material."

Clicking on a lamp, he studied her with an unmistakable gleam. He unlaced her boots with practiced hands, tossed both aside and peeled her flight suit off before stripping away his clothes.

"Nice view, Cruiser. So there's more for me tonight?"

"Definitely more. I owe you one that lasts longer than five minutes." He flung his jeans over the ottoman and stood before her in totally unselfconscious nude glory. "Unless you'd rather talk."

Talk? Not a chance. Too much turmoil bubbled inside her. She couldn't risk ending up blubbering in his lap again.

Josie stood, bare and thoroughly enjoying the appreciation in his eyes. She pointed to the sofa. "Get your naked butt over here right now."

She definitely needed to be in control of something today.

"Yes, ma'am." He dropped to the couch and stretched out, arms behind his head.

She swung a leg across to straddle his hips, draping herself over him and losing herself in the luxury of lazy kisses they'd been too frantic to fully explore earlier.

He shifted under her.

"No." She cupped his shoulders to urge him back down again. "This show's mine."

"Yeah, and I'm looking forward to that, but there's something—" he reached under his waist "—beneath my back here."

His hand reappeared with her horsy Beanie Baby

that had captured her attention because it reminded her of riding lessons with her sister. She started to take it from him but he kept it out of reach.

"I meant to ask about these when I was here before, but I got *distracted* by you." He skimmed the fuzzy toy along her spine. "Why do you have a gross of Beanie Babies in your living room?"

So much for losing herself in sex. Was his an idle question? Or a move to venture into a more personal connection? Her chest went tight as if trying to hold back sharing words.

How silly.

She swallowed hard and forced herself to speak. "The day I was commissioned, my dad gave me a new nine-millimeter to carry into battle. My sister gave me a year's worth of ammo for target practice. All my Athena Academy sisters—the Cassandras—gave me the ranks and insignias for my uniform."

"And?" He traced the toy along her shoulders over skin still tingling from the power of a release more intense than any she could remember.

"And my mother gave me a camouflage Beanie Baby. She told me I was strong and that she was proud of me. But never to forget that being soft could sometimes be the greatest strength of all."

Except that was so much easier said than done when it seemed every time she let down her guard something went wrong. So she had collected the doggone Beanie Babies on the sly and hid them in her condo until the place was damn near bursting with them. "Remember when we were talking earlier in the parking lot about my note this morning and whether or not you should go home tonight?"

The tickling softness stopped on her back. "So this was 'wham bam thank you, sir' sex?"

"No!" Everything inside her rebelled at treating him that callously. "That's not at all what I meant. That the words would come out that way is just all the more proof that I'm not thinking straight or making smart decisions. I need my objectivity back, Diego, and I can't be objective around you."

He tossed the tiny horse onto the coffee table. "Somehow I don't think you're complimenting me."

She braced up onto her elbows and searched his darkening eyes. "Are you going to go ballistic on me again if I tell you I need a little space?"

"Not as long as you tell me to my face." His jaw flexed.

"I really do need breathing room." And how strange did that sound with her naked body pressed to his? Her peaking breasts already betrayed how much she wanted him again. "That's what the note was supposed to be about. I can't think when you're around and I have a helluva lot to wade through. I need you to take a step back. Not a big one. Just enough that I can clean up my life—"

"Okay." He sat up and swung her off his lap and to the side.

Her mouth went slack. "That's it? Okay?"

He glanced sideways at her with a don't-give-a-shit blandness. "You wanted me to fight for you Thor-style?"

She'd gotten her way. She should be turning back-flips. Instead the pool of blue melancholy inside her darkened to purple. "Maybe I wanted you to be a little disappointed since this is tearing me up."

"Tearing you up inside?" His don't-give-a-shit look shifted to pure anger. "Good. Because you've damn near shredded me today."

The anger didn't soothe her pride after all. This man confused her and she hated that. "I just meant we wouldn't work together right now." Her hands fell to his shoulders. "We can still be together, like this. Let's go upstairs."

He looked down at one of her hands on him until she slid both away. "You want to segment me off into your apartment like those toys over there. Maybe once in a while you'll take me out for a ride in your car. Oh, and I'll get to have sex with you, too. Thanks, but I think I'll pass."

Every fair and P.C. bone in her body protested at the scenario he'd painted. If the roles were reversed she would be furious—and rightly so. "That's not what I meant."

"Uh-huh. Yeah, right." He hiked on his jeans. "If I just wanted sex, there are plenty of women out there who are a helluva lot less trouble than you are."

She scooped her flight suit off the floor. "As always, you're the king of tact."

Josie swept her flight suit back on, yanking the zipper up with as much speed and emotion as it had been tugged down earlier. Once she finished, she looked up to find Diego watching her with narrowed eyes. Brooding came easy to him. All his emotions seemed to flow.

Diego stalked forward until they stood nose-to-nose. "You want to boot me out of your life? Fine. But first we need some things settled. Somebody's gunning for you, Buttercup. And if my suspicions about

Wagner's crash are right, this person's not afraid to kill. Until we find out who's pursuing you so damned doggedly, you're stuck with me in the workplace. As far as in bed? I'm not feeling particularly turned on at the moment."

She wanted to argue with him. She could handle this on her own. Still, he'd put his butt on the line for her often enough and she was grateful.

A noise sounded from upstairs, stretching her taut nerves to near breaking. Diego tensed beside her.

The spare bedroom door at the top of the stairs swung wide.

"Josie?"

Diana. Josie gripped the sofa arm. Relief melted through her.

Her sister stepped from behind the door with her hand clapped over her eyes. "Are you two about finished?" She padded barefoot into the hall, gray baggy sweatsuit making her nearly indistinguishable in the dark. "If not, throw a blanket over yourselves or something because I can't stay hidden out of the way up here any longer without a bathroom break."

Josie climbed the stairs, Diego's shadow stretching as he followed her. "Jesus, Diana! You scared the hell out of me—again. I'm grateful to see you and all, but I never expected you'd be here so fast."

"I tried to announce myself, but then you two went at it so fa—"

A noise from behind gave her only enough time to spin around before—

Her bedroom door exploded open. Two masked men charged into the hall.

Guns drawn.

Chapter 17

Surprise and adrenaline jolted through Josie like a double shot of espresso strapped to a stick of dynamite.

Two men in dark clothes and ski masks charged from her bedroom, guns drawn. The sliding-glass door in the master bedroom to the garden balcony gaped open behind them.

"Stop right there." The left-handed gunman, bulky in build, swung his weapon toward Diego, stopping him halfway up the stairs.

The right-handed attacker, lean and tall, alternated his gun from Diana to Josie and back again.

Tension coiled inside Josie, ready to spring. She took quick mental inventory of the intruders. Clothes fit snugly so as not to snag on anything, as if worn with careful planning—often. Each man carried a black automatic pistol in gloved hands, a Glock for Lefty and a Beretta for Righty.

"My jewelry box is on the dressing table. There isn't much there, but take it," Josie offered in steady tones, testing their motives, hoping to speed them on their way.

Righty snorted. "We don't want to pawn any cheap rings, lady."

"Our wallets then." She angled down as if to get her wallet, trying to decide whether it would be wise to whip free her survival knife from her boot.

Her heart thudded in her ears. She could face dying, had in fact worked through the possibility in combat and test flights. But she could not lose another friend because of whatever mess she'd stirred with her test project. And Diego and Diana were so much more than friends to her.

Diego's shadow stretched up the steps.

"No farther up those stairs, dude." Lefty hauled Josie back against his bulk. No way to reach for the knife now. "I mean it. Stop, or we blow away the babes."

Diego froze, his gaze flicking from Josie to Diana. "I hear you. Just stay cool."

"Damn. There weren't supposed to be three people," Righty barked in raspy grunts swinging his gun onto Diana. "Just her and her boyfriend."

"No problem," Lefty growled with hot garlic breath. "We'll dump all three of them in the desert where the coyotes can get 'em."

This wasn't a random hit or burglary. They'd been sent. And they were apparently either stupid or overconfident. She now had no choice but to fight, since they'd removed hope of being left alive.

Lefty waggled his gun at Diego and banded his beefy arm tighter around Josie's waist. "Dude, I can see you thinking there about taking us out now, but here's the deal. You cooperate and we won't rape the

women before we pop 'em in the head." He caressed
the cold gun barrel along her temple. "You can even
be the last to take a bullet to the brain, dude, just to
make sure we're good on our word. So? We have a
deal?"

As if they could trust these bastards on anything.

But the bastards wouldn't know they were up
against women who could defend themselves. That
element of surprise would be an advantage they could
only wield once.

"So, *dude*," Diego drawled lazy and slow, swinging the attackers' attention ever so subtly to him and
buying time for the women to act. "I guess you're not
interested in cutting a deal here for my Harley?"

"Harley?" The gun slid from her temple.

Josie jammed her elbow back, pivoted, reached to
grab his arm. A gunshot exploded into the floor inches
from her feet. Scuffling sounded behind her as Diana
no doubt kicked the crap out of her opponent. A shot
blasted the ceiling. Plaster rained on their heads.

She leveled Lefty just as Diego launched forward
up the stairs, landing flat. He grappled for the gunman's hand and twisted. Cracking bones echoed with
the man's scream as he rolled to his feet.

Josie spun to her sister. Diana's hands were wrapped
around the other attacker's wrist, wrestling the gun above
their heads. She brought her knee up between his legs.

Howling, Righty tumbled forward, ramming Diana
against the wall.

Josie grabbed a fistful of his hair and yanked him
off. She slammed his head against the wall once, twice,
again until he stopped resisting. He collapsed into her
bedroom.

"Shit," Lefty said, and stumbled back from Diego's fist, nose spurting blood. Decisiveness burned in the dark eyes in the mask a second before he spun away. Righty scrambled after him.

Whipping her knife from her boot, Josie sprinted, so close, if she stretched her reach a little farther... Footsteps pounded behind her with backup.

Both masked men dove out the balcony window.

Josie screeched to a halt against the wrought-iron railing, regaining her balance, readying to scale down to the lot. She swung one leg over the barrier—

The men climbed into a waiting car and squealed away.

Damn.

She brought her leg back over and turned. "Everyone okay?"

Diego was covered in blood.

The knife slipped from her fingers and thudded to the floor. "Oh my God."

She rushed forward. Her hands hovered along him, careful not to risk touching and possibly hurting him until she knew. "Where are you injured?"

"I'm fine." He gripped her shoulders and hauled her close. "It's just blood from his broken nose. At least the cops will have a decent DNA sample to go with that license plate number. Diana?"

"I'm okay," her sister answered from beside the bed, telephone already in hand. "Just calling the cops."

"Josie?" His hands stroked down her hair again and again. "What about you? You're awfully quiet, Buttercup."

Her cheek pressed to his chest. His heartbeat slugged against her while she stared at the empty parking lot. Diana's voice relaying details to 9-1-1 broke the night silence.

They both could have died—because of her. Just like Craig.

"I'm fine." She inched out of the comfort of Diego's arms that threatened to weaken her with softer emotions. "Totally fine and completely pissed."

The bastard responsible for this was going down.

Three hours later, Josie stabbed at her supper—cashew chicken. Delivery Chinese food would have to take the place of mac and cheese for comfort tonight. Diana sat across from her at the glass-and-chrome dinette set, stirring her chopsticks through a carton of sweet-and-sour pork.

Josie's damp hair stuck to her neck. Diego had hugged her so hard he'd smeared the blood from Lefty's broken nose all over her flight suit, necessitating a shower and change into shorts and a T-shirt.

Now, Diego was showering back in her bedroom, which too easily brought to mind images of bathing with him at his place. Was that only a few days ago? Since then she'd been threatened with a court martial, arrested, released, had wild sex with Diego against a wall, been attacked by two gunmen and filed police reports.

And it was only Monday. She'd faced combat situations that hadn't given her heart as heavy a workout as it had received in the past twelve hours.

The cops had responded quickly to Diana's call, scouted the area, run the license-plate number. Stolen plates. No surprise there. Josie couldn't fault the police. There wasn't much more to go on or much else to do from a civilian angle.

Still, someone was definitely after her.

Now Diego and Diana had come into the crosshairs, as well. Especially Diego, since hadn't the men noted to expect a boyfriend? She needed to get them both the hell away from her.

"Don't even go there, Josephine," Diana ordered between bites of fried pork.

"Go where?" Josie swung her feet up onto the chair beside her.

Diana dropped her chopsticks into the carton. "You're blaming yourself for calling me and that's just crap. I'm an adult. Nobody makes me go anywhere I don't want to anymore. I'm not leaving until we have some answers for you. I don't think you're going to have any luck budging Diego, either."

She suspected her stubborn sister was right. Even as that scared her hair nearly dry, she couldn't stop a smile over Diana's not-so-subtle reference to the times a much younger Josie had hauled her baby sister around—by her pigtails, if necessary. "I still believe you should go home. But I'll try not to feel like pond scum for bringing you here."

"Well, try harder. And while you're at it, pass the pot stickers please, *Buttercup*." Diana drew out the last word with the torturously teasing emphasis that only a sibling could deliver.

And she'd thought her sister was too occupied calling the cops to have heard Diego use that silly name. Heaven forbid Diana had overheard it earlier during the sex-fest against the wall.

Diana smiled wickedly. "I'm never going to let you forget that one you know."

"I figured as much."

"So from the, uh—" Diana scooped up another pork bite, red sauce dripping onto her sweatshirt "—*activity* earlier with you and Diego, I'm guessing you're officially a couple now?"

Big-time blush alert. "Why didn't you let us know you were here right away?"

"I tried to say something, even hollered a hello once, but you two went at it so fast and, uh, loud, you must not have heard me." She snatched a napkin from the middle of the table and dabbed at her sweatshirt. "I didn't want to embarrass you. I thought I was being polite."

Her sister sure seemed to be getting a kick out of making her blush now. *Buttercup.* Josie rolled her eyes. "Well, you could have put a pillow over your head."

"I did. It helped, except for that crash," Diana continued with a wicked grin.

The picture frame.

"Okay! Okay." Josie closed her eyes, raising a hand in surrender. "I get the idea."

"Actually, I decided it wasn't a bad time for a nap. Noise from the guys breaking in must have triggered those agent instincts and woken me."

Memories of the hellish moment when the gunmen had burst in rolled back between them in a toxic cloud. Being almost certain they could kick their attackers' butts didn't stop a healthy respect for the lethal power of a gun. Any or all of them could have died so easily.

Diana's napkin wadded in her tight fist. "Are you ever going to pass my pot stickers?"

Josie thrust the box of Chinese food. "Sure. Sorry."

"Thanks, Buttercup." The need to insert levity was obviously mutual.

Josie lobbed the Beanie Baby horse at her sister's head. "Brat."

"Ouch! Don't make me come over there and hurt you."

"I'd welcome the fight."

"That bad a week?"

"The worst." Craig's death. The possible end of her career. The end of salvaging her mother's dream.

Diana jabbed inside the cardboard carton with her chopsticks and speared a doughy dumpling. "Are you upset with me for calling Diego?"

"A little," she answered truthfully. Didn't she always? Which compelled her to continue. "Although I'm starting to wonder if on some subconscious level I knew that was exactly what you would do since I couldn't bring myself to ask him for help. Is that messed-up logic or what?"

"We Lockworth women sure do know how to get mixed into some screwed-up relationships. Of course, we didn't have much of a model for a mother."

Defensiveness rolled to the fore on already plank-taut nerves. "She was sick, Diana. Isn't it time you cut her some slack?"

"Maybe you should take your own advice with Dad," her sister snapped back.

"There wasn't a damn thing wrong with him." Josie dropped her carton on the table, leaning forward on both elbows. "Just because he tried to cook us macaroni and cheese once doesn't make him a good father or a good husband. He can fawn all over Mom now that she's well, but where the hell was he when she was staring at a wall like a zombie for hours on end? And when he dumped us off at boarding school?"

Diana sagged back into her chair in surly silence.

Hell. Way to go, Buttercup. She comes to save your ass and you pick a fight.

Josie formed a time-out *T* with her hands. "Whoa. Hold on. Let's take this down a notch. We were actually getting along for a while and God knows I appreciate your help even though it scares the hell out of me having you here. Let's agree to leave the other subject alone."

"Sure. Worked in the past, I guess. Whatever you say. You're the big sister after all." Diana scraped her chair back from the table and shuffled toward the kitchen.

"Ah, come on, Diehard. I'm sorry."

"Whatever."

God, that sister of hers reverted to the sullen teenager so easily she made it tough to remember she was an adult officer.

"Hey, ladies," Diego called from the hall. "Hope y'all saved some of the Chinese for me. I'm damn near starving."

Scrubbing a towel over his wet hair, Diego ambled down the stairs, wearing fresh jeans, a clean T-shirt and a just-showered smell that watered Josie's mouth more than any box of cashew chicken. "Do you need to check on Bogey and Bandit?"

"I took care of that before I picked you up. They're with a neighbor." He smoothed her hair back with a lover's caress before continuing into the kitchen.

He'd definitely intended from the start to stay overnight, otherwise why bring a change of clothes? Her watering mouth dried up. She'd slept in bed with him twice over the weekend. No problem. Except now there was this big pink elephant in the room between them after her note and request for distance.

She watched him over the bar separating the dining area from the kitchen. Angling past Diana, he hooked the towel around his neck.

"Hey, little sister, want a—" he swung the refrigerator door wide and grimaced "—bottled water?"

"No long-necks, huh?" Diana groused.

"'Fraid not."

Josie envied his ability to call Diana "little sister" without generating a nuclear sulk in return. But then Diego had that sort of easiness with just about everyone. Even in brood mode, he didn't set people on edge—like she somehow managed to do too often.

Taking the seat beside Josie, Diego twisted the top off his water and grabbed the carton closest to him. "Any thoughts on what move you want to make next?" He set his bottle on the table. "I'm thinking we'll want to act fast since apparently somebody's upset you dodged the court martial so easily."

Josie snagged a steno pad from the middle of the table. "I agree."

Diego pointed to the paper with a chopstick before stabbing his beef lo mein. "Make sure you save yourself a sheet for your note to me in the morning."

Ouch.

Diana studied the sweet-and-sour sauce stain on her sweatshirt with exaggerated interest.

Josie ignored Diego's jab and picked up her pencil. "I guess we start with who has reason to hate me."

"Bridges." Diego's fist tightened around the water bottle until the plastic dimpled.

"Yeah." Josie wrote his name. "And if Bridges is responsible, then he's been defused now."

Diana strode to the table. "Unless he's so mad he's prepared to go for broke on revenge."

Josie frowned. "Even to the point of hiring thugs? And why? It all seems to come back to someone wanting to derail my project. Too many things went wrong for it to be coincidence—including Craig dying. What are the odds that every safeguard would fail on that flight?"

"A flight you were supposed to be on." A tic twitched in the corner of Diego's eye as he shoveled more noodles into his mouth.

"But Bridges pulled the schedule switch. So if he's the problem, he doesn't want me dead." Options churned through her head. "Unless he yanked me off the flight just to get back at me for turning him down, like I thought, and someone else was responsible for the crash."

"Two agendas?" Diana dropped into her chair. "Two people after you? That's a little paranoid."

"Thanks bunches, Diehard."

"You're welcome. Do you know for certain Bridges was the one to change the schedule?"

"Yes, um, no. I'm not sure. I could ask Zeljak on Monday since he works in scheduling."

Diana frowned. "Unless this Zeljak fellow made the scheduling change. What do you know about him?"

Zeljak? Josie mentally reviewed his file. "Seasoned master sergeant. Over two thousand hours in flight test. Family man. I can't imagine…ah, hell, I guess I have to consider everything and it all goes back to the crash. The investigation will take months, which gives somebody too much time to bury evidence." Which meant she needed to be a step ahead of them. She pushed away from the table and folded the lid on her cashew chicken, grateful for a chance to actively fight back. "What do you say we head over to the testing facility and start digging before somebody else has the chance?"

Diana leaped to her feet, the gleam in her eyes burning away any residual anger. "Who needs sleep? Diego, pack up your supper while I change into something fit to be seen in public."

Standing, Diego folded the lid on his lo mein to take along. "Just need my boots and I'll be set to go."

Her arms full of the extra cartons, Josie hesitated. Fair play made her rise up onto her toes and brush a kiss over his surprised mouth. "I really am sorry."

And she meant it. She just wasn't ready to figure out what she should do in place of note writing. They truly did have pressing concerns, life-threatening stuff and an ungodly amount of data to plow through searching for that needle in a haystack.

She turned to her sister. "Give me ten minutes to grab a fresh flight suit and switch out my patches and pockets."

With Lefty, Righty, Bridges, Zeljak and God only knows who else to worry about, she'd definitely be packing her knife tonight.

Chapter 18

Josie made tracks away from her office, folders of data under her arm, computer disks stuffed in her flight-suit pockets. Diana and Diego trailed a couple of steps behind, discussing road rallies and biker gear since apparently Diana had a secret stash of black leather to wear when she morphed into secret-agent girl. Josie rounded the corner—

And stopped short.

A light shone from underneath an office door—Mike Bridges's door. Her heart revved even as she told herself nothing would happen in the security of a military installation. If Bridges was responsible, it wasn't as if he would blast out of his office and gun them down in the corridor.

However, having already been shot at once today, she couldn't help but be on edge.

She glanced over her shoulder and shushed the biker buddies behind her. Pointing to the light under the door, she continued past but at a stealthier pace. Diego tucked in beside her and she never even heard him increase speed.

The exit loomed ahead. Closer. Just a few more steps.

A door opened behind her. "Lockworth?"

Bridges's voice stopped her. Diego damn near growled. She rested a hand on his arm and faced Bridges, keeping the healthy distance of half a hall length between them.

"Yes?" She couldn't bring herself to say sir to this man, and likely he wouldn't quibble with her.

"I would like to speak with you for a minute—if you don't mind."

"*I* mind," Diego snapped.

She did, too. "We need to leave."

Tension clouded the air and she couldn't help but notice the new droop of defeat to Bridges's shoulders. Why wasn't there any joy in this victory?

"It'll only take a minute, Captain. You can both stand right there. I'm not asking your guard dog to leave." When she started to turn away anyhow, he pressed ahead in a louder voice, "These past few days have made me do some hard thinking, life reevaluation and all of that."

"I'm glad something positive has come out of this nightmare."

"I know I don't have any right to ask you this. But would you talk to Kayla for me and tell her that I want to see Jazz?"

What the hell?

A request to see his daughter was the last thing Josie had expected to fall out of Mike Bridges's mouth and the one thing sure to make her hesitate in leaving. Could he know that and be tricking her into staying? Or did he really think she might help him? Dirtbag. "Why?"

"Everything that's happened this past week, what with Wagner's accident, the whole TV exposé nightmare, it all shook me up. Made me do some reevaluating about where my life's headed and what's important."

As much as she knew Jazz would love to have a father in her life, Josie noticed Bridges was careful not to call Jazz his daughter. A Freudian thing? It bothered her, especially since this turnaround of his was so darned fast. Bottom line, Jazz's interests had to come first.

"I can't help you. This is between you and Kayla. I'm not being petty." Even though she would really, really like to be. That doggone sense of fair play of hers worked both ways.

He stepped forward. She held up a hand and he stopped, wincing. "I guess I deserve that."

"Damn straight you do," Josie retorted, ever aware of Diego at her back. She didn't need these two men duking it out and she didn't want Bridges asking questions about the files under her arm. "I would like to think you're truly interested in being a part of that little girl's life, but forgive me if I don't have a lot of faith in you anymore. You'd better be sure before you step into Jazz's life, because losing a father's love can really mess with a woman's mind long-term for other relationships, as well."

Now wasn't that a personal-lightbulb moment?

Too bad she didn't have time to mull it over. Josie spun on her heel, leaving Bridges standing alone in the hall—without her respect or salute.

Josie punched in the cipher lock code and swung wide the door to the warehouse room for storing data on current test projects at the Palmdale military testing facility. The answer had to be here somewhere. She only needed to find it first—with Diego and Diana's help.

She didn't like that Bridges knew they were around. She liked even less that he'd seen her hauling files out of her office. They were all three perfectly legal in being there, given their clearance levels, but still she wasn't thrilled about alerting anyone to their digging.

However, it was done. Bridges seeing them gave her all the more motivation to search faster. Only someone with clearance could find them here—which, of course, didn't offer much reassurance right now.

"Jesus, Josie." Diana pivoted in the shelf-lined room, about the size of a two-car garage, as the door swished closed. "We'll be here until the next millennium going through all of this."

Binders, tapes and disks crammed every inch of wall space. Tables stretched down the middle with televisions hooked up to different viewers—VCR, DVD—to watch the recorded flight footages. And these were only the active test projects. Once a test finished, the "cold data" was catalogued, shipped out and stored in mammoth facilities.

Folding his arms over his chest, Diego lounged against a shelf. "You're the boss on this one, Josie. Give us our marching orders."

Work. Action. Already she felt more in control than she had since Craig's crash. "Cruiser, how about you start with checking the data-stream readouts. I'll review video footage." She hefted up three twelve-inch stacks of computer printouts on green-and-white striped paper. "Diehard, let's put your computer skills to work. Review the codes on the flight control program for each mission, check the algorithms."

Diana's hazel eyes gleamed with an anticipation only a computer geek could summon for such a tedious task. "You want me to look for sign errors, divide by zero errors, illogical lines of code."

"Exactly."

"And what are you and Diego looking for?"

Rising up on her toes, Josie slid free the first two tapes in the test project. "We don't have a clue. Just something that feels…wrong."

Five cups of coffee and countless hours later, Josie's face cracked with a yawn. Only the blast of air from the vent overhead kept her from falling out of her chair. The windowless room provided no sense of time passing but the clock told her the early-morning sun must be shining outside.

At the far end of the length of tables, Diana propped her cheek on her fist, scanning page after page in her latest stack. Diego sat beside her flipping through data-stream readouts while she viewed flight video segments. The lone drone of recorded flight voices echoed, control tower, pilots, sensor operators.

She stifled another jaw-cracking yawn. They'd taken turns snagging power naps through the night so the data wouldn't blur, but there was just so much of it. She drained her mug of lukewarm java.

Bleck.

Footsteps sounded in the hall. Josie's muscles tensed, every fiber of her going on alert.

Diana and Diego rose from their chairs along with her, shifting to a less vulnerable part of the room. Nothing would look amiss to an innocent person, but they would be at a better vantage point for another blast from Lefty and Righty type thugs.

The door opened. Master Sergeant Don Zeljak stepped into view, popping his chewing gum.

Josie exhaled half her held breath. "Good morning, Sergeant. You're out and about early."

"Morning, Captain. I didn't expect to see you here this early, either."

Was there a hidden meaning? But what would Zeljak have to do with any of this, even in a small way? What would he have to gain by tampering with scheduling?

He really was one of the last people she would suspect. He was one of the air force's best, the reason she'd handpicked him for her team. It would shake her confidence something fierce to learn she'd misjudged him.

"Sergeant Zeljak, you remember Morel. And this is my sister, Lieutenant Lockworth, in town visiting. They're helping me weed through data as I wrap up paperwork now that we're on hold." That sounded like a logical cover for him to relay. "What are you doing here?"

"The accident-investigation board sent me to pick up some tapes and mission data disks."

Time was running out. Josie hefted the stack of tapes she and Diego had already reviewed and passed them over.

Zeljak scanned the labels, his mono-brow bunching with his frown. "What about the tape from your initial liftoff flight? I don't see it in here. The board mentioned needing that one in particular since it was the first airborne mission."

And the board would have to wait. Josie inched to sit on the edge of the table on top of the tape in question. *Ouch.* "Hmm. I don't see it right offhand. How about I bring it up when we find it?"

"And the mission data disks? They can only find the copies, not the originals."

A couple of which were burning a hole in her calf pocket waiting to be reviewed. "I'll track those down, as well."

"Thanks." Zeljak backed out of the room. "I'll let them know." He paused. "Captain, I'm glad everything got straightened out yesterday. We need more like you around."

She wanted to believe those supportive words from someone whose work she so respected. "That's good to hear right now. Thank you, Bubbles."

Nodding, he left. The door swished shut.

"Bubbles?" Diana squawked.

"His call sign, because he's always got a wad of bubblegum in his mouth." Springing up from the table, Josie whipped the tape out from under her. "All right. Let's see why the review board really wants to check out this particular mission."

Nothing.

Josie swiped the grit from her eyes and watched the same flight for the fourth time, and still she saw nothing new or unusual. Diana had given up on the video after the second viewing and transferred her attention back to the stacks of computer codes.

Diego sprawled in a chair beside her, silently watching, processing—the tape or her? He'd been oddly silent since they'd left her apartment, other than pointing out different aspects of the flight data that might or might not compile into something promising.

Was he truly that angry with her over the note and her request for some space? She *so* stank at the dating thing—and she suffered no illusions. They had somehow shifted into the boyfriend/girlfriend realm over the weekend.

Maybe she was only nervous since she had little experience in the dating deal. Given her confidence in the workplace up to now, facing a situation where she doubted herself would undoubtedly shake her even more. And she didn't know how to handle doubting herself.

She'd been so driven during high school and college there hadn't been time for dates. Her mother hadn't been around much to offer advice about boys and men, either.

Yet, the discussion with Mike Bridges about Jazz and the importance of a father's love earlier kept echoing in her head at a time when she really needed to concentrate on this damn video footage. Although she was starting to think her instinct about watching it was off.

Another dead end.

Maybe she was simply borrowing trouble when it came to the flight and Diego, but she'd been so hopeful. On both counts. Her brain started to fog from sleep deprivation until she could have sworn she was strapped on a test-model Predator again.

She could feel the wind kissing her face, the sense of flying as it must have been for pioneer pilots. The adrenaline pump of hurtling out there in the open with nothing but a flight suit, helmet and your butt strapped to a machine you hoped would bring you home safely. Defying the elements with *your* new twist on flying.

She couldn't imagine never going up again. Just a simple spin around the flight line had been worth risking everything. Craig had been willing to die. Diego had almost died during his last mission.

Josie let the roaring sensation of flying suck her in deeper, further away from the frustrations around her as she lived out this mind flight simulator of her own making.

"Josie?" Diego's voice joined her in the sky. "You can't hide from me forever."

His rumbling words sent her mental flight plummeting back to a cold-storage room with even colder coffee. She kept her gaze glued to the video. "Now's not the time, Diego."

His hand landed on the back of her chair as he angled closer. The heat of him beside her negated the air conditioner and sent her temperature soaring.

"I understand you have pressing priorities. Hell, I've got pretty much the same ones since they involve keeping your most excellent ass alive. But eventually, you have to accept what's going on between us."

A dry smile played with her tired face. "Can't we just keep having sex against the wall instead?"

Across the room, Diana slammed aside a stack of readouts. "You two really suck at stage whispers. I'm going to find more coffee."

The door whooshed closed, sealing them in privacy.

She kept her eyes on the screen, a convenient excuse not to risk looking at him. "I meant it when I said I'm sorry for walking out on you yesterday morning. That was wrong of me. What I said about Jazz earlier and how a distant father could give a girl a complex? Well, that's me. Okay? I just need you to be patient."

Silence hung between them, cut only by the crackling sounds from the television of recorded voices in flight, her own voice on the Predator and the surreal sound of Craig's as he flew the remote.

Diego leaned on his forearms closer. "You're cheating yourself."

He studied the screen so intently she thought for an instant he was referring to the flight. "What the hell does that mean?"

"I've watched how you operate," he continued, following her lead in keeping his eyes on the TV while his scent and gravelly tones stroked her senses anyway. "You ask me to be patient. And while I'm doing that, you'll close yourself off from participating in the world around you. You have your facts lined up, but when it comes to any true emotional investment, you check out."

Checking out emotionally? Her father was the one who'd done that. Not her. She felt things—deeply— and hurt just like everyone else. She simply didn't feel comfortable making those emotions public.

Ah, hell.

She didn't want him to be right. Her gaze fell away from the screen to the stacks of tapes and DVDs, then up to him. "Your timing totally sucks, Cruiser."

With dark morning beard peppering his unshaven face, he looked more like the Diego she'd met, even with his shorter hair.

"There will never be a good time for you, Josie, because you're always going to be this driven. That's one of the things I admire about you. But are you going to continue using it to avoid the tough conversations? The past week should have taught you there might not be a tomorrow."

"You think I don't know that?" Her temper slipped past her defenses, thanks to exhaustion—and yeah, pain. "You're a fine one to talk. You've been hiding out in the desert for three years. You work enough hours to pay your bills, but I've yet to see you enjoy your job. I understand you lost your dream. There are a lot of dreams a person can lose. You just have to find a new purpose."

"Maybe I already have."

His intense opaque eyes sucked her in as surely as the flight had. It was one thing to lose herself in a solo flight away from the world. But, oh, God, losing herself in a man while he lost himself right back in her…

"No," she whispered.

"It's scary as hell, isn't it—this thing that happens when we're together? But I'm thinking it'll be scarier to walk."

She ripped her gaze from him. "I can't deal with any of this right now."

He canted away, giving her a few inches of physical space, if not emotional. "I understand what it's like to have the world rock under your feet until there's no sense of up or down—a mental vertigo as well as physical. You're right. I was pretty much a waste of airspace when you met me."

Like the video continuing in her periphery, memories scrolled through her mind of seeing him that first time. Right from the start he'd stimulated more emotion in a day than she'd allowed herself to feel in years. "Diego, I can't think—"

"Remember when I told you to quit thinking so much and feel the plane? Sometimes the same applies to life. We may crash and burn, but at least we're not just taking up airspace."

She understood him in theory. In practice however, she couldn't envision things being quite that clear-cut. The old Josie/Josephine war cranked into high gear within her, so she stayed silent.

"Yeah, you're probably thinking now that I'm a damned fine one to preach. I'm still not where I should be in life, but finally I'm feeling like I have a compass again." He gripped her chin and turned her face toward him. "You did that for me. The vertigo that smacked my life as hard as my ears? It's leveling back out for me since knowing you. I'd like to do the same for you."

He tempted her and scared the spit out of her all at once. God, this man cut her no slack.

But then hadn't she done the same with him?

She wanted to lean forward and kiss him, but he'd put everything right out there in front of them until simple kisses weren't possible between them anymore.

Slicing the tension, whistling sounded outside the door, Diana announcing her arrival before stepping inside with three steaming cups of coffee. "Sustenance for the troops."

Exhaling hard, Diego stood. "I'm going to stretch my legs. Thanks for the java, little sister."

Diana stayed blessedly silent for once, setting the cups down silently.

"Thanks." Josie smiled without looking up. She feared her emotions would be visible for her sister's agent-honed eyes to perceive. She needed time to let Diego's words settle and, damn it all, she didn't have time.

Everything inside her was raw and out there, frustrated and scared that maybe, just maybe, he was right. She didn't want to be that exposed and vulnerable. The video screen was much safer terrain at the moment. She continued to stare at the screen scrolling the Predator images from the night flight.

And then she saw it.

Something she'd missed before. Just a flicker of light that niggled at her. She hit review and backed up, watching slower, closer. The light grew larger, brighter, shining through a window...of the mission-planning building. Had somebody been working late or just left a light on? Such a small detail, but God, she didn't have anything else.

Josie clicked on the sensor operator's second-camera view, bringing a close-up angle inside the window. Inside the room, someone sat at the AFMSS—Air Force Mission Support System. The computers for planning missions, cutting the very flight control disks that rested in her thigh pocket.

Still could be nothing, she cautioned herself. People worked late.

She zoomed again. What if she found Bridges there? What would that mean for Kayla and Jazz? Josie blinked to clear her vision and her objectivity, finding...

General Quincy?

A spider tingle started up her instincts. He had the

proper clearance to be there, but no readily obvious motive for going alone so late.

Questioning a general's motives was scary territory. They would need serious backup before rolling out accusations. Thank God for Diana's intelligence connections so they could dig deeper into General Quincy's past. Luckily they would just need to shuffle across a few streets over to the intelligence building.

"Diehard? Your security clearance is pretty high, right?"

"You could say that." Her wry answer bounced back.

"Good." Adrenaline pumped double time because, heaven help them, they were about to question a general. But before doing so, they would need some hard facts. "Because we're going dark once the Palmdale facility quiets down tonight."

Chapter 19

Dark blanketed the roads linking the Palmdale testing facility buildings.

Urgency humming through her, Josie steered around a corner, closing in on the intelligence building. An afternoon spent crashing at her place had offered little more than restless tossing and a quick shower while they waited for Diana's clearance to be okayed.

They'd placed a call to Diana's unit security manager to verify her clearance status for *their* unit security manager here. Since Diego had top clearance for his testing work, there would be no problem gaining access to the vault.

Fast was good. Now was even better with Lefty and Righty sorts on their tail and God only knows who else.

Diego sprawled in the passenger seat beside her, one foot resting on his knee. "Got any ideas why a general would be gunning for you, Buttercup?"

"It still doesn't make sense," the ever-logical Josephine insisted. "Sure the man isn't big on women in the service, but this method of dealing with things goes to the extreme. Although if he wants me out of the way, the whole unreasonable house arrest makes more sense. But why would he kill Craig?"

"Maybe he meant to kill you," Diana chimed from the back seat. "Remember the two-agendas theory? Bridges grounded you out of spite, not knowing someone planned to down the plane. Craig died in your place."

A burning started in Josie's stomach that had nothing to do with too many cups of coffee and thirty-six hours of little sleep. The need for revenge seared.

Diana leaned between the two seats. "If this was deliberate, how could someone shut down the entire system? I searched those codes. There's nothing there."

Diego tapped his boot heel. "What about a virus?"

Diana snorted. "That almost seems too simple. Spin the idea out more."

"We could have been looking too hard by assuming the bad guy here is smarter than he really is." Streetlights glinted off his coal-black hair. "If it's Quincy, maybe his technical knowledge is outdated from too much time at a desk. Although sometimes the simple answer can be brilliant for its sheer ease in implementation. What do you think, Buttercup? Workable?"

"A horrific thought, but yes, it would then be possible."

Diana draped her arm over the seat. "How would someone place a virus in both the remote control program and on the Predator's override control program? Logistically, that's tougher to pull off."

Josie shook her head, turning into a parking spot outside the windowless brick building. "It's the same disk."

"Wait." Diana tapped Josie's shoulder. "I thought there were two different mission data disks that went in at the start of each flight."

"No, there's only one disk. In the old days, the software versions and hard drives were more complicated. But now things are more streamlined." Josie tugged the key out of the ignition, twisting to face her sister while she explained. "The mission data disk is loaded first into the remote control station. Then the same disk is loaded in the test Predator so that override controls can act just as the remote would, if needed. That way we're always certain the data is compatible. During a test, we do use a new disk for each mission though, because we're always making modifications."

Diana sagged back. "So if the copies were made prior to the virus being introduced, they won't help us. Where's the original disk used on the last mission?"

"It went down in Craig's pocket. It's the responsibility of the pilot going up in the craft to load the data." She patted her calf. "I even still have the disk from my last saddle mission right after I returned from Red Flag tucked in my day runner."

Diego scrubbed a hand over his shorn head. "We have a possible who and how. Now we just need a why with some proof."

Josie swung wide her door, pulling up the seat for

Diana to climb out. "If it's Quincy, hopefully we'll find those answers here."

Diana stretched, her hand pressed to her stomach. "I'm sorry, Josie, but I have to confess that, unlike you, I'm a mere mortal. Leftover Chinese food from your fridge just isn't cutting it anymore. Can I have your keys? You and Diego can read up on the Quincy dude to your heart's content while I run and grab us all a bite."

Diego leaned his forearms on the roof. "Think again, little sister. You're not going out there alone."

Diana cranked a brow. "Excuse me?"

Josie tipped her head toward Diana and whispered, "Thor."

"What?"

"He's gone into Thor mode. He figures we're safer locked up here in a vault than out there alone for Lefty and Righty to pick off."

Little sister struck a pose in the halo of a lot light, black leather pants and silky shirt full of attitude. "If I want to ride a bicycle through land mines to buy hamburgers, I'll do it."

Diego strutted around the front bumper to the two women. "I'm sure you will. But being practical, as well as Thor-like, I'll point out that you are more adept at computer wizardry than either of us. It makes sense for you to work with Josie while I brave the land mines for our food. Or if you're insistent, we can all go out to eat since I'm not overly pleased with leaving you two alone at all."

Diana's pose and attitude melted. "Damn, Josie. Don't you hate it when they're right? Fine. I'll take a double-double from In and Out Burger."

"Got it. Josie?"

Josie stared at the two of them, so damn grateful for their help and humor even in the middle of this hell. They really were a lot more fun, help—comfort—than a room packed with Beanie Babies.

"Josie? Supper?"

"Oh. Uh. The same as Diehard, please." She held up her car keys. He reached to take them and she curved her hand around his. "And be careful."

"I'm a hunter-gatherer. No problem." He dropped a quick kiss on her mouth before prying the keys away. "I'll meet you both inside in less than an hour."

She curved her fingers into her empty palm, which still carried the heat of his skin. For a guy who claimed they could steady each other's worlds, Diego sure shook her foundation on a regular basis.

"Earth to Josie?"

She startled. "Yeah? I'm here."

"Uh-huh."

Foreboding gripped her as she watched her Mustang disappear around the corner. Damn it, he was just going for hamburgers. She would see him again in an hour or so. Wasn't she the one who'd insisted she could think better without him around?

She'd just proved herself wrong.

They couldn't afford to be wrong about this. Josie tucked beside Diana in the elevator descending to the basement vault. If the lead on Quincy turned into a dead end, they were screwed, with no other options and nothing to look forward to but possibly a never-ending search while watching over her shoulder for Lefty and Righty sorts.

Diana and Diego would have to go back to work soon. So would she, for that matter. God, when had she become so defeatist? They *would* find something here.

Ding. The elevator jolted. Expectancy tingled along exhausted nerves.

The doors swished open to the hall and Muzak. The low-playing music was ever-present in high security areas as an additional safeguard to mask conversations from listening devices.

She stepped into a hall empty but for the unit security manager. She strode toward the mammoth safe door leading into the SCIF—special compartmentalized information facility.

"Good evening, Sergeant." Signing in, Josie added to the manager, "Lieutenant Lockworth's unit security manager's okay should be on your screen now. Of course I'll vouch for her, too."

The unit security manager checked the laminated IDs clipped to Josie and Diana. "Working late hours, aren't you?"

"So we don't have to fight for the computer."

The unit security manager laughed. "Where's the third party you mentioned?"

"He went out for supper. He'll check in with security when he gets back."

"In and Out Burger?"

"You know it."

"Hope he brings an extra double-double."

"You can be sure to search him." Josie keyed in the cipher lock code and opened the vault room.

Cinder block walls absorbed noise, a sound sweeper also at the bottom of every door. Computers and screens filled the room, some data stored on hard drives, some on the disks filling cabinets in the pristine room.

With a low moan of appreciation, Diana settled behind the mainframe. She stroked the keyboard like a lover. "Oh, baby, with a setup like this, finding what we need will be a piece of cake since we know where to start looking. My guess, we'll be ready for a celebratory feast before Diego gets back with those burgers."

After the endless night before spent poring over tapes and readouts for a lone clue, they could use speedy results for a change.

Diana clicked in codes and passwords, bringing up the secured green screen. "What do you want to try first?"

Josie leaned closer. "Let's go for what seems obvious. Start with John Quincy's bio."

Diana typed. The screen filled with lists.

"Ugh. He's been a busy man. Refine the search to…" Josie closed her eyes and thought, scrolling through everything she'd learned about Quincy over the past months. Her mind hitched on the night at the bar, when she'd seen Quincy in the parking lot with Bridges. What had the general said?

He used to work tests at Palmdale back in the Dark Ages.

"Close in on his testing experience a couple of decades ago."

"Done."

The computer searched and…

"Hmm…I've got an interesting hit." Diana scanned the screen. "Quincy used results from something called Cipher in his testing."

Josie angled over her sister's shoulder. "But wait, the guy who killed Rainy is also called the Cipher."

"Yeah, too damned coincidental for my peace of mind." Diana's fingers flew over the keyboard. "And it also refers to the lab numbered thirty-three that I had so much trouble tracking down before. This mentions experiments with audio frequencies and how when Quincy transferred here, he applied the results to conventional tests."

Josie sagged back against the workstation. Well hell. Another snippet to pass along to Kayla that might help them discover why Rainy had been murdered. And another sign that Quincy wasn't squeaky clean after all.

"Ohmigod," Diana gasped, pointing to the screen. "Look at the dates. He worked tests here the same time as our mom."

Working with acoustics and audio frequencies. Their mother's specialty.

A dark premonition crept up her spine. "When he mentioned being stationed at Edwards and also running tests out of the Palmdale facility, I never considered he would have been stationed with Mom, and he didn't mention knowing her, much less working projects together. You'd think he would mention that."

"That is strange. Could be something. Could be nothing."

A swish and rustle alerted Josie a second before a voice—

"Or it could be exactly what it looks like, ladies."

Josie shot from her chair, Diana launching to her feet, as well. General Quincy stood in the open doorway, the unit security manager nowhere in sight.

Ah, crap. The premonition exploded into all-out certainty.

The general's eyes darted around with frenetic speed, his gray-blond hair spiky as if from harried fingers. An automatic pistol with a silencer shook in his hand. "You Lockworth sisters are almost as good at sniffing out things as this old birddog. But then I guess that's how I got my call sign."

Birddog. General. Killer. It didn't matter which she called him. He had a gun trained on her and a crazed look to him, as certifiable as anything she'd seen in the hospital ward where the military had once tried to lock away her mother.

Any thoughts about not hitting a senior officer went out the window—well, if there had been one in this dark room in the bowels of intelligence. Her only concern was how to stop the maniac without him shooting her or Diana.

Quincy advanced a step deeper into the vault room. "I'm sorry to have to do this to Zoe Lockworth's beautiful daughters, but I'm afraid you must be silenced. Both of you."

Feigning submission, Josie dropped back into her chair, letting her arm fall to her side. If only she could get to the knife in her boot. Diana gripped the edge of the table. To steady herself? Or search for the alarm?

Quincy tut-tutted. "You can forget about activating the alarm. I disabled it and sent security off. I'm a general, after all. I can redirect as many people as I want to any area."

He patted the land mobile radio sticking out of his pocket. His flight suit looked unusually wrinkled, as if he'd slept in it. "And this will alert me should anyone report suspicions to the SPs. Granted, I didn't have much time to plan, thanks to your eluding my gunmen friends. But then, a gifted leader adapts and takes decisive action quickly. Important in battle, don't you agree?"

Josie gulped back her fury at this man's gall, his total lack of concern for the people who followed him. She would gladly show him battle soon enough when she kicked his ass.

Her sister stepped forward, obstructing Josie's path, forcing her to wait. "Why would you do this?"

Frustration itched. Was Diana working an angle? Pulling some intelligence officer mind game? Distracting him to get closer or stall for help?

"Sir," Quincy snapped.

"What?"

"You will call me sir, Lieutenant Lockworth. Is that understood?"

Diana nodded. "Yes, sir."

"Why did I do this? For recognition of course. This should have been my project, my success all those years ago."

Josie blinked, waiting for the other shoe to fall, but…nothing. That was it? Why would anyone risk everything to log credit for what in the big scheme of things was one small project? There had to be something else, or this guy was seriously more bent than she could imagine.

Josie inched her hand lower, her calf back farther, survival knife only millimeters away from her fingers. "Okay then," she said in her best rational-Josephine voice. "Let's be reasonable. There has to be some kind of deal we can make."

"Deal?" Quincy whipped to face her, anger mottling his distinguished face into purple mania. "You had your chance to deal, Zoe."

Zoe?

Diana gasped. Josie faltered.

Her flesh crawled at the horrible realization. "My mother. You wanted my mother."

"Of course I want your mother," he explained as if to a moron. "Your father was never worthy of Zoe, just look at how he never made general. Hoyt Lockworth lost his drive to move up the chain after your mother's tragic breakdown and swapped career paths. That proves he was weak. Your mother deserves a leader like me."

What a different image of her father this man relayed, showing Hoyt Lockworth as overwhelmed and grief stricken rather than too distant to be bothered with a troublesome wife and kids. Had her perceptions of her dad been skewed by childhood misperceptions?

As much as she wanted to process all Quincy was throwing her way, she needed to focus on reaching for her knife and straining her ears to listen for reinforcements. Later she would work through the implications of the general—Birddog—confusing her with her mother. It only provided further proof the man was deranged—and therefore all the more dangerous.

One fingertip grazed the top of her survival knife. When the opportunity arose, she could sweep her hand in to snag and throw in a flash. Meanwhile, she would let the general ramble and wait.

"You should have worked with me, been with me, Zoe. Instead you stayed with that loser, a man who never even made general because he was too busy trying to play nursemaid to those brats of yours. Now I'm taking charge."

He steadied his gun level with Josie's chest.

She stopped moving. Immobilized muscles bunched. He couldn't actually plan to shoot? She trained her eyes on his trigger finger, ready to strike at the least twitch.

His arm moved away from her. She sighed—then realized he wasn't lowering his weapon.

He was shifting aim. Targeting Diana, his eyes narrowed. His finger twitched.

"No!" Josie launched toward her baby sister.

A second too late.

Quincy shot. The silencer hissed.

Blood blooming on her black shirt in a fatal mockery of so many stains before, Diana crumpled to the ground.

Chapter 20

"No!" Josie screamed.

Rage spun her around to Quincy. Her hand moved by instinct, securing the knife in her grip as she leaped.

She took Quincy down onto the carpeted floor with the force of her charge and fury. He crashed onto his back, eyes stunned wide. He thrashed with bulk and frenzy, a punch knocking her sideways. She gripped, her fingers twisting in his flight suit. His leather name tag dug into her hand, Velcro loosening, the tag ripping free.

She flung it aside, regained balance. Her nails clawed at his face as she anchored his head, her knee jammed against his chest. Josie pressed the knife edge to his throat.

All movement ceased.

Emotions howled inside her, dark and ugly, the

need for revenge. This man had killed Craig, her sister and done God only knows what to their mother. Even in her rage, Josie couldn't miss how cleanly the problems in her test program mirrored her mother's.

Josie had feared repeated mistakes. Quaked at coincidence. Now she seethed at the traitorous deceit.

Quincy stared up at her with fanatical intensity in his hollow blue eyes. "Your sister isn't dead, but if you kill me, she *will* die."

She couldn't believe anything he said. He'd gone off the deep end. But what if…

Josie eased back on the blade while holding it in place. "Talk. And make it fast, because I can justify a self-defense kill so easily."

Too easily.

"I only shot to wound. But the bullet I used is hollow," he explained with a strange calm, "filled with an amnesia drug. I only planned for her to forget what happened. However, the longer she goes without the antidote, the more of her memory she'll lose."

He was smart. His whole story could be a lie. But she couldn't afford to gamble with Diana's life, and as reason trickled in, she couldn't justify murdering him in cold blood.

Diana moaned behind her. Relief stunned Josie with images of her sister, all of seven years old again, racing across the countryside on her horse with her pigtails sailing.

And in that scant moment where she'd let emotions creep in, Quincy flipped her.

His gun pressed to the center of her forehead. "Drop the knife."

The first beads of real panic trickled over her like

Chinese water torture. Her fingers relaxed, releasing the knife with a thud.

Quincy scooped it up and tucked it in his boot, keeping his gun trained on her. "Good. Now listen. You *are* going to die, but if you do this right, your sister can live. I was being straight about the amnesia drug, if not the need for an antidote. When she comes to, she won't remember a thing about the past forty-eight hours. Everyone will assume you shot her before you killed yourself—another Lockworth lady going crazy. But at least your sister will be alive to console your parents."

Like hell. She wouldn't let him win that way. Not when he'd hurt so many people. Diego would be back. She needed to do her best to make sure he didn't walk into an ambush—and to leave him a clue. Hysterical laughter threatened. Too bad she couldn't leave him another note.

She couldn't even allow herself to consider him being hurt—or worse. That would bring debilitating fears, emotions she couldn't risk.

Josie scanned the room, searching.

The general's name tag lay just a few inches away, where she'd tossed it during their scuffle. If she could just plant it somewhere on Diana so it would be clear the man hadn't simply dropped it some other time. It wasn't much, but Diego already knew they were looking into Quincy.

Meanwhile, knowledge was power, because she would live, damn it, and anything she learned would help bring this bastard down in court. She inched up to sit, ever aware of that gun and its amnesia bullets trained her way. Losing her mind, living out the horror of what her mother had experienced, threatened her more than death.

"How do you intend to kill me?" She inched her hand closer to the name tag while locking eyes with Quincy so he wouldn't look away.

"We'll get to that soon enough. Now stand up." He waved the gun. "Move it, Captain!"

"Please, just let me check on my sister." She leaned forward, faking a need to balance with her hand so it landed on top of his name tag. "I'm not going without reassurance she's alive."

Quincy rolled his eyes. "Women and their damned emotionalism. Fine. Say your goodbyes."

Her fist closed around the incriminating square of fabric and Velcro. Yes. At least one victory in this hellish situation.

Josie leaned over her sister, pressing a kiss to her forehead. "Hang in there, Diehard."

With her body shielding her from Quincy's line of sight, Josie folded her sister's limp fingers around the name tag. Please, be enough. If the worst happened, at least Diana would know her own sister hadn't done this to her.

Josie rose slowly. "Where are we going?"

He swept his uniform once, twice, again even though he'd long since swiped away any dust from his fall to the floor. "There's still one test Predator left. You were so grief stricken over the failure of your project, you went off the deep end. The mission data disk I've prepared will disable your override controls and fly you into a mountain—if fighter planes don't shoot you down first."

"Fighters?" She searched the room for a weapon, a

room that was deliberately left bare for security reasons. Nothing but computers and files surrounded her.

"Captain, I'll have to share my concern that you've gone crazy like your mother and may plan to crash the craft into downtown L.A." He gripped her arm, gun kissing her temple. "Now walk."

As much as she hated leaving her injured sister, she wanted this nutcase and his gun away from Diana. Hopefully Diego would be back with their food and would question why security out front was lax. Even if he couldn't stop Quincy, Diego would discover Diana and the name tag. Soon, please.

She needed to keep Quincy talking, voices being the only advance warning she could offer Diego if he was already on his way. She would walk a fine line between keeping Quincy chatty and irritating him. Her gut told her, though, that he was married to his specific plan for killing her. He wouldn't want to deviate.

The elevator opened. Empty. Disappointment squeezed.

Quincy shoved her inside. "I told you no one's around to help."

He took his place beside her, only a few inches taller and leanly muscular, but with a crazed strength she wasn't sure she could combat.

Talk. Get in his whacked-out head and gain as much arming knowledge as possible. "Damn it, you killed Craig Wagner by introducing that virus in the mission data disk."

"No. I only placed it in the remote booth's disk. I was careful when Bridges flipped the schedule. If your program had worked as it should, Wagner would have flown out of the problem with his override controls.

You would have looked like a fool when your remote control flying failed. But Wagner would have safely landed. His death is a tragic loss to the air force that I never meant to happen."

The overconfident idiot. He hadn't realized she used the same disk for both the remote booth and the craft. His "brilliant" virus had killed an innocent man. The senselessness of it all threatened to weaken her. She refused to bend.

A hunch prodded her to push. "Do you really expect me to believe that when you started killing long ago?"

"You don't know what you're talking about, Captain." The elevator door opened again and he jerked her into the hall.

"The hell I don't. What about the pilot who died during my mother's test program?"

"Your mother's test failed. Those things happen. That a pilot died in the accident was yet another tragic loss to the air force." He swung open the back exit and escorted her through to a dark and empty parking lot. He truly had sent all help away. His car waited, parked inches away.

If she got inside, her odds of living decreased significantly.

She stood her ground with nothing but stars and wind for backup. "Bullshit, *sir*. It was no accident. I think you made the crash back then happen in just the same way you killed Craig."

"You know as well as I do the technology is different now than it was back during your mother's testing days. It couldn't have happened in the same way."

"So you didn't mean to murder the pilot working

my mother's test, either?" Anger clawed higher, begging for release. It was really getting tougher not to risk entering that pissing-him-off territory. "You really are an incompetent fool."

Quincy yanked her closer, his sweaty upper lip close enough for her to see and smell fear seeping from him.

He jammed the pistol into her gut. "Oh, I most certainly did mean to kill him. I reprogrammed the hard drives, just a subtle change in the controls. In the end, the pilot thought he was turning twenty degrees. In reality, the plane turned twenty-five. The evidence exploded with that self-righteous bastard."

A couple of degrees on the right mission could fly a craft into a mountain or straight into the ground. Her mind's eye replayed in horror the test prototype exploding on the runway. That poor pilot. Accidental death was bad enough. "Why?"

"He was going to tell her how I felt."

"What?"

She'd wanted answers for her mother, but this went beyond anything she could have expected. Her brain struggled to review what she knew about the crash that had ended her mother's career. Not the test data that Josie had memorized in flight school, but the personalities. Damn it all, she'd been so focused on the dry data, she'd missed the explosive dynamics of the people involved.

"If he told Zoe I loved her, that would ruin everything. I needed to win her over slowly. She was married so I couldn't make an overt move. That would be dishonorable and against regulations. I became her co-worker on the project, her friend, as well, so I would be in place to pick up the pieces when her marriage dissolved. I'm certain it will one day. Then she'll come to me and I'll divorce my wife for her." His eyes glowed with a maniacal passion. "You look just like her, you know. I still have a picture of her from our days here together in California."

Bile burned her throat. His hand gentled on her arm and stroked absently, gun still bruisingly deep in her tender flesh. One inhale could kill her. "When I go to console Zoe over the loss of her child, finally she'll see that I'm right for her. I'll make sure her daughter's project—hers, as well—succeeds. Because of my modifications, of course. We'll hold a special ceremony in your honor."

He released her arm and fished out his key ring. He activated the trunk release. "Get in."

Into the trunk? Survival instincts recoiled.

Josie considered forgetting about odds and the gun in her gut and just fighting it out here even though he was strong, trained and well armed. But if she lost, her sister would be helpless to whatever Quincy went back to do. She couldn't risk the confrontation.

Staying cool and giving Diego time to return offered the most hope for Diana.

Folded inside the general's trunk, Josie choked back claustrophobic fear. This wasn't any tighter than a cockpit, no darker than a night flight.

Of course, in a plane she had a stick and throttle to control her future. Here she had dark and stuffy air with exhaust fumes gagging her. Worse yet, he'd tied her hands.

Industrial carpet abraded her cheek, her head

crammed into a nook behind the fender. She'd tried shouting for help. He'd turned a sharp corner in retaliation and slammed her head against the side, nearly knocking her out. If she passed out, he could kill her before she woke.

Josie struggled to loosen the bonds on her wrist. Inching and twisting, she searched in the dark for something to chafe the rope against. Still nothing. Any hopes faded of pretending to still be bound and then overpowering him.

The car jerked to a stop, jolting her. She cracked her head against the metal interior again. Pain exploded through her brain. Sparks lit behind her eyes.

Footsteps sounded. The trunk popped. Overhead lights blinded her long enough for him to reach in and yank her up by the arm. Her numb legs collapsed under her. She hated the helplessness most of all.

Blinking, she cleared her brain and eyesight. They were outside her testing hangar, still at Palmdale, thank God. He really did plan to strap her to her remaining test Predator.

It was dark, late and abandoned. Even if someone saw him, no one would be in the least suspicious until she took off—and then it was very likely she would be shot down by her own air force.

Punching the access code into the door, he escorted her inside the hangar. Their footsteps echoed in the cavernous metal structure. A dim halo of light silhouetted her gray-and-white sleeping craft.

She pressed a hand to the cool side, eyes gliding along the expanse of wings. She'd been so proud of the crafts and the chance to clear her mother's name. It couldn't end like this.

Quincy opened the access panel and slid his data disk into the slot behind the pilot's seat. "This will fly the craft with my plan, while locking out your override controls."

She would be helpless to stop the crash, with no parachute as backup. Real fear kicked in with the childhood memory too close to the surface, of watching the crash in her mother's project. The smell of burning flesh roiled through her again. The sirens from just last week at Craig's accident—no, his murder—shrieked in her mind.

Josie balked.

Quincy leveled his gun at her. "Climb on, or I'll shoot you now and your sister will die. The sooner you take off, the sooner I can drive back to the intelligence building, *discover* her and call for help. Once I do, then I can report how you went crazy, confessed that you'd hurt your sister and then stole the plane at gunpoint before I could stop you." His fingers caressed the claw marks she'd left on his cheek, his eyes glassy with a crazed fanaticism. "That will explain these."

She was afraid Diana might die anyway without help soon. But what did Josie have to fight back with? She didn't even have her keys to stab at him if she could get free. She only had her wallet, a tube of orange-tryst lip gloss and her day-planner calendar.

Her day planner. With a flight data disk inside. Hope flickered.

Could she actually free her hands and slide in the new disk while in flight?

Hiss. A bullet spit from Quincy's gun. Cement spewed beside her foot. Shards stung her leg.

"No more waiting, Captain. Board your craft."

Okay. Her odds were better on the Predator than against a crazy gunman.

She climbed onto the Predator, sinking into the modified saddle seat with familiar ease and an unfamiliar dread. Quincy secured her harness, strapped in her legs and fit a helmet over her head without the benefit of a connected headset. She would be out there in the open sky with no way to communicate. Her legs locked tighter around the fuselage.

He opened the hangar doors and let the preplanned flight data take over. The craft hummed underneath her, a thrill she'd worried about never experiencing again, not knowing worse fears awaited her.

She had a plan. It would have to be enough. Because more than her own death, she feared her sister's—and leveling Diego's world if he lost another wingman.

Burger bags in his fists, Diego elbowed the down button on the elevator. His instincts were getting a workout this week, and now he couldn't shake the sense that Josie was in trouble. He'd feel a helluva lot safer when they rejoined forces. This solo crap was for the birds.

He understood he couldn't hang with her 24/7, but…nothing. He didn't have a logical reason for how he could stay closer or what he could do differently. Josie wasn't the type he could wrap in a cotton cocoon and he wouldn't change a damn thing about her.

Except maybe that prissy nature—which could actually be sexy sometimes when it challenged him to ruffle her.

The doors parted to reveal…

The vault door, cracked open. Where was security? Instincts jumped into an overtime workout. His heart kicked up to compensate.

He cleared the elevator, fears hammering as fast as his pulse. Had the gunmen found them here after all? How in the hell would they have gained entrance? And if they were in there, they would have already heard the elevator. Any element of surprise was gone now. "Josie? Diana?"

A moan sounded from inside. Feminine and injured. Bile burned his throat all the way up to his brain.

The sacks of food dropped unheeded to the floor. Diego shoved the heavy vault door the rest of the way open and found Diana sprawled and unconscious. Blood saturated her shoulder.

He shot across the room and dropped to his knees beside her. "Diana? Diehard?" He pressed his hand to her neck, felt a steady pulse. Thank God. He peeled aside the blood-soaked shoulder of her shirt to check her wound, a clean shot but bleeding like a son of a bitch. "Come on, little sister, wake up, damn it."

Where the hell was Josie? Seconds pounded past in his head. He needed to call for backup, but phones weren't allowed in the vault and his cell wouldn't work from the reinforced cellar. "Hang on, little sister. Just hang on."

He launched to his feet again, raced up the stairs and called the security police on his cell phone. Back in the vault, he shrugged out of his jacket and mashed it to her shoulder in counterpressure. He resurrected his best officer bark and commanded, "Lieutenant Lockworth, wake up."

Her lashes fluttered open, eyes glassy. "Morel? Ouch. You're hurting my shoulder."

Relief dulled the edge of fear. "Yeah, little sister, it's me. Where's Josie?"

"I dunno. Where's the Chinese food? Josie better have saved some of those pot stickers for me." She pressed her clenched fist to the floor to brace up, flinching from her injury. She looked down at the blood, went ghost-white and sagged back. "What the hell?"

"Just hold still."

Pot stickers?

Damn. The injury must have scrambled her head. "Keep thinking. What do you remember right before you fell asleep?"

Footsteps pounded in the hall. Thank God for quick response. Security police swarmed the room, followed by General Quincy.

Quincy? The very man Josie had brought them here to investigate.

The general's proximity jangled more alarms and plenty of rage. Diego took a closer look at the man, who had a land mobile radio clenched in his shaking hand. Something definitely wasn't right. The normally composed general had a serious case of bed head to match a rumpled mess of a flight suit. His eyes darted with frenetic intensity.

And two distinct fingernail scratch marks tracked down his cheek.

The man seemed oblivious to it all as he strode inside with the expectation of authority, unaware that even the SPs were eyeing him with suspicion.

Shit.

Was Josie already dead? The horrifying thought almost rocked him into reckless motion. If he flew at Quincy, the cops would haul him off. Josie needed help and his calm. "Where is she?"

"Captain Lockworth?"

"Yes, where is she?"

"Zoe's out working on her test."

Zoe? "Uh, sir, that's Captain Lockworth's mother." More than strange, this guy was plain wacko.

The security cops exchanged frowns.

"Diego?" Frowning, Diana groped behind her.

"Yeah, little sister." He reached for her elbow. "Steady now."

She extended her arm, fist opening to reveal a name tag from a flight suit. He didn't need to read any further than Birddog.

His eyes flew to Quincy's flight suit—devoid of a tag.

The man's crazed look, the name tag left behind, his coincidental appearance here and now…Diego didn't doubt for a second. Josie had left the unmistakable message behind that Quincy was indeed guilty.

Diego scooped up the incriminating tag and, just as he'd felt the plane all those years ago, he could feel Josie's strength in the message she'd somehow managed to leave behind during what must have been a hellish encounter. God, he loved that hardheaded woman. How could he not?

Rising, Diego passed the tag to the nearest SP and nodded toward the general. They needed to detain, if not arrest, this guy before he got away. Military police weren't hamstrung by as many legalities as civilian cops. Military police were bound by the Uniform

Code of Military Justice, not the Constitution. Thanks to Josie's fighting spirit, they had more than enough cause to hold the man temporarily.

The SPs closed in, flanking Quincy. "General, we need you to come with us."

"Of course." He threw back his shoulders with overblown dignity. "I'm happy to help with the investigation into Captain Lockworth however I can."

Tension burned through Diego until he was so damn taut he could snap. The need to find Josie pounded through him. He would not lose her. Failure was not an option.

Diego approached, leash on his rage short, fear alternately feeding and restraining the urge to pummel information free. "Where is she?"

"She stole an aircraft—the remaining test Predator." Quincy's hand gravitated to his face and stroked along the scratches in an eerie caress. "She wants to prove her theories, you know. I'm afraid I couldn't stop her insanity."

Diego rasped in air. There was a chance she was still alive. Relief slashed through him.

"Although I imagine fighter planes will have to shoot her down, if she doesn't crash first."

Fresh horror cut through him. What had Quincy done to Josie's Predator?

But she was alive.

She had to be. He would focus on that because he couldn't accept the alternative. He thought he'd been sent to hell three years ago, but that was nothing compared to what his world would be like if Josie died.

Diego sprinted past the security police. There would be time for statements later.

For now, he had to keep F-16s from blasting her out of the sky. And then pray she could outfly whatever Quincy had thrown her way.

Chapter 21

If she could just fly.

Wind and low-lying clouds tearing at her through the murky night, Josie sawed the binding ropes against the edge of the useless control panel in front of her. Agony knifed up her blood-slicked wrists. She pressed harder, unable to gauge her progress in the inky sky. Stars hung closer to her face at the higher altitude, the moon behind her.

She had the old data disk in her flight suit. She had a chance and damned if she would lose it. Emotions she couldn't even waste time restraining pummeled her as hard as the wind.

How much longer before Quincy's flight plan crashed the craft? Or until fighter planes overtook her?

She shuddered. She had to get free, maneuver herself into position and then wait three minutes for the new data to load. Doable. It offered at least hope for survival, and more of a chance than when Quincy's gun had been pressed to her forehead.

The knot inched. She could swear it had. If only her wrists weren't swelling. She jerked harder, blood lubricating the nylon rope.

Her hands pulled free.

Pain screamed through her fingers. She didn't have time to so much as shake control back into her flaming hands. Praying Quincy had been lying, she grabbed the stick and pumped it.

Nothing happened.

The Predator continued to fly Quincy's preprogrammed plan. The override controls were truly locked out. Her fists balled along with the urge to scream. She would have to install the disk stored in her flight suit pocket—easy enough to do on the ground. Not so simple at eight thousand feet in the air.

She smeared the slippery blood on her legs and unzipped her pocket. Carefully. God, she didn't even want to think about dropping the disk into the void of air below her. She shivered from the image more than the cold of altitude. Fumbling, searching, finally her fingers closed around the disk.

The access door for the disk was aft of the saddle— a far back and dangerous lean that would threaten the Predator's aerodynamics. She would have to hope Quincy's autopilot disk was programmed to compensate for weight shifts and the wind battering her.

She angled back, unable to see, only gauging by numbed touch. The center of gravity adjusted aft, as well. The Predator's nose pulled up. The slipstream noise lessened. Everything inside her shouted in protest.

The craft decelerated.

Her fingers tight around her only chance, she leaned forward to drop the nose and speed up again, farther still to build speed so she could afford to bleed off some when she moved back again to insert the disk.

Josie twisted, reached. Speed decreased. *Hold. Hold. Hold.* She willed the craft to obey her.

She pried the release open, then leaned forward fast, a second to spare in stopping a stall. The disk stayed in her numbed grip.

Okay. Almost there.

Gasping slow breaths to steady her heart—God, she couldn't afford to pass out now—she built speed again then strained her arm, tighter, farther. Adrenaline and nerves stretched as taut as her extended arm while she tried to keep her body planted as much in the seat as possible. She was so close. Even considering failure threatened her with lethal shakes.

Hand steady, she felt for the slot. Noise decreased. *No.* Just another couple of seconds.

A thumping sounded along the wings, wind battering rather than flowing, destroying the craft's natural aerodynamics.

God, one more second.

The disk jammed home.

Air exhaled as fast as her hand slapping the Read button. She only needed three minutes more for the data to load and re-enable the onboard controls. She brought her arm forward.

The Predator stalled.

Total silence enveloped her. Even the wind dwindled to more of a stroking breeze from an anonymous lover.

"No!" She threw her weight forward to counterbalance but didn't get to centerline fast enough. A wing dipped in sync with her lean from popping in the disk.

The stall morphed into a spin.

"Damn it!" she shouted to no one as the aircraft wrapped into violent revolutions.

Given the three minutes needed to reload…she calculated rates of speed, spin, descent. Even if she gauged her altitude correctly, by the time she regained control, she would be…

Too low to recover.

She was going to crash.

For the first time, the very real fear of failure slapped as her body cycled toward the ground. *No. No. No!* She had too many things left to do. Stop Quincy. Clear her mother's name. Be with Diego. Watch his hair grow again and love him. God, how she loved that wild and reckless man who cut her no more slack than she gave him.

Robbed of even sight in the dark, her senses spun until vertigo slithered its insidious stranglehold around her. Vertigo. Leveling worlds. Diego's words earlier came back to her.

Vertigo.

Leveling.

Feel the plane.

Her instincts shouted a solution, a scary as hell and totally illogical solution. She started the math required to prove it could work, but she didn't have time to compute.

Sometimes an aviator had to feel the plane.

Shutting down doubts, she reached for her seat belt. She leaned forward, out over the fairing. Her butt lifted from the safety of the seat. Farther forward she angled, no parachute to save her if she slipped, flung from the gyrating craft.

And in an odd way that empowered her—just her out there with the elements, no safety net. She had to win.

She *would* win.

The air rotated into a hurricane vortex beneath her. One look threatened to shake her loose. She fixed her eyes ahead.

Her arms wrapped around the fuselage, inching her body forward, shifting the center of gravity with her in increments while the Predator spun like a child's top. Much more and the wings could suffer stress cracks.

Breaks.

Her thighs screamed at the strain of locking her in the steely grip to keep her from flinging off. She held tighter, kept her eyes forward in spite of the gyrating forces working to peel her skin from her body.

The spin slowed.

Still the craft dropped but not as fast, the wings able to glide again. Would it be enough? Seconds ticked by. She tucked her head to the side, staring back at the panel, waiting for the green light signaling data load completed.

Go!

The light flashed. The engine restarted.

Her arms numb, her muscles screeching from exertion, she eased herself closer to the saddle, dropped back into the seat to straddle the fuselage. Her hands closed around the stick.

The aircraft responded. She had control. She exhaled, heart hammering in her ears. Damn Quincy and his insane plans.

Josie applied pressure to the opposite rudder to arrest the spin just as Diego had done in the simulator to stop her descent. The craft followed her every instruction as perfectly in tune as she remembered. *Yes.*

Although she wasn't risking her second chance just to log some extra flight time. She was getting her butt back on ground. ASAP. There would be time to celebrate later.

She nudged the stick forward, a little more, careful of the dark and the threat of mountains, since she didn't have a clear idea of where the hell she was. The night sky parted to reveal rolling dunes. No pretty runway landings for her. She would settle for that smooth stretch of dried-up lake bed less than a mile ahead.

Josie pulled back on the throttle, ground coming toward her at a nice sedate pace instead of a flat spin crash. The gear skimmed the desert, puffing a cloud of sand as she rolled to a stop. She sat and let the quiet reality roll over her along with the grit. She was alive.

She tipped back her head, belting out a war cry that must have reverberated to Reno and back.

Two F-16s circled overhead, lights blinking alongside the stars in the night sky. How long had they been there? Had they been with her in the air? She'd been too focused on survival to notice. And thank God they hadn't shot her down.

Her position had been noted, however, and rescue would come soon. She would only have to sit tight and wait.

She had no idea how long she watched the fighters

maneuver overhead. She simply lost herself in the magnificence of their flight. For years, she'd flown for her mother. From this point forward, she knew she would fly for herself.

Taming the sky was now *her* dream.

A rumble in the distance pulled her attention from the sky. Rays of sunlight fingered from the horizon with the first hints of morning, purples and oranges painting the stark desert. A military Suburban eased into view. Instincts told her Diego was in the passenger side. Nothing would have stopped him from being here for her or from taking care of Diana's safety.

Those awesome instincts also told her she wouldn't hesitate to walk into his arms. Emotions—full, out there and free—empowered her more than years of restraint through logic.

She hefted herself from the seat and swung over to the ground. Her boots pounded solid earth. Her knees rocked a little, but a flattened hand against the Predator steadied her, her eyes already locked on Diego stepping from the Suburban.

Then she was running, her knees working just fine. Diego met her halfway, his arms banding around her. Hard and oh, so hot. She buried her face in the crook of his neck.

She'd beaten the odds for her second chance. But would her sister be as lucky? "Diana? Quincy shot her—"

"I know," Diego answered against her hair. "I found her when I came back."

"Is she okay?"

"She'll need a few stitches. And she doesn't remember anything that happened for the past few hours, but she appears to be completely okay otherwise."

Just as Quincy had said. Thank God. "What about General Quincy? He needs to be sto—"

"I got your name tag message and the security police have him under house arrest—actually more like a psych watch. I hope to God you've got some concrete evidence to nail that bastard."

"Damn straight, I do." Josie eased back to stare up at him, morning sun behind his shoulders casting his face in shadows. "I guess I have you to thank for keeping the F-16s from popping me."

"You can thank me later."

All shadows aside, she could see his smile.

His hands stroked over her hair. "I don't know how the hell you got onto the ground, but I'm just so damn grateful you're here."

She smiled right back. "I just felt the plane."

His rumbling laugh wrapped around her. "When you figure something out, you go all the way."

"I'm all about giving a hundred percent." And wasn't that another lightbulb moment? Time to give one hundred percent in her relationship with this man, as well, because, by God, he was right. Something incredible happened when they were together. "I love you, Diego Morel."

Oh, yeah, she could definitely see his smile— wicked, wonderful and lowering toward her face for a kiss guaranteed to send her soaring.

"Love you, too, Buttercup."

Four days later, Josie and the remaining modified Predator descended toward Palmdale's runway, her test project back on track now that Quincy's tampering had been proved and cleaned away. Her test budget was tight due to the recent delays and crash, so the powers-that-be wanted things up and running again immediately. Down days meant precious and limited dollars burned.

And after the hellish experiences that had come her way with the crash and horrific night flight, it was more important than ever that she crawl back in the saddle right away. Rock solid, she'd logged another flight mission.

The nose gear kissed asphalt, gliding to earth and slowing. Her headset blasted with cheers from the control tower, the remote pilot and the sensor operator, Zeljak.

"Yippee ki yay, mo-fo," she shouted in honor of Craig Wagner, the hokey cheer a new tradition she intended to ingrain in all her test programs. They were, after all, the last of the real cowboys.

Or *cowgirls.*

Josie went through the routine of parking procedure calls through her headset while the Predator skated down the runway onto the tarmac. On a small set of bleachers, a group of nearly forty gathered to watch and celebrate—higher-ups from Palmdale and nearby Edwards.

Her reporter friend, Tory Patton, had flown in at her request to cover the event, giving the air force and all of Athena Academy grads positive press to counteract anything Shannon might manage to wrangle out into the public eye. Although Shannon Conner's name was pretty much mud in the broadcasting industry lately, after her piece about Josie and Bridges had been so firmly disproved. Not that Josie harbored any illusions that a bad reputation would keep Shannon down long.

Josie scanned the runway, which bustled with activity—and celebration. The fight had been a tough one these past weeks, but she wasn't a quitter. None of the Athena women were, and they would apply that collective determination into finding justice for Rainy. Josie scanned the crowd in front of her. Meanwhile, she owed it to her friend's memory to savor life.

The craft slid to a stop. Sweeping off her helmet, Josie deplaned amid applause and cheers, her sister's uninhibited whistles and whoops ringing out the loudest in the gusting wind.

Diana was still in town, suffering no ill effects other than the short-term memory loss. She would never know all that Josie had gone through trying to save her. For the best. Josie didn't want gratitude or big sister/little sister politics. She looked forward to them working on that equal friendship they'd only just begun to build.

Josie studied the crowd, searching for Diego by Diana and found…

Hoyt and Zoe Lockworth?

Her parents.

The surprise gesture touched her more than she would have thought. Crying right now would *not* be cool, but God, it was good to see them both waiting there for her.

Helmet tucked under her arm, she strode forward, waving to her smiling family. A memory of her graduation day and her mother's Beanie Baby gift came rolling back, along with an understanding of what her mother had meant about the importance of being soft as well as strong.

Just as she'd learned in the air four days ago, it was all about balance.

Josie grinned back at the face a mirror image of her own, with a few years added. "It works, Mama."

"I know, baby." Her mother tucked a stray hair behind Josie's ear with a familiar maternal gentleness she'd missed so often as a kid. "I couldn't be prouder of you. Thank you."

Hoyt Lockworth hooked an arm around his wife's shoulders. "I always knew this would fly. Congratulations to you both."

Her father's love for his wife shone in the morning sun and for the first time Josie saw it with adult, wiser eyes. Now that she'd had a taste of how intense love could be, compassion kicked into overdrive. Being up on that craft rigged to crash would have been a cakewalk compared to imagining Diego in danger.

"Thanks, Dad." She stepped into his hug, her mother's, too, then Diana's.

Okay, maybe one or two tears would be cool in light of giving Josie and Josephine equal time these days.

And where *was* Diego? Still holding hard to the perfect moment, she scanned and finally found him a few feet away, with Tory now, feeding her information without ever once taking his eyes off Josie.

Yes, he was giving her the space she'd asked for only a few days ago—without ever leaving. Of course she couldn't help but think telling him she loved him and then jumping his bones repeatedly the second they were alone may have given him a hint that she didn't have any plans to run away.

In fact, she wanted to run *toward* him.

She eased out of the family hug, the warmth remaining. "Mom, Dad, I'll be back in a minute. I want to introduce you to someone."

Not a bad plan since she would be meeting Diego's parents over the New Year in a short vacation down to Mississippi.

She tucked through the crowd, smiling her thanks and shaking hands. She backed a step, bumping into a body blocking her way.

"Josie?"

She tensed. What was Mike Bridges doing here? She spun to face him.

He raised his hands in defensive surrender. "I'm not here to spoil your day and the last thing I want is another pounding from your scowling boyfriend over there. I'm leaving in the morning, but I wanted to see that everything went well with the flight."

Bridges seemed sincere and there was really no need to cut him, literally or figuratively. His career was basically over. Even if he managed to stay in the service, he would never be promoted again due to his admission to hitting on Josie. He had nothing to gain by being here.

Unless he was bucking for her help with Kayla again. "Have you called Kayla?"

"Not yet, and I'm not asking you to play intermediary. Just still working up my nerve." His gaze skimmed over to the big brass in attendance and back again. "I hear you're top of the list for being the new detachment commander. Congratulations. You deserve it."

She'd heard the same rumors, but still couldn't wrap her brain around it. The job went to majors or lieutenant colonels. But apparently the position would shortly be hers—a challenge she embraced. "Thank you."

Nodding, he turned to leave.

She still couldn't bring herself to call him sir. That was a sign of respect he would have to earn back, if he ever could. But maybe his call sign might not be a bad middle ground. And a fun jab, too. They'd always called him Boss around the detachment because he hated his real call sign that tied into his last name, Bridges. "Hey, Brooklyn?"

He winced. "Yeah, P.C.?"

"Good luck with that phone conversation."

A hint of his old charm returned with his smile. "Thanks."

"I wish I could say I meant that for you, but I really mean it for Jazz."

"And that's why you'll make a great commander. Fair and impartial to the end."

Scowling, Diego peeled away from Tory's side and started toward them. Thor alert. Bridges held up a hand.

"No worries, Cruiser. I'm not sticking around for the party." Spinning away, Bridges retreated, climbing into a military truck and out of her life.

Diego strutted toward her, pure sauntering sin in jeans, boots and a T-shirt. His shoulders stretched leather tight, a brown jacket today. Finally he'd tugged out his old flight jacket to wear for what he called Josie's special occasion. He'd vowed he wasn't planning on returning to the military, and she believed him. He didn't need to. He was comfortable in his skin and the new path for his life.

After his work with her on the project and the crash, Diego had been approached again with old offers renewed from contractors about signing on for real, rather than just consulting.

The salary offers were beyond complimentary.

Of course Diego had never been about the money. He was, however, all about the challenge. And the programs he could head for government contractors designing new military aircraft were most definitely cutting-edge challenging.

He was ready to move forward.

And so was she.

"Great job up there, Buttercup."

"I just let the guy in the remote booth do his job. Zeljak even captured some great footage of the nudist colony."

Diego winked. "Hey, if you want to see a hoo-hah—"

"Is that a personal invitation?"

"You bet. The minute the partying's done here."

Yeah, she loved this wild man who'd roared into her life and demanded she be Josie, Josephine, P.C., Buttercup, all worthy parts of herself.

Finally, Josie, who'd always given one hundred percent, understood how to accept one hundred percent of herself. "I'm looking forward to an hour-long sweat with you in the sauna so we can—" she gave him a slow, sultry once-over "—talk. You never did tell me how you performed that *lomcevak* maneuver in a Christian Eagle biplane."

"How about once we get naked together in the sauna I'll show you instead?"

Her stomach already flipped in anticipation of the soaring thrills she and this man could experience together.

Even with both feet still on the ground.

* * * * *

Books by Catherine Mann

Silhouette Bombshell

Pursued #18

Silhouette Intimate Moments

Wedding at White Sands #1158
*Grayson's Surrender #1175
*Taking Cover #1187
*Under Seige #1198
The Cinderella Mission #1202
*Private Maneuvers #1226
*Strategic Engagement #1257
*Joint Forces #1293

Silhouette Books

*Anything, Anywhere, Anytime

*Wingmen Warriors

ATHENA FORCE

Chosen for their talents.
Trained to be the best.

Expected to change the world.

The women of Athena Academy
share an unforgettable experience
and an unbreakable bond—until
one of their own is murdered.

The adventure begins with these six books:

PROOF by Justine Davis, July 2004

ALIAS by Amy J. Fetzer, August 2004

EXPOSED by Katherine Garbera,
September 2004

DOUBLE-CROSS by Meredith Fletcher,
October 2004

PURSUED by Catherine Mann, November 2004

JUSTICE by Debra Webb, December 2004

**And look for six more Athena Force stories
January to June 2005.**

Available at your favorite retail outlet.

**Bestselling fantasy author Mercedes Lackey
turns traditional fairy tales on their heads
in the land of the Five Hundred Kingdoms.**

Elena, a Cinderella in the making, gets an
unexpected chance to be a Fairy Godmother. But being a
Fairy Godmother is hard work and she gets into trouble by
changing a prince who is destined to save the kingdom,
into a donkey—but he really deserved it!

Can she get things right and save the kingdom?
Or will her stubborn desire to teach this ass
of a prince a lesson get in the way?

*On sale November 2004.
Visit your local bookseller.*

BOMBSHELL™

COMING NEXT MONTH

#21 SISTER OF FORTUNE—Lindsay McKenna
Sisters of the Ark

An ancient artifact had plagued Vicky Mabrey's dreams
for a year, and now she had to find it—with the help of
an enemy from her past. Vicky couldn't stand the sight of
Griff Hutchinson, but they had to work together to find the precious crystal—before it fell into the wrong hands and destroyed
the people Vicky loved.

#22 JUSTICE—Debra Webb
Athena Force

Her best friend's killer was dead, and so was police lieutenant
Kayla Ryan's best lead to find her friend's missing child. Now
Kayla had to work with a lethally sexy detective to find the person who'd sent the assassin, and to bring him to justice.
But she couldn't shake the feeling that someone was watching
her every move.... Was the enemy closer than she'd ever suspected?

#23 NIGHT LIFE—Katherine Garbera

Sasha Malone Sterling had given up the dark life of a spy to
be a wife and mother. But the agency had called her back
for a mission she couldn't refuse: bringing in a rogue agent.
She was the only one who could catch him—because the
agent was Sasha's own estranged husband, and no one
knew him better than she did.

#24 HOT CASE—Patricia Rosemoor

Detective and confirmed skeptic Shelley Caldwell couldn't have
been more different from her naive twin sister. But when her
twin found a body, drained of blood, that later disappeared,
Shelley was eerily reminded of an old case that still haunted
her. The old trail was heating fast—and to follow it, Shelley
would trade places with her twin and enter the dark world of
Goths, wannabe vampires and maybe even the real deal.

SBCNM1104